"Whatever has happe~~ned~~ ~~can be smoothed~~ over. I've come back ~~... ~~ Far wealthier than S~~o~~ ~~... ~~ duke or earl in Lond~~on~~ ~~...~~

Her face remained impas~~sive~~ ~~as she scanned the room~~ filled with items of great wealth. All obtained for her.

At last, she lifted her sad eyes to him. "I never cared about money. I would have rather had you all these years, so I did not have to make the choices I did."

"I did it for you," he protested. "For us."

Her lips pulled into a mirthless smile. "You did it for yourself."

Author Note

In *How to Wed a Courtesan*, Evander is trying desperately to win back Lottie's affection. One way he tries to do this is through flowers.

However, flowers were not always readily available year-round in England, especially during 1816, when this book takes place, which happened to be a particularly rainy and cold year. Which brings us to the hothouse flower.

Hothouse flowers were grown in something like a greenhouse, though it wasn't the type that you and I are used to today. These structures would have been built of brick or stone with large multipaned windows in them. Glass was taxed heavily then, which meant that owning a hothouse for plants would have been extraordinarily expensive, and it was why hothouse flowers really could only be purchased by the very rich.

What was terribly romantic about those hothouse flowers was how much the meaning of flowers were incorporated into bouquets back then. The emotion flowers are meant to evoke has always fascinated me, and I had a wonderful time with Evander utilizing these wonderful bouquets to his ultimate advantage. I hope you enjoy the play of flowers in this book as much as I did when I wrote it.

MADELINE MARTIN

How to Wed
a Courtesan

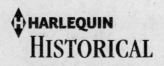
HARLEQUIN
HISTORICAL

HARLEQUIN®
HISTORICAL™

Recycling programs
for this product may
not exist in your area.

ISBN-13: 978-1-335-40721-4

How to Wed a Courtesan

Copyright © 2021 by Madeline Martin

This edition published by arrangement with Harlequin Books S.A.

For questions and comments about the quality of this book,
please contact us at CustomerService@Harlequin.com.

Harlequin Enterprises ULC
22 Adelaide St. West, 40th Floor
Toronto, Ontario M5H 4E3, Canada
www.Harlequin.com

Printed in U.S.A.

Madeline Martin is a *USA TODAY* bestselling author of historical romance novels filled with twists and turns, steamy romance, empowered heroines and the men who are strong enough to love them. She lives a glitter-filled life in Jacksonville, Florida, with her two daughters (known collectively as the minions) and a man so wonderful he's been dubbed Mr. Awesome. Find out more about Madeline at her website, madelinemartin.com.

Books by Madeline Martin

Harlequin Historical

The London School for Ladies

How to Tempt a Duke
How to Start a Scandal
How to Wed a Courtesan

Visit the Author Profile page
at Harlequin.com.

To John Somar, who inspires so many of my heroes and whose consideration and patience are unmatched. It's with him that I have been lucky enough to find my own happy-ever-after.

Chapter One

June 1816, London, England

The ring on the table required an answer.

Lottie turned away from it so abruptly that the hem of her skirt snapped against the Brussels weave carpet in her parlour. Her pulse beat heavily in her ears.

This was what she had wanted. Years ago. When she'd been a girl. But she was no longer that girl. She was a woman.

One who understood the effects of love.

One who had sacrificed far too much.

She hadn't even opened the box yet. Not that it mattered. The jewel within was of little consequence. She had a good deal of wealth. She could purchase her own bloody ring.

What mattered was what it stood for.

Everything.

She'd had a ring on her finger once before and its presence there had scored her heart with what ought to have been eternal love. How wrong she had been.

Evander's timing had been planned to perfection. Lottie had completed all her lessons that day—instruction to the women of the ton, who came to her to learn the art of seduction and flirtation. After all, why else would they come to a former courtesan.

Not that Lottie had wanted their life. What vicar's daughter did? But then she'd had little choice in the matter. She'd offered too much to Evander in her youthful infatuation and ruined her prospects for anything else.

It rattled the soul to know what one must do to get by. To protect those one loved.

That was why her decision was so hard now. When the fantasy of love warred with bitter reality. When desire arose despite obligation. When society stood in the way of dreams that could never be.

There was no other man in her life. Her protectors were a thing of the past. Their financial support was no longer necessary now she had established herself as an educator of the ton's ladies.

Those rumoured to be under her instruction received extraordinary attention at balls and soirees, and their suitors were endless. Those on the outside assumed her lessons were of a sensual nature. In truth, Lottie's focus was always on the lady—on teaching her to accept herself.

All of which comprised the reason she should send the ring back to Evander. The Earl of Westix did not need a woman of ill repute at his side, mingling her tarnished reputation with his esteemed reputation.

She snatched the box off the cool marble tabletop, just beneath yet another glorious bouquet of the hothouse flowers Evander insisted on sending. Irises and white tulips this time. Just as beautiful as they were unwanted.

The box with the ring in it was cold against her palm and she found herself prising it open, doing to the little box what she had only recently been able to do to her heart.

Nestled within a nest of glossy black satin was a small diamond ring, winking up at her. She staggered back, as if at a blow to her chest.

Her expectations had settled on something large and grand—an opulent bauble befitting the Earl, who had seen the world and gained a fortune. This stone was a modest little thing, almost a chip. Once upon a time, it had been the most beautiful ring she ever seen. She'd thought it lost for ever when she'd thrown it across the drawing room at Comlongon Castle, and had bade the bit of jewellery good riddance. Yet here it was once more, begging for a piece of herself she could not give. A piece of herself which could not exist.

Because all that was left were memories of better times, of beautiful places, of a love that was innocent and precious, of things that could never be.

And things she could not stop herself from wanting.

Chapter Two

August 1809, Bedfordshire, England

Music tinkled with refined elegance through a ballroom dripping with crystal chandeliers, where candles shone from gilt sconces and reflected their golden light throughout the room. It was beautiful in a way that was nearly indescribable to a girl like Lottie, who had spent her life in a small village in the vicar's cottage with her father.

The borrowed gown she wore—pale blue satin, with gems sewn into the delicate fabric—sparkled as if it too was as otherworldly as the scene glittering before her.

'Is it everything you thought it would be?' a familiar voice asked.

She spun around and beamed up at Charles, the only son of the Duke of Somersville, a man whose station meant she ought never to associate with him. Except that his manor was near Binsey, the village where she'd lived. They'd spent every summer together before such a thing as class had ever entered Lottie's thoughts.

And now he would be leaving on his Grand Tour, trekking across the world as his father once had, gone for who knew how long. This was Charles and Lottie's last hurrah together, and he had declared it would be grand.

That was why he had insisted she accept his aging aunt's offer to visit her sprawling estate in Bedfordshire.

Lady Hasgrove was a wealthy widow who had always found Lottie's companionship agreeable. This ball her neighbours had put on, two nights after Lottie's her arrival, was undoubtedly part of his scheme, and it was proving to be nothing short of magical.

'This is more than I ever thought possible,' Lottie confessed, unable to stifle her awe. And how could she in such an exquisite setting?

He chuckled. 'I knew it would please you.' His blue gaze, clear and brilliant, quite similar to her own, flitted about the room. 'Any suitors as yet?'

She laughed at that. 'Surely you jest? I'm hardly the type of woman to draw men. And you know I did not come to Bedfordshire to—'

'Lord Folton, I demand you introduce me to this divine creature.'

They both turned at the sound of Charles's title to find a tall, lean man, impeccably dressed in a tailored black jacket and a green waistcoat that made his eyes the most stunning shade of jade. His auburn hair was combed neatly to the side and he wore a smile that revealed straight white teeth.

Lottie's heart stuttered off its beat.

The men of the ton were all handsome, with their fine clothes and manners and the air of sophistication they bore. But the one standing before her put them all to shame.

Charles lifted his brows at Lottie, as if to gloat because he'd expected this. No doubt she'd hear of it later.

'Miss Rossington, this rapscallion is Evander, Baron Murray. His father, the Earl of Westix, and mine are in the same adventure club.' Charles shifted his attention to the gentleman. 'Murray, may I present my dearest friend, Miss Charlotte Rossington?'

'Miss Rossington.'

The Baron's attention focused on Lottie and her breath froze in her chest, trapping her in a moment of sheer bliss.

He lifted her gloved hand to his lips as he bowed to her. '*Enchanté.*'

His smooth voice and the genuine interest in his searching stare sent tingles racing over her skin.

'It's a pleasure to make your acquaintance,' she said, in a voice far softer than usual.

'Would you believe this divine creature hasn't a single name on her dance card yet?' Charles nudged Lord Murray.

Heat scorched Lottie's cheeks, but before she could chide Charles for his blatancy Lord Murray spoke up. 'I wish I could fill the whole of it with my name.'

'You can fill at least the first space.' She glanced up at him through her lashes and found him grinning down at her in a way that made her pulse race.

'The set has already begun.' Lord Murray glanced up with a pensive expression. 'It would appear we have quite a wait until the next.' He gave a beleaguered sigh. 'I supposed we'll have to keep one another company until it begins. More's the pity.'

A wink followed his lamentation, indicating that he was no sorrier for it than she. In truth, she wanted to know everything about this man. His father was the Earl of Westix, that was what Charles had said. The name was indeed familiar, as Lord Murray's father was oftentimes brought up alongside Charles's.

'Shall I fetch you a glass of lemonade?' Lord Murray asked.

As much as Lottie enjoyed the refreshment, she did not relish losing Lord Murray's company after having just become acquainted.

She shook her head. 'No, thank you.'

'It's for the best. Lady Pensville is notorious for watering down her drinks.' Lord Murray gave an exaggerated grimace.

Lottie, who had always been raised to be honest and generous with compliments, while being silent on complaints, covered her mouth with her hand in horror. 'You shouldn't say such things.'

He lifted his shoulder with an uncaring shrug. 'Well, it's true. You can try it, if you'd like to see for yourself.' He indicated the linen-covered table, where a large crystal punchbowl sat. The liquid within did appear rather clear.

'Well, now you've recommended it with such alacrity...' She laughed and shook her head.

'Ah.' He held up his forefinger. 'You're afraid you'll have to lie and tell me you enjoyed it, aren't you?'

There was something taboo about his nonchalance, the way he so casually broke the rules she had tiptoed around her entire life, that it left her giddy.

'Are you blushing?' he teased. 'I dare say you must have the moral compass of a vicar's daughter.'

'Perhaps that's because I am a vicar's daughter.' She grinned at the mention of her father's profession.

'If all vicar's daughters were as lovely and sharp-witted as you, every man in England would attend church.'

'Every man in England should attend church,' she argued.

'Yes, but then they actually *would.*'

She laughed at such a brazen statement.

'I assure you, Miss Rossington, I do not jest.'

'Do you always speak what's on your mind?' she asked, genuinely curious and inexplicably drawn to his cavalier demeanour.

'I do.' He lifted a brow at her. 'Everyone should.'

She caught herself before issuing forth a scoff at that. 'Even women?' she countered.

He leaned closer, bringing with him a pleasant sandalwood scent. 'Especially women. How are we ever supposed to understand you if you never share what is going on in those pretty heads of yours?'

She twisted her fingers absently as she considered this. Her father had always permitted her to speak her mind with him, and obviously she'd always done so with Charles. However, she had been cautioned from doing so among others, lest she come across as a hoyden.

'Like now, for example.' Lord Murray studied her, his head tilted to the side in an almost dreamy fashion. 'You're thinking something poignant. I can see it in the lovely crystal blue of your eyes. And yet you are saying nothing.' He leaned as close as he could, which scandalously bordered on the inappropriate, and whispered, 'Tell me.'

All the air seemed to be sucked from the room in that moment. Lottie wrestled to keep her wits about her with this charming rogue. 'I was instructed in my youth that men do not care for intelligent women.'

A spark glinted in his eyes and he straightened, relinquishing the space around her once more so that she might draw a proper breath. Or at least as much as the bodice of her gown would allow. Being borrowed, it was made for another woman's body and was a bit on the snug side.

'If you are as intelligent as you are beautiful, perhaps I ought to propose this very night.' He grinned at her—a boyish smile that hooked itself into the deepest part of her chest.

'If you are as honest as you are charming, I might just consider such an offer.' She had never been coy, but he encouraged a daring boldness in her. And she liked it. Just as she liked his appreciation for her intellect. That was a rare thing indeed.

He laughed. 'You truly are enchanting.'

'Coming from a man of blatant honesty, I take that as the highest compliment.'

'As well you should,' he said, nodding favourably. 'As well you should.'

The music in the hall tapered to a close and the people around them shifted in preparation for the arrival of those returning from the country dance.

'Dare I ask what the lady thinks of me?' Lord Murray turned his attention away from her as he posed the question.

'I am not so bold with my honesty,' she replied airily. 'I suppose you shall have to wait for my assessment.'

He turned back to her with an exaggerated look of pain. 'You slay me, madam.'

'Patience is a virtue.'

She recalled the words her father often said to her, more as a reminder to herself than to Lord Murray. For she was impatient and always had been. Even now, a restlessness stirred within her. She longed to know more about him. And wondered how she might see more of him.

It was foolish, of course.

Lord Murray was the first man to ask her to dance— the first who had even paid her a modicum of attention. She would be a ninny to cast her heart his way when she knew nothing of him.

For his part, Lord Murray was not at all put off by her answer. Instead, his eyes twinkled with a mischievousness she enjoyed more than she ought to admit.

'Yes, but dancing is preferable by far to patience.' He offered her his arm. 'Shall we?'

She slipped her hand into the warm crook of his elbow, near enough to him now to make out the warm sandalwood notes of his shaving soap she'd caught earlier.

He led her through the opening notes of a cotillion. 'Do you attend balls often?'

'I must confess, this is my first.'

His mouth fell open as they danced apart and towards

other partners. When they returned to one another, he appeared much chagrined. 'Then I suppose any hope of finding you at a ball in London would be impossible?'

'Unfortunately,' Lottie replied with genuine disappointment.

'If you were in London I would find you at every ball. I'd parade you through Vauxhall Gardens and ensure everyone saw you sitting at my side in my family's box at the opera.'

It was fascinating, how he described it. 'Goodness, that does sound exciting.'

'You would love it.' He twirled her around in the dance.

Her gaze met his, even as the room around them seemed to continue to spin. 'I want to hear of it all.'

'In Vauxhall Gardens a whistle blows at night, and lanterns as far as the eye can see all light up at once.'

She could imagine the spots of light flickering to life amid a sea of darkness and smiled. 'Tell me more.'

He went on to sweep her away into another world of grand entertainments in London and summers spent at the family castle in Scotland. Lottie had always cherished her life in Binsey, and had never once thought it dull. At least not until now, as she heard of the splendour to be found beyond the cottage.

As she listened to the velvety rich detail being painted in her mind, she could not help but be dazzled as Lord Murray swept her away into another world—one she had never been party to until this night.

While she did dance with other men that evening, the cotillion was not the only dance set Lord Murray claimed. He secured her for a country dance later, though the steps were so lively there was little talking to be had. Still, they laughed and smiled, eyes locked, her heart racing throughout.

Facing the end of the evening, and her time in his presence, had been difficult. For this ball had been the most magical thing ever to have happened in her life. And Lord Murray the most fascinating man she'd ever met.

Never had she known someone whose speech, for better or for worse, was so honest. A refreshing change from the polished conversation she tiptoed around every day. He filled her mind with the experiences he so eloquently described and easily drew her in with his infectious grin. And, while she would never wish away her happy life in Binsey, she couldn't help but hope to see Lord Murray again.

Evander, Baron Murray, heir to the Earldom of Westix, floated on the proverbial clouds the day following Lady Pensville's ball. In the past years there had been several ladies who had caught his eye as he'd sought the woman he intended to wed. He'd even called on a few of them the day following a dance, with flowers in his hand. But never had he selected a bundle with more nervous care.

It was ironic that he should meet such a woman just as he was due to return to Westix Manor in Southampton, to aid his father following the Earl's return from India.

Evander considered the flowers on the padded seat beside him. Daffodils for his regard, pink carnations for his affection, and a few sprigs of myrtle to signify love and marriage—a play on what they'd spoken of the night before. However, as he drew his curricle to a stop before Lady Hasgrove's sprawling estate he thought better of his decision and plucked out the sprigs of myrtle.

They lay scattered over the rocks lining the curved drive like large flecks of snow. What was worse, removing them left the bundle of flowers woefully apparent of their absence. It looked no better than the miserable weeds he'd plucked at Comlongon Castle in Scotland for his mother and sister when he'd been a boy.

Damn.

He kicked himself for not having gone with roses or tulips or bloody lilies. Hyacinths, even. Anything more typically in fashion and more appealing.

He jumped from the carriage with the intent of reclaiming the small white flowers when a cheerful voice broke through the silent country morning.

'Good day, Murray.'

Charles, Lord Folton, offered him a congenial grin as he made his way up the path to where Evander was preparing to climb the stone steps.

'Might I hazard a guess that your visit has something to do with a certain lovely vicar's daughter?'

Evander drew up short at the sight of the other man, leaving the white flowers where they lay, limp and discarded.

When Folton had implied the night before that no one had claimed a space on Miss Rossington's dance card, Evander had assumed this duke's heir had no interest in the stunning young woman. But if he was calling on her now, after the ball where he too had shared a dance with her…

Lord Folton cocked an eyebrow at the bunch of flowers, whose slender stems had become rather warm and wilted in the cradle of Evander's palm. 'I dare say Lady Langston will be quite put out at what you have no doubt done to her garden to obtain those.'

Evander gritted his teeth. In truth, he had gone to the garden at the Langston estate, where he was staying with a friend from university. He'd been too eager to see Miss Rossington and hadn't wanted to bother with attempting to find someone who might sell hothouse bouquets in the country.

He flicked a glance at the sad little flowers and sighed. 'It was a notion best left to the foolishness in my head and not put to application.'

Folton laughed. 'You aren't the first man to lose his head over Miss Rossington.'

'Aren't I?' Evander levelled a gaze at him, with the intent of seeking out the truth then and there.

Folton held up his hands in a surrendering gesture. 'Not me. Miss Rossington, while admittedly beautiful, shares a friendship with me that is not even remotely romantic. She is more sister to me, as we are both without siblings and became something of that for one another as children.' He clasped Evander by the shoulder. 'I merely meant the many country hearts she has inadvertently broken in Oxfordshire. She never even realised the poor lads had an interest in her.' He shook his head in sympathy.

Evander had been so taken by Miss Rossington, so consumed by her, he had not thought even to ask if she had a beau. 'So there isn't anyone she favours back in...?' *What the devil was the name of the village?*

'Binsey,' Folton supplied. 'There isn't. And I've never seen her take note of any man's attention.' Folton gave Evander's shoulder a squeeze and released his grip. 'Until now.'

A thrill surged through Evander. She had certainly shown an interest in him. Though she had danced with several others, he'd noted that with them her smiles had been less bright, her blushes less frequent and her demeanour more reserved.

'Come, I was on my way to see to my aunt.' Folton led the way up the steps to the massive entrance. 'How long will you be staying at the Langston estate?'

'I leave later this afternoon, I'm afraid,' Evander replied with genuine regret. 'It would appear both our fathers are just returned from India. Mine has summoned me back to our Southampton estate to assist him with some items he's collected.'

'I see.' Lord Folton spun about, heading in the opposite direction. Away from the large house.

Evander frowned in confusion. 'What the devil? Where are you going?'

'I will call upon my aunt later, as I remain in Bedfordshire several days more.' Folton turned back to regard Evander. 'For now, I leave you to Miss Rossington without my company. You are forewarned: my aunt has a tendency to fall asleep at tea.' Folton winked and made his way down the path with a cheeky wave. *'Bonne chance.'*

Evander held up his free hand in acknowledgment of the good wishes.

As he made his way to the steps his nerves jangled. Ordinarily, he was fully in control of his faculties. A man who was put off by nothing and sure of himself in nearly every way. At least until being in the radiance of Miss Rossington.

She was exquisitely lovely, but it was her wit that made her shine so brilliantly in his eyes. That and the way her eyes lit with wonder as he'd shared stories of London and Scotland. There was something in the starry-eyed way she'd watched him that made him long to take her to those places, to drape her in the finest silks and let her feast on the finest foods, drink the richest wines.

The butler showed Evander into the large manor, and led him to the drawing room to wait for Miss Rossington with his pathetic bunch of weeds. The room was an odd green colour that resembled asparagus, with small tables cluttered with a multitude of figurines set atop bits of lace that had gone yellow with age.

The door opened and Miss Rossington entered with Lady Hasgrove. Evander's heart snagged in his chest. A stream of morning light shone in from the window like a beam from the heavens, falling over Miss Rossington as she smiled up at him.

'Lord Murray,' she said, in that delicate voice of hers.

He'd thought several times about what he might say to her when he saw her again. Now all those carefully scripted greetings slipped from his mind, replaced instead by an awed reverence for her extreme beauty.

She was sheer perfection, in a white muslin gown that offset the creaminess of her skin and her glossy dark hair, which she'd twisted into a simple knot. Women were oft so very complicated in their hairstyles these days. There was an elegance to the lack of adornment of Miss Rossington's appearance which allowed her natural beauty to shine through all the more.

'Miss Rossington,' he managed, 'You look well.' Remembering his manners, he offered a short bow to Lady Hasgrove, whom Miss Rossington was helping to a plush settee. 'Good morning to you, Lady Hasgrove.'

The older woman nodded at him once she'd settled back on a cushion with a needlepoint rose, her eyes already beginning to droop.

Miss Rossington smiled and indicated a chair across from her. Spots of pastel colour dotted the sleeves of her dress at her wrists. Small stains caused most likely by paint of some kind.

Noticing his attention on her sleeves, she quickly pulled her hands into her lap. 'Would you join us for some tea?'

'Yes, thank you. And I brought these for you.' He held out his carefully selected bundle of flowers.

As her crystal blue gaze fell on the bouquet he saw the flowers through her eyes. The frail stems had given way to the weight of the bulky flowers and now hung in defeat around his fist.

'I suppose they could use some water,' he muttered. 'Perhaps I ought to have brought roses. But they seemed far too ordinary a flower for such an extraordinary woman.'

She accepted them and carefully hid her stained sleeves

behind them. 'Water will do wonders for them.' After ringing for a servant, she studied the bunch of flowers as he took his seat. 'I rather like your selection.'

He settled into the thickly padded pink velvet chair. 'Do remember I asked you for your honesty. It is admittedly a sad bunch of weeds.'

'Not at all.' A wistful smile touched her lips with such sweet joy he felt a mirror reaction pull at his own mouth.

'They remind me of home. I have carnations planted under my window that bid me good morning every day.' She ran her fingertip over the waxy yellow petal of a daffodil. 'Your regard.' She touched the pink carnation next. 'And your affection.'

A pretty flush of colour touched her cheeks and she kept her eyes demurely fixed on the flowers, before looking up at him with a boldness that struck him in the most delightful way.

'I can think of no bouquet more perfect.'

A servant entered then, and took the flowers from her to put them in a vase. In that moment he was grateful for his choice of floral arrangement and the way it made her shine. Most women of the ton would regard his choice with an upturned nose. But not Miss Rossington. She was as pure and gracious as she was beautiful. A woman who made him long to shower her with gifts and affection.

There was no one quite like her, and he swore that despite his imminent departure he would find some way to put himself in her path once more.

Chapter Three

Rain pattered against the windowpanes, the droplets melting into one another before trickling down in fat wet trails against the glass. Lottie looked outside to the slick cobblestones, wishing she'd heeded her father's warning to bring an umbrella. Or at least take the carriage.

'It's coming down something fierce.' The shopkeeper of Notions, the local haberdashery, narrowed her brown eyes behind her spectacles, looking at the whipping rain. 'If you wait until three, Mr Williams will be about and can see you home.'

A swift glance at the clock on the side table indicated to Lottie that it was only just now half past two. Back home, there was still a button to reattach to Father's favourite jacket, some tidying up to do and dinner to be made.

'Thank you, Mrs Williams,' Lottie said politely. 'But a bit of rain isn't anything I can't handle.'

Mrs Williams withdrew some more paper, this one shiny with wax, and bound it round the length of lace she'd just wrapped. 'I know, you need to be returning to your father. It's a shame he never sought to remarry. You know, the miller's eldest daughter is looking for a husband.'

Lottie accepted the parcel from the woman and thanked her—not for the marital suggestion for her father, a woman two years younger than Lottie, but for putting the lace in a waxed wrap so it wouldn't be soaked by the rain.

'Are you sure you won't wait?' Mrs Williams asked with a slight frown.

'It's truly fine.'

Lottie thanked her for her consideration and slipped out of the shop into the deluge of driving rain. The chill of the downpour was enough to rob her of her breath. To think that morning it had been warm as she'd walked into the heart of the village to purchase some lace for a gown.

She angled her head so that her straw hat kept her from being pelted in the face. Not that it did much good.

All at once a shadow appeared and the rain came to an abrupt end. She looked up to find an umbrella open over her head.

Someone had come to her rescue. Most likely Mr Williams, returned early from his tasks.

'Mr Williams, that is—'

Whatever else she might have said died on her tongue as she turned her head and realised her saviour was not, in fact, Mr Williams at all.

No, this man was taller, but just as familiar.

Lord Murray.

He grinned down at her, his green eyes bright against the dull grey sky. 'Miss Rossington,' He spoke loudly to be heard over the rush of rain, which was now drenching him as he held the umbrella for her. 'Please allow me to drive you home.'

'You're getting all wet,' she exclaimed.

And he was—truly. His auburn hair had gone dark with a thorough soaking.

He indicated the carriage parked only a few feet away. Rather than argue, she allowed him to guide her towards the carriage and scrambled inside with as much decorum as anyone could muster when attempting to flee a deluge. He joined her on the opposite seat and snapped the umbrella closed, keeping it tucked into the corner opposite her. Not that any additional drops from its surface would matter when she was already in such a sorry state.

Her fingers went self-consciously to her hat, which felt to be wilting over her face. Embarrassment scorched her cheeks and made her cast her gaze to where her hands were clasped in her lap.

She had spent a considerable amount of time hoping to see Lord Murray again, wishing that somehow they might once more be drawn together. But as the months had gone by she'd given up, assuming the whole of England was far too large an area for fate to place them in one another's company once more.

Yet now here he was—and she looking no better than a drowned mouse.

'Thank you.' She lifted her focus from the sprigged pattern on her gown to Lord Murray, who openly stared at her.

'By God, Miss Rossington, you are truly the most beautiful woman in the world.' His cheeks coloured with a flush and he gave a self-deprecating laugh. 'Forgive me. I ought to have asked where you should like to go.'

His compliment took her aback, robbing her of all thought. All breath. All everything. She didn't want a destination. No, she wanted to spend the entirety of that rainy afternoon in his company, opposite him in the carriage. Their proximity was such that the clean sandalwood notes of his shaving soap prickled at her awareness.

'I… I was going home,' she replied, offering him the direction, which he relayed to the driver through a small sliding hatch.

The carriage lurched forward as rain popped along the top of the cabin.

'I didn't think I'd ever see you again,' she admitted, studying him now as openly as he had her.

His thick auburn hair, his high cheekbones and regal nose were all the more apparent in the shadowed interior of the carriage. He smiled at her, and her heart did that strange thing where it seemed to stumble over itself.

He was even more handsome than she remembered.

'I was hoping to find you.' He put his elbows to his knees as he leaned closer.

Heaven help her.

'You came here looking for me?' Only when the words were out of her mouth did she realise how foolish she sounded. Of course a baron did not go out of his way to seek out the daughter of a parish vicar.

'If I was a clever man, I'd have done exactly that.' His forefinger reached out and tentatively stroked the damp fabric against her knee. 'But my father has kept me running around England and I haven't had an excuse to come here. Until now.'

That spot went immediately hot. Indeed, the rest of her did too. It was a delicate touch—a brush more than anything. It might have been an accident. But she knew it was not. And that was why it affected her so viscerally.

Especially as she wanted him to do it again.

'I'm here to claim some items from the Duke of Somersville,' he said.

'I believe he is in London now,' she replied. 'And Lord Folton is unreachable, as he is off exploring the world on his Grand Tour.'

'So it would appear.'

There was a hardness to his tone that took her aback. He must have noticed her surprise, as his expression immediately softened.

'Forgive me. There have been some unpleasant issues that have arisen between our families since our fathers' return from their last expedition. It would appear there were some duplicitous dealings.'

Lottie frowned as she tried to puzzle over what the Duke of Somersville might possibly have done. 'I'm sorry to hear it.'

He shook his head. 'It's nothing I wish to lament over— not when I'm in such fine company.'

A pleasant rush of giddiness replaced her concern for the Duke. 'Will you be in Oxfordshire long?' she asked, trying not to sound as hopeful as she felt.

'Now that I've found what I was truly hoping to find, I believe I may stay a little longer than intended.'

This time the understanding that he was indeed referring to her pushed all thoughts of the Earl of Westix and the Duke of Somersville from her mind. Surely it wasn't anything a letter between friends couldn't mend. Not when their fathers had been so close for so long.

The carriage pulled to a stop before the small rectory Lottie shared with her father. It was a lovely cottage, white washed with a thatched roof, and flowers grew beneath the windows, vegetables in a small garden beyond. Trees surrounded it on all sides, lending the home a modicum of privacy.

But, while she enjoyed the cottage, never had she been more disappointed to see it so quickly.

If this carriage ride opposite Lord Murray went on for the whole of her life she would not have cause for complaint.

'I should like to see you again,' Lord Murray said.

She longed to sit on the cushioned bench for ever, speaking to him thus. 'I should like that very much.'

At least there would be tomorrow, or whenever their schedules allowed time to see one another.

The door to the coach opened, revealing the footman, standing in the ceaseless rain. Lottie flashed a shy smile at Lord Murray before quickly exiting the carriage so the poor man would not need to remain in the elements.

Once more the umbrella appeared over her head, and Lord Murray walked alongside her up the narrow footpath.

'When may I see you next?'

The urgency of his question matched her own longing as she scrambled for an answer.

The next day was to be dishearteningly busy. As all her days seemed to be. There was tea with several ladies from her father's parish, as well as preparing soup for those who had recently been struck with a sniffling, sneezing illness that had spread through the village. Then, of course, there was mending and housework and cooking.

The day would be full.

Except…

'I go for a walk every morning,' she said tentatively.

Of course on her walks she was entirely alone. Which would mean they would be alone together. But it was only one walk. Where was the harm in that? If discovered, they could easily say they had happened along the same path.

Lord Murray's smile widened. 'I'll be there.'

'At half past ten.' She spoke quickly as they neared her door. 'I usually follow the stream behind my home.'

'I'll find you.'

They stopped on the footpath, facing one another beneath the protection of the umbrella as the rain continued to drive down, pattering against the waxed fabric. For the briefest of moments the umbrella dipped lower as Lord Murray leaned down and brushed his mouth over hers.

She almost thought she'd imagined it, dreamed it with the extent of her hope, except that when he straightened there was a besotted grin on his lips.

'Tomorrow, my beautiful Miss Rossington,' he said, in a low, intimate voice that made her pulse spike.

'Tomorrow,' she agreed, and slowly backed away, opening the door to her home.

As she closed it behind her she could think of little else but how much the time between now and when she would see him would drag terribly.

Fate had brought them together once more.

Evander met Miss Rossington the following morning, where she waited for him in the dappled sunlight near a swiftly running stream. Her white muslin day dress was demure, with a modest neckline that showed off the graceful litheness of her frame, and her straw hat covered enough of her face to protect her from the sun. Her lovely blue eyes lit up when she saw him and she waved.

There was something about the way she looked at him, with her entire focus fixed on him, that made him realise no woman had ever made him feel as she did. Perhaps that was why he'd found an excuse to come to Oxfordshire and seek out the small village of Binsey.

He'd meant to do it sooner. Truly he had. Except there had been the estate to visit, to ensure all was running well while his father travelled about, and appearances to keep in his father's absence. The Murray name was Evander's legacy and needed to be upheld, no matter the burden to him. And it was one he gladly shouldered.

Besides, he was here now, with Miss Rossington, and wasn't that all that mattered?

The forest was still damp from its thorough soaking the day before, but the clear blue sky overhead promised beautiful weather.

'Good morning, Miss Rossington.' He offered her a bow.

She laughed and caught his hands, drawing him upright. 'Please do call me Lottie. You're far too dear to address me as Miss Rossington.'

'I should like that very much,' he replied earnestly. 'As long as you promise to call me Evander rather than Lord Murray. It's so very stuffy with formality, isn't it?'

'Evander...' She twisted her fingers, a habit of hers recalled from their prior meeting.

'That's better.' He offered her his arm, giving way to the stuffy formalities he'd just disparaged. But this was a way to be closer to her, to breathe in her delicate, powdery floral perfume and let the warmth of their bodies whisper against one another.

'That's what I've always loved about the country.' Lottie said wistfully, her face hidden in profile by her bonnet.

'What do you mean?' he pressed.

The bottom of her gown was damp from the dew on the long grass and small dot of pink showed against the muslin. Something like paint, as before when he'd seen her.

'I love how everything here is much more relaxed.'

She looked up at him, revealing her face once more. Bright blue eyes, fair skin, full red lips. He was struck anew with the force of her beauty.

'Charles always speaks of the rules in London and they sound terribly suffocating,' she continued.

'Indeed, they are,' Evander agreed. 'I would never be allowed to walk with you as we are now. Alone. It would ruin you.'

'I'm glad we're here, then.' She smiled up at him.

'As am I,' he replied.

And indeed he was. Glad that he had found Lottie after far too many months of thinking of her, and that they were now alone, somewhere he might once more sample the sweetness of her sensual mouth.

Though their kiss had been brief the day before, it had not left his mind—the softness of her lips, the heady sweet scent of her, the incredible yearning it awoke within him.

'And how do you find Binsey?' she asked. 'After all the fine places you've been.'

'I can honestly say there is nowhere else I'd rather be.'

'Not even travelling around the world like your father?'

He shook his head. 'I've never had the desire for a Grand Tour. Not when there are so many things to see to in England. I believe I shall leave the rest of the world to him and enjoy my time here in Binsey. Tell me, what is it that occupies your days here?'

Colour warmed her cheeks beneath her bonnet. 'It's a far simpler life than what you've told me of life in London. I care for my father and see to his parishioners, whom I take tea with and help care for should they be in need of anything.'

'I doubt it's as simple as you claim.'

'Well, there are the gossips to contend with.' She gave him an exasperated look. 'You would be surprised how much havoc bored women can wreak.'

'Oh, I understand entirely, as there are far too many bored women in London.' Evander grimaced, thinking of how the ton could destroy a reputation with a string of well-placed gossip. 'What do you do for yourself? For pleasure?'

She gave a self-deprecating laugh and put a hand to her face, obscuring it. 'I'm afraid my life here is rather dull.'

In truth, he was surprised at such a response. He'd assumed a woman of her wit and charm would have droves of friends to meet up with, for sewing circles and ribbon curling, or whatever it was that ladies did with one another.

'But you paint,' he said, by way of encouragement. He'd gone on about London and Scotland for an age at the ball all those months ago. He wanted to learn more about her.

Lottie blinked. 'How did you—?' Her gaze caught on the slight pink stain on her skirt and her eyes widened. 'Oh, I didn't realise...' Her entire face went as pink as the small stain. 'Yes, I… I am apparently a very clumsy painter. Just watercolours.' She lifted her shoulders and shook her head. 'It is nothing terribly exciting.'

'I think it sounds fascinating,' he replied. 'What did you last paint?'

She paused and bit her lip. 'A sunrise,' she replied at last. 'I woke one morning before the sun had fully risen and found the sky stained with the most brilliant colours. A blaze of red-orange at the centre and mixes of purple and pink, with gold tones colouring blue-bellied clouds. The trees were but shadows in the foreground, as though giving way to the splendour.'

Her gaze fixed on the clouds now, as though she was seeing what she described. Evander certainly was, in his mind's eye. In the discussion of her painting, he'd found a passion awoken. She might downplay her pastime, but it was of great import to her.

They neared the place where he had met her—where they would soon part ways.

'I should love to see your paintings sometime,' he said.

She blinked her eyes open and twisted her fingers against one another. 'You would?'

'Yes, of course.' Before he could stop himself, he reached for her flushed cheek. 'I want to know everything about you.'

Her lashes fluttered downward as his fingers gently caressed the softness of her skin. They were close enough for him to recall the sweetness of her mouth, the headiness of that moment of their first kiss. He shouldn't, he knew. Not when they could be happened upon by those gossips she had mentioned.

Except that as he began to pull away she lifted her chin and rose up on her toes to press her smooth lips to his.

He closed his eyes and met her with a chaste kiss that set his heart pounding. After all, he hadn't kissed her. She had kissed him. His mouth captured hers, guiding her towards a deeper kiss, a delicate brush of their tongues that made her gasp and left him aching and hard.

It was then he knew the kiss must end.

'I wish to see you again,' he said.

Her brow furrowed. 'I'm afraid I stay rather busy.'

She looked at the ground, and for a fraction of a moment Evander feared she might tell him she could never see him again. The thought of being deprived of her brilliance would be a devastating blow.

'But I walk this path every day.' She lowered her lashes and turned her head away, hiding her face behind the delicate wall of her straw hat.

He put his fingertips under her chin and lightly brought her face, and her attention, back towards him. 'Then I shall meet you every day so that we might walk together. If you will allow me to, of course.'

Her eyes searched his and he fell headlong into the endless blue. 'I would love nothing more.'

Before he could stop himself, he kissed her once more, eager and swift, before bowing his departure and promptly exiting, lest he never leave. It was far too easy to bask in the company of Miss Lottie Rossington.

He met her again the following day, and the day after that, and the one following that. On and on he met her until three weeks had gone by.

In that time, he learned a lot about Lottie. Like how she and Lord Folton had become so close, how he'd been there to comfort her when her mother died. Admittedly the platonic way Folton cared for her made Evander find the other man less distasteful, despite his father the Duke of Somersville's selfishness against Evander's own father.

And Evander finally got to see her paintings—a blend of drawing and watercolour paints—after much encouragement. She had downplayed her skill considerably. Every painting she showed him was lifelike—as though it had been taken from reality and imprinted directly onto the page.

Evander shared details about his own childhood as well—how he and his sister had been close, until their father had struck her and Evander had stepped up to put a stop to it. He'd been promptly sent away to school, and when he returned, he found the occupants of the house cold and reserved in their reception of him, including his sister Eleanor.

He'd never spoken of it to anyone before that day, but somehow confessing it all to Lottie on one of those sunny mornings when they walked along the stream was so easy to do. There, amid the overgrown grass and wildflowers, he shared his heart. And she accepted him for exactly who he was.

That was why he fell in love with her. Or rather one of the many reasons why he did. She sparkled more greatly than any enticement London had to offer. Her wit made him laugh, and anything that made her solemn tugged at a tender place he hadn't known existed within his heart.

He had become so enamoured of her he had postponed the meeting with his father's steward to go over his report on the estates—something Evander had never once done since he assumed the task after completing his time at university.

She was beauty and kindness, altruism and grace, wit and sensuality—on and on the list went, with every reason why she was so remarkable.

He realised one morning, when he was bidding her farewell, that their small kiss had blossomed into something deeper, more intimate. She gave that delicious little hum in the back of her throat, as she always did, and held tight to him as their mouths parted to stroke tongues. Evander's body was on fire with longing, but it was more than that, something far purer than simple carnal lust.

He didn't want to leave Binsey. He didn't want to leave her. The world that had meant so much to him only a month ago paled in comparison to the resplendent joy of her company. He wanted a lifetime of her.

The realisation dawned on him in a moment, and he did not shy from what had been unearthed in his own heart.

Love.

He straightened with the intent to tell her. She pulled him back towards her with a little whimper of protest and arched into him.

'Lottie,' he said raggedly.

Her eyes flew open. 'Forgive me. I didn't want you to stop kissing me. I wanted—I want—so much more.' She flushed shyly and looked away. 'Do you think that's terribly wicked?'

'Nothing about you is wicked.'

Truer words had never been said. No innocence rivalled that of Miss Charlotte Rossington.

He longed to draw her towards him, to tug off her bonnet and smooth his hands down her glossy hair in reassurance. And in the same moment, he had the nearly overwhelming urge to show her exactly what 'wicked' entailed.

'Even if I like your kisses?'

She licked her lips, the gesture unintentionally erotic.

'Even if I find myself imagining what more there is between a man and a woman.'

His groin twitched in reply. He shifted his stance lest she see exactly what she did to him.

'Especially all that.' He hesitated only a moment before speaking the words that had been in his heart since he'd first spotted her that first rainy day when he'd come to Oxfordshire. 'I mean to make you my baroness, Lottie.'

Her eyes went wide. 'You...want to...?'

'I want to marry you,' he said, with all the vehemence of young love. 'I will see your father to ask formally, of course. That is...if you want to marry me.' The sense of confidence which had guided him down this path faltered. 'Do you?'

Lottie smiled up at him. 'Of course I do.'

Her reply, while positive, was not as exuberant as he'd hoped and cast doubt on his joy. 'Are you certain? I would never wish you to agree without your full heart.'

'You have my full heart.' She took his hand and pressed it to the centre of her chest.

Except that it wasn't her heartbeat he felt beneath his palm, but the round plumpness of her breasts. It was all he could do to keep from shifting his touch upon her to cup them, caress them, until that little hum at the back of her throat gave way to a moan.

'It's only that I don't wish to leave my father.'

She released Evander's hand and he withdrew it from her bosom with great reluctance.

'I'm all he has.'

'I will be purchasing the Huntly Estate, where I've been staying,' he replied, grateful he'd already spoken to Lord Enders about the possibility the prior week. 'He is a good friend, and knows I have a strong reason to remain in Oxfordshire.'

Before he could say another word Lottie gave a cry of joy and threw her arms around him. She kissed him again and again and again, until his head swam.

'I am so eager to wed you.' She nuzzled her lips against his neck, just below his ear. 'To walk proudly on your arm, to share my life with you. To experience all the things that exist between a man and his wife...'

Good God.

'I shall speak with your father tomorrow morning,' he said, in a low, intimate voice.

And that was exactly what he did—as soon as it was appropriate for the vicar to receive a caller with the intent to formally request her hand, so that Miss Charlotte Rossington could become his wife.

Chapter Four

Never had Lottie's home felt so achingly small. She paced the drawing room like the caged lion she'd once seen at a travelling fair.

Another peek out through the doorway revealed that the hall remained empty. Not that she wouldn't have heard the door to her father's study open. She strained for every sound she could make out. While she could detect the baritone of two male voices, they were far too muffled to decipher what was being said.

Surely her father would allow Evander to wed her. Why would he not? And yet they had been in the study for a considerable amount of time.

She huffed out a sigh and stared at the blank page before her, the intended watercolour image locked within her brain, held captive by the many thoughts flying about within.

A door swung open, followed by the heavy thud of Hessians over the glossy wood floors.

Lottie's breath caught. They were finally done.

She rushed to stand in the doorway and caught sight of Evander. He wore a splendid suit, cut and tailored to frame his lean, strong body to perfection. Simply looking at him made her yearn to press her palms to his powerful chest.

Soon.

Soon they would be wed, and they would seal their adoration with the intimacy meant to exist between a married couple. The ache between her thighs pulsed with anticipation. She shouldn't long for such things, she knew, and yet she could not stop herself from wanting that part of him any more than she could stop her heart from loving him.

Evander drew closer, leading the way before her father. Except it was not a joyous expression on his face as his eyes met hers.

Confusion gripped her.

His brow was furrowed, his mouth pressed in a hard line. He appeared...angry? Disappointed?

He discreetly shook his head at her.

No.

No?

Lottie remained rooted in place. Had her father rejected Evander's request for her hand in marriage?

'Lottie, please go to my study,' her father said in a stern tone. 'I'll speak with you once I've shown Lord Murray out.'

She studied Evander one final time, noting the way he stared after her as though he thought never to see her again, and a tender place within her chest split open. The pain of it was excruciating. She clutched her heart, though it did little to soothe the agony, and rushed to the study to collect herself before her father's return.

Her efforts were in vain. By the time her father joined her fat tears had left spatters on the white muslin of her lap.

He rubbed a hand over his thick hair, still dark despite the occasional threads of silver. 'Come now, Lottie,' he said in a soothing tone as a handkerchief appeared in front of her.

She sniffled miserably and accepted the piece of linen. 'I love him.'

'How do you even know him?'

'I met him at a ball when I was in Bedfordshire. And we…' She winced at her next confession. 'We have been walking every morning together.'

He father's brows lifted incredulously. 'You've been sneaking—'

'No,' she rushed in. 'At least we didn't mean to. The only time I could spare to see him was in the morning, on my walks. I didn't… It wasn't meant to be duplicitous. It was entirely innocent.'

Or mostly, at least. Aside from those kisses that had scorched themselves on her mind.

'And you think this means you know him?' Her father had never spoken so sternly to her.

'I do,' she said with finality. 'And I love him.'

'Love.' Her father's kind brown eyes filled with sadness. 'You have known the gentleman for, what? A month?'

Heat scorched her cheeks. 'Three weeks. But it's been enough—'

'You don't know what love is.'

There was a hardness to his tone that snipped away the end of her argument. She couldn't stop the tears from welling in her eyes. Astonishment left her mute—that this man, who had always been so tender and considerate, this man who listened so patiently to others problems, should be so resolute now. When her heart was pinioned by his decision.

Her father looked around the small study, lined with shelves of well-handled books. The room was careworn by his constant work, and spotless through Lottie's housekeeping efforts. But even its familiarity brought no comfort to her now.

He splayed his hand on the surface of his desk. 'I told him my answer is no.'

A sob erupted from her. 'How could you?'

'I'm saving you, Lottie.'

'Saving me?' she cried.

Her father moved away from the desk and crouched before her, so he was at eye level with her, the way he'd done when she was a girl. The way he did with parishioners who were in need of counsel.

'He was going to buy Huntly Manor so we could be near you.' Her voice had taken on a pleading tone, but she didn't care. She would get on her knees and beg her father if she had to. 'Because he knew I didn't want to move away from Binsey. From you.'

'You don't understand how these men of the ton behave.' Her father frowned with more displeasure than she'd ever seen him react with.

'They do not care for innocent girls the way a man ought to. They act on their own whims, do what suits them. He may love you now, but likely will not in the future. These men are spoiled. Fickle. If you marry him, you will be headed for heartbreak.'

Lottie was crying openly now, unable to hold back the flood of tears. 'My heart is already broken,' she said raggedly, between gasps of breath.

'Better now than when you have truly fallen in love.' He took her hand in his and gently patted it in consolation.

'He isn't like those men,' Lottie said, in an attempt to sway her father.

'Every man of the ton is.'

Something bitter glinted in her father's gaze. Who was this man who was so full of spite and anger? Wasn't he the one who always told her to give everyone a chance? To allow them to show their character before drawing conclusions based on a short association? And now he was slotting every titled man into a prejudged category. Including Evander.

'Lottie, I forbid you from seeing him.' Her father straight-

ened and stood upright. His right knee popped in protest.
'I've likewise informed him to stay away from you.'

'No, Father—'

'I forbid it,' he roared.

Lottie froze at the foreign sound. Never in all her life
had her father raised his voice to her, let alone shouted as
he did now.

His brow wrinkled as if he were in pain. Or perhaps
he'd realised what he'd done.

'Please go to your room,' he said in a softer tone. 'This
discussion is over and will not be revisited.'

Lottie pushed herself up from the chair and ran from the
study, not stopping until she was face-down on her mattress, letting her heart shatter into a million tears.

Evander waited in the woods the following morning,
with a small wooden box in the palm of his hand. The
Reverend Rossington would most certainly not approve
of Evander's plan. But it wasn't Reverend Rossington's
agreement he needed now. It was Lottie's.

If she would see him.

An ache squeezed in his chest and made it difficult to
draw breath.

What if she refused to see him and he never had her in
his life again?

The thought was too horrible even to imagine. Not when
they had grown so close…when she had so thoroughly
rooted herself into his very soul.

In the time Evander had come to know her, he had
found her to be the quintessential obedient daughter. She
did not speak her mind unless there was something positive of note to say, she sacrificed the entirety of her life
to the betterment of others, and she worried often about
what people might think of her—far more than she should,

in Evander's opinion. And she obeyed her father without question.

Would she see Evander now? Or would she send him away?

A shadow stretched over the bend in the path at the exact time it always did and his pulse rushed in his ears.

Lottie.

He stepped from the trees and remained where he stood, waiting for her to see him, holding his breath to ascertain her reaction. If she seemed disagreeable, he would do as her father demanded and leave Oxfordshire, never to return. Though, dear God, it would be like cutting out his own warm, beating heart to do so.

However, if—

She gave a little scream and clamped a hand over her mouth. Before he could gauge if that was a good thing or bad, she ran at him. The bonnet flew from her head and the hem of her muslin gown kicked out around her white-stockinged calves.

His emotions soared higher than they'd ever gone before. He met her halfway and she threw herself into his arms and clung to him. She was heaven in his arms, her familiar scent a perfume more intoxicating than the finest wine. This woman who had almost been snatched from his life for ever was now in his arms. He held her to him in an effort to confirm she was indeed real, that this was not some apparition of hope.

'I thought never to see you again,' she whispered against his chest.

'And I you,' he said into her cool, smooth hair. He breathed in her fresh, delicately floral scent and longing slammed into him, powerful and potent.

'There is a way we can be together,' he said urgently.

'Come this way, so we won't be seen.' She grasped his hand and pulled him towards the trees as she scanned the area around them. 'If someone had happened upon us before our meeting could have been easily explained. But now...'

Now their meeting would be seen as what it was—a direct defiance of her father's wishes. And she had done that for Evander.

They disappeared into the woods, the sun overhead blotted out by the thick canopy of leaves and the scent of damp earth lingering in the cool air around them.

He reached for her, drawing her close to him. Her eyes were red-rimmed and swollen, as though she had been crying for the better part of the night.

'Lottie, your father does not approve of our union,' Evander said.

'I know.' Her eyes became glossy with welling tears. 'But I... Evander, I can't imagine my life without you. It's like trying to imagine living without one's heart beating.'

Her admission echoed deep in his own soul. She understood. *She felt the same way.*

'You don't have to be without me,' Evander said.

She searched his face, anxiety evident in her tensed brows. 'What do you mean?'

'We could run away together.'

She sucked in a breath and took half a step back.

He caught her hand and gently pulled her towards him once more. 'I will purchase Huntly Manor, as I said, and we will reside there once we return from a swift jaunt to Scotland.'

'Scotland,' she repeated slowly.

'Gretna Green.' He whispered the words as the scandal they were. Everyone knew the relaxed laws of Scotland made for swift marriages—most especially those unions with which the parents were not in agreement. 'Comlongon Castle is nearby. We can stay there several days before returning.'

Her slender fingers twisted together, and he could see the uncertainty within her.

'Your father loves you,' Evander said. 'He'll forgive you and we'll be here when he does—at Huntly Manor.'

'That's brilliant.'

A smile blossomed on her face and he knew she'd made her decision. She nodded. That was the moment he had been waiting for. He withdrew the wooden box from his pocket and knelt in the layer of leaves which crackled beneath his weight.

'Marry me, Lottie.'

He opened the wooden box. The ring within was small, a poor declaration of the enormity of his love. But in an area such as Oxfordshire there were few esteemed jewellers to be had.

'Say yes and we will make plans to run away tomorrow morning.' He indicated the ring sheepishly. 'And I will obtain a proper ring for you when we are next in London.'

She put her hands over her face and squealed with joy. 'I love it exactly as it is.'

She plucked the gold band with its chip of a diamond from the satin lining and slid it onto her finger, admiring it before beaming up at him.

He grinned, his heart near bursting from its confines. 'Is that a yes?'

She nodded, fresh tears welling in her eyes. 'Yes.'

He laughed with his joy as he got to his feet and opened his arms to her. She leapt into them, knocking them both backwards. He wrapped her in his embrace as they tumbled to the soft forest floor, their mouths finding one another's as they kissed first in joy and then in passion.

Desire took over as he gently eased them over, so he lay atop her, his forearms bracing his weight over her body as their mouths and tongues caressed and teased. His body raged with a need his fist could no longer slake.

But not until they were wed. It would be only days before they were true husband and wife. He would do this properly.

Before he could push himself off her she parted her legs beneath him, cradling him against her centre and arching up towards him so their pelvises fitted together. There was no hiding the force of his arousal with such intimate closeness. Though layers of clothing separated them, her eyes widened with surprised delight.

'Lottie, I should go.' He pushed away from her and got to his knees.

She remained where she lay, beneath him, leaves clinging to her dark hair as she shook her head. 'No, please.' She reached for him, drawing him back down to her. 'I almost lost you yesterday. I thought you gone this morning. I *need* you.'

He resisted, but only slightly, understanding exactly what she meant, understanding that overwhelming desire to claim what had nearly slipped through her fingers. The matched need within him was so strong his body trembled with the force of it.

'Please.' She gazed up at him, her brilliant blue eyes heavy-lidded with desire. Her breasts pushed up as she lay on the ground, the soft, round tops visible above her neckline.

He had a decision to make in that moment—one that would either seal their fates in body and spirit, before they could do so in law, or give them the more prudent option of walking away, waiting.

He knew what he wanted. And, oh, God, how he wanted it. More so than anything else he'd ever wished for in his life.

Yet still he hesitated.

'We'll be wed soon.' Despite his protest, he did not get to his feet.

'We will.'

The hem of her gown had ridden up to reveal shapely calves in pristine white stockings and she watched him with open desire. But more than all that, it was what she said next which finally broke his tenuous hold on his control.

'I love you, Evander.'

Those beautiful words were offered so softly and with such earnestness that it dragged him straight back to her.

'Lottie.' He leaned over her. 'I love you.'

She smiled up at him and cradled his cheek in one slender palm. He leaned over her once more and claimed her mouth, his body on fire with the need to express physically the words he'd just said. For theirs was a love no other could possibly understand, a love greater than any to have existed before. And their bodies cried out in equal measure to their hearts, longing for the power of such feelings to be properly expressed.

Chapter Five

Lottie could not cease her kisses with Evander. Each one proof that he was still with her, that he had not gone, that he would be her husband. Her *husband*.

Mere minutes before, she thought never to see him again, never to hear the timbre of his voice, to relish his vivid stories, witness how his eyes sparkled when they caught hers. Now he was here with her, all of him consuming all of her in the most glorious fashion, a testament to the incredible love glowing between them.

His weight was comfortable against her. More than comfortable, it was titillating. It brought a closeness unlike any other, and proof of his affection for her rose hard and insistent through layers of cloth, where it nudged against her most intimate place.

She had always been a good girl, doing all she was told, never veering from the demanding constraints that framed the life of a vicar's daughter. Now she gave herself permission to tear through those constraints, granted by the weight of that simple, elegant ring now encircling her finger.

She was to be Evander's wife.

She kissed him, open-mouthed and bold with the stroke of her tongue. His hands moved from her face down the column of her throat and his lips followed, leaving a trail of sensual heat. He cupped her breast in his hand and his fingers found her nipple through her stays.

Pleasure prickled from his ministrations at her bosom and tingled through her whole body. Before she could acknowledge what she was doing, her hips were rocking against Evander's weight, nudging his hardness against her soft centre. The action built up a delicious friction that made her yearn to be closer still.

'By God, you're the most beautiful woman in all the world,' Evander murmured against her neck. 'I love you, Lottie.'

He took her earlobe gently between his teeth as he began to move with her, in a careful flexing rhythm that made him pant in her ear. There was something erotic about being close enough to him that his heavy exhalations sounded in her ear, his face nuzzled against her sensitive skin.

One of Evander's hands shifted to her hip as they began to undulate in earnest. The column of his desire ground into her and made the hot ache between her thighs almost unbearable.

She needed this. Him. Them together for ever.

Each time she elicited more than a breathy exhalation Evander put his mouth over hers in a kiss meant to muffle the sounds of her excitement.

The brush of his fingertips swept up her calf to just above her knee, where her garters were tied. His caress met her naked thigh and then stopped, hesitating.

Disappointment crashed down on Lottie. They had come too far to stop now. She wanted this man who would be her husband in every way.

She put her hand over his and met his gaze. 'Make me your wife in body.'

'God, Lottie.'

He said nothing else as his fingers slowly inched up the hem of her white muslin gown until it tipped over her knees and fell against her upper thighs. His fingertips brushed over the juncture between her legs. She gasped in surprise at the exquisite rush of pleasure, and Evander's mouth closed over hers as everything around her faded away, her focus fixed on that glorious sensation.

The way he teased her most intimate area elicited cries and moans she could not stifle, sounds that melted between their lips. A strange tightness wound through her body, as if she was on the cusp of exploding.

Evander drew his hand away and worked at his falls, hasty as he unbuttoned the placket of his trousers. She did not see him as he freed his manhood, but she felt its hot, fevered weight as it rested against her sex.

'Are you certain?' he gasped.

Lottie looked into his face. His eyes were bright with desire, his cheeks flushed with a need that matched her own. 'I love you, Evander. I will always love you.'

A muscle worked in his jaw. 'God, I love you. More than I ever knew possible.'

He shifted over her and their gazes locked on one another as he slowly pressed the hardness of his longing against her entrance. His movements were careful and slow as he pushed in and withdrew, edging further into her each time.

Sweat shone on his brow, evidence of his restraint that was echoed in his trembling body. 'I think this may hurt.' He grimaced.

Lottie opened her mouth to ask what he meant when he clasped her hand in his and thrust into her. A sharp pinch cut through the haze of her pleasure and made tears sting her eyes.

He kissed her then, tenderly and with all the affection she'd ever dreamed of. And it was through the immense love between them that the discomfort began to ebb and something far, far more enjoyable took its place.

Their bodies were perfectly fitted together, locked as close as was possible, unified by love. The heat of desire warmed through her and rippled outward, so she was soon hot and panting once more: Evander flexed his hips into her as their pelvises met again and again.

That tightening sensation was back. Too much to bear this time. It squeezed at her awareness until she was trapped by the pressure. When she thought she could stand it no longer, whatever it was snapped, and the most glorious waves of pleasure washed over her in time with Evander's thrusts.

His pace increased into hard jerks until he stopped suddenly, thrusting deep into her. He gritted his teeth around a groan and his hardness twitched with the same uncontrolled spasm her sex had made during the peak of her release.

They remained where they were for a long moment, savouring their union, basking in the glow of their love, dragging out the last vestiges of bliss from their coupling before he lowered himself over her on his forearms and pressed his brow to hers. Together, their ragged breaths and racing hearts began to even out. The heat between their bodies cooled to a languid warmth and Lottie was struck with the longing to curl her body against his and sleep.

'I didn't hurt you too badly, did I, my love?' Evander lifted his head to regard her.

She shook her head. 'It was incredible.'

'I love you, Lottie Rossington, with all my heart.' He smiled down at her. 'Soon to be Lottie Murray, my baroness.'

If he said those words to her a thousand times a day she would never grow tired of them. 'I would listen to you tell me you love me for a lifetime.'

'I'm happy to hear it, for I plan to tell you every day from here on forward.' He nuzzled his nose against hers and then his mouth brushed hers. 'Ready your things, my darling. Tomorrow we will leave at dawn for Scotland, to become husband and wife.'

'I'll be ready,' she promised.

Giddiness tickled through her veins. Tomorrow they would be well on their way to being man and wife. Their joy today a precursor for their happy life together.

And her father would forgive them.

Wouldn't he?

A shiver of trepidation eased its way down her spine. It was followed by the first whisper of unease in the back of her mind, but she quickly hushed it. With a love such as theirs, nothing could ever go wrong.

Happiness was a ray of sunshine that did not often cast its warmth over Evander. Now the whole of him practically shone with it.

He left Lottie with the ring on her finger and the promise to return the following day. There would be much for him to prepare before their departure. A horse and carriage would need to be arranged, as he could not in good conscience take Lord Ender's.

And while he was on the topic of Lord Ender, he would need to write to his old chum and settle on a price for the manor in Oxfordshire. Evander had been sincere in his promise to ensure Lottie would always live near her father. A similar note would need to be sent to his father's solicitor, to procure the necessary funds for purchase.

Evander's steps were light as he made his way the long distance to Huntly Manor—a journey he gladly took every day for the purpose of seeing Lottie. Indeed, he was nearly buoyant as he made his way up the long flight of steps to the exquisite home.

The butler opened the door before he could even reach for the handle. The man's mouth was turned down. More so than normal, and he had a propensity to be the dour sort.

'My lord, you received an express just after your departure.' He offered a heavy envelope to Evander, with a thick, red wax seal at its centre. 'I was informed to advise you of its urgency.'

Evander accepted the envelope with a nod of thanks, and waited for the butler to depart before breaking the seal and unfolding the letter.

It contained only two lines, written in his mother's elegant, looping script.

You must return to London immediately. Your father is dead.

Chapter Six

Evander returned to London with the expediency his mother had requested. Though he'd wanted to see Lottie prior to his departure, his conversation with her father the day before left him with little choice but to write her a quick letter, to be delivered while he was en route to Westix Place.

The grand townhouse in London was silent upon his arrival, and his mother and sister were both as dry-eyed as he. There had been little love between the Earl of Westix and his family, any sense of affection discarded before it could ever begin to take root.

And so it was that Evander embraced first his mother, whose bland expression indicated no true sense of mourning, despite the severity of her black gown. Next came his sister, Eleanor, who had that quiet, tucked-in look she had acquired in his time away at school. Never again had she been the laughing, playful girl he had spent hours running wild with through the Scottish countryside.

He'd been tempted in the past to attempt reparation, and now wished once again that he could do so. But it was not the time. Not when their father's estate had to be seen to. Not when Evander would have to fill the Earldom and ensure his sister and mother were well cared for.

He had been tempted to tell them of his intention to wed Lottie, but the oppressive silence in the house would sully such happy news. And so it was that he resolved to tell them once his father had been buried.

Through it all, at the forefront of his mind, was Lottie and the way she'd looked at him when she'd said she loved him, with her entire heart open and pure and loving. Recollections of the pleasure they'd shared rose in his thoughts and the cries of her pleasure echoed in his ears.

How must she have looked when she'd received the news of his hasty return to London?

He grimaced even to consider it.

His father's funeral was a solemn affair, with barely anyone in attendance—only him and the estate's solicitor, Mr Edsby. Whatever wedge had been driven between his father and the Duke of Somersville, along with the other members of the adventure club, must have been deep, as noted by their poignant absence.

Evander had difficulty summoning up sorrow for his father's passing. The man had been irascible, short-tempered and cold. There had been nothing about him to endear him towards his children. Not after he'd punished Eleanor. Guilt inhabited the place in Evander's chest that sorrow usually occupied upon the passing of close family—an emptiness that he could not fill with a genuine feeling of loss.

Mr Edsby wasted no time encouraging a discussion with him in the study at Westix Place following his father's funeral.

The solicitor, who had overseen the legal affairs of the Westix estate for years, sank into the large armchair in front of the desk and pulled out several sheets of paper from his glossy leather briefcase. 'Would you like a drink before we begin?'

Evander shook his head, realising it would be best to discuss numbers with a clear head.

Mr Edsby considered the stack of papers and lightly touched them with his fingertips, his expression one of obvious discomfort. 'It would perhaps behove you, my lord, to have a bit of brandy in you for this discussion.'

'Very well.' Evander went to the small table which held his father's best liquor and splashed some into a glass. 'Would you like one?'

'Please,' Mr Edsby answered without hesitation.

Evander poured one for him as well, and returned to the desk, both glasses in hand. He offered one to the solicitor, who drained the drink in one swig.

Apprehension tightened in Evander's gut.

'Come, now,' Evander said with forced lightness. 'It can't be all that bad.'

Mr Edsby closed eyelids withered with age behind his spectacles. He gave a long exhale and opened his eyes once more. 'Forgive me, my lord, but it can.'

Worry squeezed at the back of Evander's neck. Were there perhaps some issues with the estate in Scotland? Or with the manor in Southampton ?

'Out with it, man,' Evander prompted. 'You cannot leave me in suspense.'

Mr Edsby's thin chest puffed out with a great breath. 'You've almost nothing left.'

Evander blinked, certain he had heard the old man incorrectly. 'I beg your pardon?'

'Your father had a great many debts,' Mr Edsby began. 'Your steward, as you know, simply provided your father with funds when they were requested. I am not certain the late Earl was aware of the plight into which he had plunged his family.'

A great many debts?

Evander tilted his glass to his lips and drained the brandy as the solicitor had done. It did nothing to ease the tension in his chest. He'd had many dealings with his father's steward in overseeing their land. Never once had he mentioned dwindling wealth.

A sudden thought prickled through Evander like crackling ice. If there were no funds remaining to pay his father's debts, he could not afford to purchase Huntly Manor. He could not make good on his promises to Lottie.

She deserved better than this. She deserved to be mistress of a grand estate while draped in the most fashionable gowns, visiting the finest establishments London had to offer and seeing an opera every damn night if she chose to do so.

That was what Evander had intended to give her. Now he could offer nothing but debt and a future of ruin.

Rage filled him all at once, for the father who had shirked his responsibility towards them for years in favour of his damnable adventure club, traipsing around the bloody world for trinkets while they all grew colder and more distant at his behest. And now this—to be left with nothing but the Westix title, which would, at best, give them only a few more months of living on credit.

Suddenly his father's recent obsession with a missing ruby made sense. The Coeur de Feu was doubtless worth a fortune—one that might recompense their own, which had been so frivolously spent.

'Bollocks he was unaware,' Evander muttered.

'I beg your pardon, my lord?' Mr Edsby lifted his brows.

Evander shook his head, putting aside the bitter remark. 'I need to think. Surely there is something that can be done?'

'If I may be so bold, my lord…?' Mr Edsby let the suggestion hang in the air, waiting for permission.

Evander regarded the solicitor with desperation. 'By all means.'

'You are still in possession of *The Adventurer*—the vessel the former Earl used in his travels. I am also aware he took considerable notes on his journeys.'

Mr Edsby turned in his chair to regard the shelves filled with his father's journals, all stamped with that ridiculous adventure club compass.

'I will not waste what little we have left and push my family into further ruin by leaving them to travel around the world myself.'

Evander took the other man's glass from where it had been set on the edge of the desk and marched across to refill them both. If ever there was a call for a considerable amount of brandy, it was in this moment.

'You misunderstand me,' Mr Edsby said. 'Your father went for fame.' He accepted the glass with a grateful smile upon Evander's return. 'Fortune is far easier to come by across the ocean.' His forehead wrinkled. 'If you went with that purpose in mind, I believe you would find yourself quite a wealthy man once more.'

'What of my mother and sister?'

'Ah, now that matter is in good order.' The solicitor set aside his drink to rifle through a stack of papers. Finding the one he needed, he plucked it from the pile and regarded it through the lenses of his spectacles. 'Lady Westix had a trust set up in her name after she married your father. It has sufficient funds to cover her expenses for at least five years—six if she is frugal.'

His mother was not frugal. Nor was Eleanor. Five, then. Maybe even four.

Could Evander truly find a way to make a fortune through his father's compendium of travel notes?

He reconsidered the notebooks with renewed interest.

Two days later, he had his answer. Based on his father's reporting, and that of his fellow club members, who had all marked various locations throughout the journals, finding opportunities to make money abroad was not difficult. By Evander's estimation it would take approximately six months. At most a year.

After explaining circumstances to his mother, he received her blessing. Both of them agreed to keep the matter from Eleanor, who would hopefully remain oblivious until his return.

Now he need only tell Lottie of the delay that would keep them from being together for a little while longer. Surely once she realised fortune would be at the end of the long wait, and she would be a wealthy countess, she would understand.

The days Lottie spent without Evander seemed to drag on for the span of a lifetime.

She continued her walks at the usual time every day, in the hope he would eventually join her.

The bend she rounded reminded her most of him. It was where he would wait for her in those weeks they had walked together and fallen in love. And near the place where they had given themselves to one another in body as they had in soul.

It made her breath quicken to think of it—how he'd touched her, how their bodies had joined so completely, creating sensations of love unlike anything she had ever dreamed possible.

Nearly a fortnight of walking around that notable corner of the trail had passed before she encountered a wonderfully familiar sight. A tall gentleman with auburn hair and a lean, muscular frame.

She cried out when she saw him, and raced the short distance into his arms. He wrapped her in his strong embrace, filling her with sensual notes of sandalwood that brought a swell of such joy and affection it seemed as though her heart would burst.

It was only when he had held her for a long time that she remembered to put aside her elation at seeing him out of respect for his father's death. She had wept for Evander when she'd read his missive about the Earl of Westix's sudden death. She couldn't imagine what life would be without her own father, who had always been such a pillar of support. Without him, she would be lost.

When Evander finally released her she looked up him, unable to ignore the lines of fatigue and stress showing on his face. Her chest ached with empathy.

'I'm so sorry,' she said gently.

One might think she would be adept at consoling the bereaved, being a vicar's daughter. But she never knew exactly how to respond—for was there truly any one thing that could be said to ease the enormity of such loss?

She wished she could have been in London with Evander, to offer comfort. But at least he was here now, where she could help him heal.

Rather than offer dull platitudes, she folded her hands around his, as if she could cradle away his hurt.

He seemed to understand what she meant by the gesture and gave her a sad smile. Her brave, wonderful Evander.

'Lottie...'

His gaze settled on the ring on her finger—the ring she only dared wear on these walks, when she might see him. Otherwise she left it on a chain that hung beneath her gown and rested against her heart.

He ran his thumb over the winking diamond and sighed. 'I have to postpone our marriage.'

Her head snapped up and she regarded him with shock. These were not the words she was expecting to hear.

'What is it?' She tried to stuff down the welling panic inside her, the fear that he might be slipping away. The fear that all the happiness she'd amassed in the time she'd known him was simply ephemeral, to be whisked away on the first hard breeze. Surely their love was made of stronger stuff than that.

He swallowed and looked away.

Her heart clawed up into her throat. Something was horribly wrong. 'Tell me, my love.'

'My darling, it appears my father has spent all of our fortune,' Evander replied at long last. 'I'm, as it were, quite poor.'

Lottie frowned, uncertain what that had to do with postponing their elopement. 'That doesn't matter. I've never had wealth. Being with you was never about improving my station. I want to be your wife out of love.'

'And what kind of husband would I be to offer you nothing but debt in return?'

The tears blazing in his eyes told her how very much that fortune meant to him—how much a pauper's life for his new bride would not do. She was nearly ready to protest again that it didn't matter, when she realised he was also no doubt concerned for the welfare of his family.

'Your mother and sister?'

He shook his head. 'My mother has a trust that will see to them both for some time.'

His gaze travelled around the sunny path, taking in the cheerful little stream, the thick forest where he'd laid her in the crackling leaves and claimed her with his love.

Her gown had been stained from the grass and dirt beneath them that day, but she hadn't cared. It had been a worthy sacrifice for what they had shared then. What was still strong between them now.

'I would be just as happy living in a cottage with you,' she said. 'Perhaps happier, if I'm being entirely honest.'

'I promised you Huntly Manor so that you would be near your father.' He ran a hand through his rich auburn hair. 'I cannot afford it now. I refuse to wed you into a sinking earldom.' He regarded her earnestly. 'It should not take long. Perhaps six months. A year at the most.'

Lottie grasped his hand and held onto it as if she might physically keep him there with her. 'Please don't do this. Don't go.' He had only recently come back into her life. The thought of him gone once more was a visceral ache within her. 'Please don't leave me.'

'I have to.'

He stroked her face with his hand, a tender caress she felt in her soul. 'I promise I will be back as swiftly as I can, to return to you.' His finger brushed her ring. 'To make good on my intent to marry you. Properly. The way you deserve.'

'Please don't do this.'

Tension lined his brow. 'I must.'

Lottie closed her eyes and a hot tear ran down her cheek. 'I love you.'

'And I love you.' Evander wiped it away, his touch gentle. 'I will be home before you can even miss me, to provide you with the life you deserve.'

But that wasn't true. She missed him the moment he walked away from her on that familiar path that would remind her of him for ever.

And she didn't stop missing him.

Indeed, the ache of his absence hurt more and more as time went on. Most especially when, mere days later, a carriage accident robbed her of her father and plunged her world into complete darkness.

And she missed Evander with an even greater poignancy when the new vicar moved into the only home she'd ever known and she had no choice but to carve from life whatever future she might forge for herself.

She never stopped missing him, even as time went on and hope faded into a dismal, useless thing.

Chapter Seven

May 1814, Comlongon Castle, Scotland

It was impossible for Lottie to be at Comlongon Castle and not think of Evander—especially when he'd spoken of it so often. Enough that she could see it perfectly in her head, as though she'd been there before herself.

Even if those cherished conversations had happened four years ago.

Many presumed Evander dead at this point, though he hadn't been declared so legally. For her part, Lottie wavered between grief at the idea of him being gone for ever and pain that he was indeed alive but had long since forgotten her.

Be he lost at sea, or in some remote land she would never walk upon, his absence had been extraordinarily lengthy.

Especially when she had needed him most.

Seeing this castle was an agonising reminder of the man she had loved. Yet she put it all aside for Charles and his new bride Eleanor, now the Duke and Duchess of Somersville by their recent union. Lottie would not ruin such a joyful moment of celebration.

Except Evander wasn't gone.

He stood before her now, as regal and handsome as he'd ever been. His hair was a little longer, the auburn streaked with gold, his face etched with lines she hadn't seen before. The brilliant green eyes she'd always loved had lost their sparkle. But then, so too had hers.

Her thoughts splintered in a thousand directions in the room that was filled with fine heavy wood furnishings and stacks of boxes in every corner. A treasure amassed, no doubt.

Disappointment kicked her hard in the heart. He had left her for that treasure. Four long years and not one word. It was a betrayal of the worst kind. Her suffering had been at his expense, and he had been here in Scotland, living in his castle.

She couldn't even think as her body moved of its own volition, marching past the new Duke and Duchess of Somersville to where he stood. He watched her the way someone might regard a ghost—with fascinated shock. Perhaps that was why he did not move as she reached out to slap him.

Her palm struck his face, the connection as loud and sharp as a gunshot in the stunned silence of the room.

Evander slowly raised his hand to his cheek where she'd hit him. It had been hard enough to redden his skin and leave her palm stinging.

'Lottie,' he said, his voice so familiar it dug into her chest like a butcher's meat hook. 'I'm so sorry...'

The woman she was before would have felt guilty for striking him. Rather, she never would have slapped him. But she wasn't that woman any more.

'You lied to me,' she said harshly, unleashing all those years of pain. 'You swore to come back for me and you never did. I waited—' Her voice caught.

There was more to say. So, so much more. Except that her spirit gave out before she could continue.

Charles flew past her, his arm cocked back with intent. There was no time to stop him before his fist landed on Evander's face.

Lottie cried out in surprise at this violent outburst.

Eleanor rushed forward and grabbed Charles's jacket, drawing him back by the scruff as one might have a misbehaving pup. 'Charles, explain yourself.'

He staggered back, his eyes burning with hatred. 'He ruined Lottie, Eleanor. She was a vicar's daughter—a woman with many prospects. Your brother seduced her and abandoned her.'

And there it was—the entirety of Lottie's social demise laid out like soiled laundry on wash day for all to see and judge. Her eyes prickled with tears but she stiffened her back, steeling her resolve against the power of her emotions. After all, she had withstood far worse.

'If he hadn't robbed her of her virtue before her father died,' Charles continued, red-faced with rage, 'she wouldn't have had to—'

'Charles.' Lottie put a hand on his arm. 'I believe this is a conversation I ought to have with the Earl myself rather than see my scandal aired so publicly.'

He glowered at Evander. 'Very well,' he said through gritted teeth.

'You and your wife ought to be shown to your rooms.' Lottie tried to force a smile, but her lips quivered with the effort. 'You and I can leave this discussion for later. For now, I would like a moment alone with…' She caught herself before she said his Christian name. '…the Earl of Westix.'

Charles' valet indicated the closed door. 'Shall I summon the butler to show you to your rooms?'

Charles hesitated, looking uncertain and altogether thoroughly ruffled.

Evander bowed to Charles. 'If you'll excuse me, Your Grace? I would very much like to speak to Lottie alone.'

A muscle worked in Charles' jaw. 'If you hurt her, I'll kill you.'

Evander's flat green eyes found Lottie's. 'If I hurt her in such way again, I'll kill myself.'

'Evander!' Eleanor gasped in horror.

But Evander wasn't looking at his sister. He was still focused on Lottie as he spoke. 'I have committed many egregious wrongs, sister. And for all of them I'm heartily sorry.'

The butler entered the room and politely asked Charles and his new wife to follow him. This time neither protested, and both finally left the room.

The door to the study clicked closed, confirming the departure of Charles and his new wife. An indication Lottie was now alone with Evander for the first time in four years.

Since he had abandoned her.

She stared at the door for a long time, not wanting to turn her attention back to Evander, too frightened by the onslaught of emotion doing so might elicit.

'I suppose it is safe to assume you did not receive my letters,' Evander hedged.

Finally, she turned to him. Hurt welled anew, the way blood beaded on a freshly picked wound. His right cheekbone was red, where Charles had punched him. Another blotch appeared on his opposite cheek, where she had slapped him.

'What letters?' Lottie whispered through numb lips.

'I sent two.'

'Two?' she asked incredulously. 'Two…in four years?'

Evander grimaced, enhancing those new lines on his face. 'I was rather focused on my task. I meant to send more. Truly, I even wrote several…' His voice tapered off.

Rage and hurt and confusion roiled through her thoughts

like clouds gathering before a powerful storm. After everything she had given up…after what she had lost, he had only bothered to send two letters.

She stepped back as tears welled in her eyes. She couldn't do this. Not now. Not when he had so unexpectedly reappeared in her life. There needed to be a moment of reconciliation to allow her mind to fully wrap itself about the understanding of what was happening.

'Lottie, please.' He reached for her. 'I had no idea you'd never received them.'

'Two letters?' she said sharply. 'For all the time I waited. For everything—'

For everything she'd had to become beneath the burden of a woman's shame while he'd jaunted around the world with a man's freedom. For the soul-blistering pain of what she had so recently lost.

Her stomach churned with the urge to be sick. She clasped her arms around her middle and drew in a shuddering breath.

'I had not anticipated my journey would keep me away for so long.' He stepped towards her and hesitated, as though debating if he ought to reach for her again. 'I predicted my return to be much more expedient.'

She was tempted to nod as if she understood, to be agreeable in the way women were instructed to be. Except she did not understand.

'Six months,' she said, with a clear memory of that long-ago conversation when he'd left. 'A year at most.'

He winced. 'Lottie, please forgive me.' His hand came to rest on her back.

The touch was like a bolt of lightning, cracking through her shock. It ripped away the surprise of seeing him for the first time in four years and left her once more at the mercy of her turbulent sentiments.

Forgive me.

So much pain. So much loss. So much that could never be reclaimed.

'God, Lottie, please forgive me,' Evander repeated, in a gentle voice that stoked a memory deep inside her—one that did not want to be coaxed to life.

He had spoken to her gently thus before. When he had loved her.

'You want my forgiveness?' A bitter laugh choked her. She was acting like a madwoman, no doubt. Perhaps she ought to care more about how she came across. But she'd cast aside decorum a long time ago. When she'd had nothing left. Nowhere to go.

Evander had asked for her trust and then he had abandoned her. Ruined her. And now he wished for her forgiveness?

Suddenly she did not feel compelled to laugh so much as to cry, to give in to the wild, desperate sorrow that clawed inside her like a beast.

'I love you, Lottie.' He held his large hands out, not reaching for her but imploring, the same way his gaze did. His palms, once smooth, were now callused. 'I've never stopped loving you. There's been no one else this entire time. In heart. In body. There's only ever been you.'

In body.

She sucked in a pained breath. Where he had been faithful, she had not. But then she hadn't been able to afford such a luxury as fidelity. Not when her hopes of being a governess in London were dashed with her realisation of the importance of a referral.

She'd had no choice but to become a dancer in the opera. The pay, however, had not been nearly sufficient. She'd managed to make do, but when payment of the physician's bills became necessary, there was not nearly enough money.

A fresh squeeze of agony gripped her. There had been

many offers from men who'd sought to become her protector. She'd held them off for as long as she could. At least until…

'I did this for us,' Evander was saying. 'For our future. So we could marry, so I could provide you with the life you are worthy of.'

The life she was worthy of.

He'd meant his words to soothe her hurt, but he was unintentionally thrusting the blade deeper. Whatever life he had planned for them together, she was no longer eligible for it.

'It's later than we had expected, I know, but I have never stopped wanting you as my wife.' He lowered himself to the carpet on one knee before her and lifted his hands in expectation for her to put her fingers to his. 'Marry me, Lottie.'

She shook her head, unable even to work a single word into her throat.

'Please.' He gestured around the room where he kneeled, indicating the crates and wooden pallets stacked throughout the well-appointed study. 'I did this for us. For you.'

She shook her head again, her eyes filling with the tears she'd been resolved to keep from him.

'Good God.' He pushed up to his feet in a smooth motion. 'You're already married, aren't you?'

'Who would marry me?' she asked bitterly. 'I'm ruined.'

He jerked back as if she had slapped him again. 'Don't say such a terrible thing, Lottie. What we did was… It was beautiful.' Some of the hardness in his eyes softened as he gazed at her with affection. 'It was love.'

That word was almost laughable. Love. It sat in her mind like a ghost.

'Perhaps that first time was,' she replied slowly.

Confusion pulled at his brows. 'I don't understand.'

Her heart thundered in her chest like galloping horses

over hard-packed dirt. She would hurt him with these words, but he had to hear them.

Two letters. In four years.

Yes, that steeled her resolve.

He frowned. 'We only ever—'

She lifted her brow and he sucked in a breath.

'There is someone else, then?'

'There have been a few,' she replied levelly.

He cleared his throat. 'I'm afraid I don't quite understand what you're saying.'

'In order to survive these four years…' She squared her shoulders and met his gaze with all the power of her unguarded emotions, letting him see the hurt and the rage and the soul-shaking misery of what she had lost. 'I had to become a courtesan.'

Evander stared incredulously at Lottie. Her lovely face remained impassive, her pale blue eyes simmering with what appeared to be a challenge—as if she were daring him to contradict her.

'I beg your pardon?' he said as his thoughts tangled around the words that came out of her beautiful mouth.

'You heard me,' she accused gently.

He nodded in concession. He had. Only he wished he had not.

'What happened?' He ran a hand through his hair, rubbing his scalp beneath as though it might clear some of the tension from his mind.

'My father died not long after you left. It was a carriage accident. His death was quite unexpected, as I'm sure you can imagine, considering how hearty and hale he'd always been.' She looked away and swallowed, clearly pained by the loss even now.

Evander flinched at the enormity of such news. His own father had been a surly man, but Reverend Rossington had cared greatly for Lottie, always ensuring she had all she needed, and praising her accomplishments. He had been the foundation upon which her entire life had been built. And he had kept her from falling apart when her mother died. Well, her father and Charles—but then Charles had been gone as well, on his Grand Tour.

The power of her loss ached in Evander's chest. Once upon a time he would have been able to curl her into the embrace of his arms and hold her against him to help ease her hurt. Now the stiffness of her shoulders indicated she would not welcome such comfort.

Instead, he hovered awkwardly near her. 'Lottie, I'm so sorry.'

She turned away, severing any chance of a connection between them and shielding her emotions. 'My father worked hard to give me a good life—harder than I realised. When he died, there were only enough funds left for me to get by for a while on my own. But...' She paused and swallowed, giving a slight shake of her head. 'But there are few jobs to be had for a woman—especially in a village. And, of course, I didn't plan to marry, as women usually do for security. I had no choice but to go to London for employment.'

Her fingertips moved over the glossy surface of his desk, and she averted her gaze. Purposely, no doubt.

'There are not many jobs available to a woman at all, as it happens.' There was an underlying hardness to her tone. 'Even in London.'

And so she had become a courtesan. A woman who sold her body to the highest bidder.

The fault did not lie with her, but with him. He should have held tighter to her and her love, but instead he'd left her to total ruin.

His hand curled into a fist, and he wished he could kill every man who had touched her. Or beat his younger self for having only ever sent two letters and not realising the lack of reliable post.

The letters he had sent had been long and carefully written over months, as he continued to postpone his return with each new issue that sprang up. And there had been plenty. His father's dealings had been steeped in deceit and dishonesty. It had been Lottie's goodness which had kept Evander just in his interactions, knowing she would not want wealth at another's expense. Except such work had taken too long and had apparently cost far too much.

'Marry me, Lottie,' he said again, with determination this time.

She turned to him, staring at him as though he'd suddenly sprouted horns. And maybe in her mind he had.

'You can't be serious,' she said.

'I assure you, I am.'

Tears filled her eyes and welled in his heart. 'I'm ruined, Evander.'

'I don't care.'

'But you will.' She pressed her lips together as she attempted to collect herself. 'I am a pariah. I have had lovers among the ton, men who have paid me well for my company. And through a turn of luck, thanks to your mother, I have been able to move on from such endeavours to something that has gained me even more notoriety.'

He did not ask for clarification, certain he did not want to know.

'I instruct ladies of the ton in the art of love and flirtation.' She lifted her chin. 'It is far better than my previous situation.'

His shoulders relaxed. There, now. That wasn't so dreadful. 'Whatever has happened can be smoothed over. I've come back a wealthy man, Lottie. Far wealthier than Somersville or any other duke or earl in London.'

Her face remained impassive as she scanned the room. It was filled with items of great wealth. All obtained for her.

At last, she lifted her gaze to him. 'I never cared about money. I would rather have had you all these years, so I did not have to make the choices I was forced into.'

'I did it for you,' he protested. 'For us.'

She shook her head and gave him a sad smile. 'You did it for yourself.'

She turned from him then, and desperation built in his chest as he searched for some reason to detain her just a while longer. Even if their conversation circled round and round without conclusion, it would still provide him with the opportunity to be with her. To hear the sweetness of her voice and gaze upon her beauty. And she was still beautiful. Perhaps more so.

The slenderness of her frame had filled out with curves even the high waistline of her fashionable gown could not hide. In the years since he had left she had obtained an undeniable confidence. She held herself with certainty, no longer a shy, innocent vicar's daughter, but a woman who knew the power of her appearance.

She was truly a sight to behold, in a pale blue gown that set off her striking blue eyes and made her black hair look glossy as silk.

'I love you,' he said vehemently. 'I always have.'

She stopped and turned back towards him slowly. 'Not enough.'

Before she could leave again, he added, 'I always will.'

She withdrew something from a long silver chain about her neck and tugged at it with a severe jerk, snapping it free. With shaking hands, she pulled off some charm.

'You don't even know me.'

In a swift move, she threw the thing at his feet. The bit of jewellery bounced off the toe of his Hessian. He bent to reclaim it as she walked away.

It was then he realised it wasn't a charm at all, but a small ring with a chip of diamond, still warm from where once it had rested against her heart.

Chapter Eight

Lottie's father had been right about the men of the ton after all. His words had echoed in her mind often when she was with the men who paid for the right to keep her. Men who were given freedom and wealth and time, with no purpose save to delight in the pleasures of life and privilege. And there were many pleasures to be had.

Yet she had foolishly thought Evander was different. She knew now he was not—he was as guilty of greed as so many others were of lust.

Rage kindled inside her anew, hot and bright like the first flames of a fire licking over dry kindling. All-consuming.

He had no idea what he'd done to her. She'd been kind when she glossed over it in their discussion, but now she did not feel so kind.

Not bothering to dress, she tied her dressing gown closed. The back of her neck still stung from where she'd snapped her necklace free, the chain having sliced through her tender skin when she'd wrenched it off. She didn't bother to look in the mirror before departing her room. After years of spending so much focus on her appearance, she knew well how she looked.

Golden light limned the door to the study, as she'd expected. With the newlywed couple locked away in marital bliss, there was only one other person who could be up as late as she.

She pushed open the door without bothering to knock, and Evander started where he sat before the fire.

His confusion melted away upon seeing her and he immediately got to his feet. 'Lottie.'

She strode into the room, letting the door slip closed behind her as she did so. 'I trusted you.'

Those three words had propelled her from her room and they echoed in her mind like a chant, driving her towards this moment when she could hurl them at him. But they did not flow from her lips with the ire she intended. They came out broken and hard. Like her.

'I trusted you,' she whispered hoarsely, the second attempt even more pathetic than the first. 'I was an innocent girl, a foolish country chit with nothing, and you *left* me.'

Evander pulled in a soft intake of breath as if she'd slapped him again. 'Lottie, I—'

'No.' This time she found her voice and her protest rang out in the room. 'It is my turn to say my piece.'

'Of course.' Evander remained standing by the chair, not moving towards her, though she could tell from the way he leaned forward that he wanted to.

'Do you know that even after a year went by I still thought you would come back?' she asked. 'I still look at men who pass me on the street and wonder if they're you. If you'd returned and I'd somehow missed it.' She shook her head to clear the tears before they could start. 'London is not the way you described it,' she added bitterly. 'Not when you are at its mercy rather than holding its reins.'

She turned from him and went to a small table with a decanter, pouring two glasses of fine whisky.

'I was paraded through Vauxhall Gardens like a purchased doll.'

She strode to him and pushed the glass into his hand. He accepted it, but did not drink, his eyes wide and brimming with hurt. Good. It was his turn to feel the teeth of that bite.

She did drink. With a swirl of the amber liquid and a delicate tilt, she drank a mouthful and let it burn all the way down.

'I experienced the opera as a dancer, with men gazing lewdly down my bodice and offering to share my bed. And when I was fortunate enough to find myself off the stage, and in one of those coveted boxes, I did not have the luxury of actually watching the opera.'

He swallowed.

'You think you understand what I went through in your absence, but you do not,' she said. 'It is impossible for you to possess even a modicum of understanding for what I endured as that year you promised came and went. I found myself in terrible desperation, and the one place where I sought help…'

Her voice clogged. She should tell him. Now.

'The choices I faced when I realised…'

Tell him

Except doing so was impossible. She could not salvage enough of her heart to do so.

'God, you must hate me,' Evander whispered. Tears clung, unshed, to his lower lashes.

'I don't hate you,' Lottie said, more softly than she liked. She stepped closer and the scent of sandalwood caught her awareness. The subtle notes of his cologne struck her like a blacksmith's hammer, knocking her back to when they had been young and in love and she had been lost in naïve happiness.

He still smelled the same.

Pain crumpled in her chest. 'I could never hate you.'

And she could not—not when she still loved him.

She wanted to fall towards him, to feel his arms around

her once more and see if they were still as strong as they looked. For years she had been her own pillar of support. How would it feel to allow someone else to offer fortitude?

Her resolve was faltering. She couldn't stay here. Coming had been a mistake.

'But I can never forgive you,' she said sharply. 'Nor can I ever trust you again.'

Evander opened his mouth, but she set her glass aside and started to walk away. She'd said what was needed. At least most of it. There would be time later for the rest. When she found the courage that had failed her so terribly just now.

She opened the door and his voice interrupted her departure. 'I'm sorry, Lottie.'

I'm sorry.

It truly was a paltry consolation. Words so empty they could never fill the void inside her.

She pushed out of the study and made her way to her bedchamber, half expecting he would come after her.

And perhaps even half hoping.

Evander stared at the closed door. The cut crystal glass had gone warm in his palm and the click of the door latch still seemed to echo in the room, tangling with the memory of what she'd told him.

His stomach coiled into a sickening knot. An opera dancer. So that was how it had all begun for her.

He knew Lottie better than anyone. Or at least he had. She would have waited for him, steadfast and loyal. No doubt becoming a dancer was the last resort after she'd clung to several more months awaiting him. And after such employment, finding a reputable husband would be difficult.

He saw suddenly how little choice she'd had. How little choice he'd left her with when he'd abandoned her.

She had trusted him. And he had failed her.

Her ruin had been entirely his fault.

He gave in to the weakness softening his knees and sank onto the chair. Tempering his instinct to go after her took everything he had. But his presence, he knew, would not be welcome. She had made that much clear. No matter how much he wished to be with her.

She had looked at him incredulously earlier, when he'd said he would still marry her, and had declared she was not worthy of the title of Countess.

Except it was Evander who was not worthy of her.

His gaze found its way to the glowing embers in the hearth. She had said he had reclaimed his wealth for him, not for her. Was that truly the case…?

Egypt was bloody hot in August. Evander had thought the Nile Delta would be cooler than the dry, baking sun inland, but he had underestimated the humidity that left a perpetual sheen of sweat slick across his brow. The letter under his hand was blurred where the dampness of his palm smeared the ink as he wrote. It was one he had been working on for several months. To Lottie.

Three years had passed. Two years longer than he'd anticipated. He'd sent a couple of letters to her, both composed as this one had been, over several months, written in the snatches of time between negotiations, meetings, research and exploration.

But he would be home soon, after this latest discovery of artefacts. Ancient jewellery of hammered gold and carved precious stones made up an assortment of rings, necklaces, bracelets and collars.

He had taken care to diversify his wares, with spices, fabrics and goods from other locations. There was enough to fill his coffers.

But he needed to ensure they would never again run dry.

And there was good coin to be had in artefacts.

His father had known that.

The thought made his heart slam harder. The last thing he wanted was to be like his father.

Irritation teased at the back of Evander's neck, the way it always did when he thought of his father. He wasn't like the former Earl, damn it.

Evander focused on the letter. The ink had been smudged beyond legibility. With a growl of frustration, he balled it up and tossed it in the rubbish bin beside his desk. He was tired of being away from England, away from Lottie.

His chest compressed as her image swam in his mind. Beautiful, innocent. The woman he would make his wife upon his return.

Was the treasure he'd accumulated enough?

She needed the very best in life. He would offer her nothing less. Diamonds, silks, furs, estates that would make Huntly Manor look like a cottage. Anything her heart desired.

Determination fired through him. After this haul he would be done. Or perhaps just one more. To ensure the family fortune was never in jeopardy again.

A knock came at the door and his guide entered with an apologetic bow. 'Forgive me, my lord, but it appears the authorities require approval prior to allowing you to depart with your findings.'

'More?' Evander tried to keep the irritation from his voice. 'The last "approval" took nearly six months to obtain.'

Bassel tilted his head. 'If I may, my lord, a proper bribe might be sufficient to avoid such approvals.'

In the past, Evander had immediately declined such considerations. But now he hesitated. He couldn't afford

*another six months of waiting. His father had done it. And
Evander had been gone so very long from Lottie.*

*However, it was the thought of her that made him recon-
sider the temptation of bribery. She was a good-hearted
woman who would never want a fortune that was obtained
by underhanded dealings.*

Evander tugged his stare from the fire and scrubbed a
hand over his face. He could have returned earlier if he
hadn't been so dogged in his determination to have great
wealth. In truth, he had far more than he had expected.
He'd kept his estimations low, to avoid falling short on
what he'd hoped to achieve. But in fact he'd more than
doubled the number he'd set in his mind, was closer to
having tripled it.

He'd told himself he'd done it for Lottie, but had he?

Was he just like his father?

Without thought, Evander let his hand wander into his
jacket pocket and he slipped the cold band of metal onto
the tip of his smallest finger. He withdrew the ring he'd
given to Lottie when he'd proposed all those years ago.
The small diamond chip winked at him in the firelight.

She had kept it all these years.

Hope flared anew within him.

She still loved him. Or at least she had before she'd realised how obsessed he'd become with his findings—like
the former Earl had been, hunting treasure with dogged
determination.

In truth, it was perhaps the first time Evander understood his father's devotion to obtaining dusty relics and
stones. But it was in that moment Evander also knew he
was not like his father. Because he would not allow himself to be torn from those he loved to obtain more. Rather
the opposite—he would do whatever he could to make
things right.

He shifted his focus towards Lottie. No matter what it took, he would fight for her. While, regrettably, he could not change the past, he had some control over the future in how he acted and what he did.

He vowed to make things right with her—to win back her broken trust even if it took finding every splintered piece and carefully piecing it together. After all, there was no worthier cause than the love of Miss Charlotte Rossington. And he knew that better than anyone else.

Chapter Nine

Evander finally returned to London, having stayed longer in the country than intended. In truth, he had intended to return to London long before, but his mother had been ill. Gravely so.

There had been a chilling moment when he genuinely feared he had lost her. The physician had arrived swiftly, and had managed to revive her, but the memory had seeded itself in Evander's mind and rooted there—a reminder of how ephemeral life could be and how tenaciously one must hold on to those one loved.

Not only was he reluctant to leave her side, he knew she felt more at ease with him nearby during her recovery. Even if he had already been home for more than two years.

His mother had become a changed woman in the time when he'd been off re-establishing their fortune. There was now a softness about her, a quiet affection that touched her eyes, whereas before she had been cool and unaffected. He had noticed the same in Eleanor.

Whatever had transpired within them, he knew it had much to do with Lottie and her lessons with Eleanor. His sister had evidently been Lottie's first student at her scandalous school for ladies.

Evander walked up Fleet Street and stopped in at Aphrodite & Cherub. The fresh perfume of hothouse flowers greeted him, as well as the cheerful bidding of the shop girl. The young woman appeared within a second, her blonde hair bound back in a simple twist, as she always wore it, and she regarded him with large doe-brown eyes.

'Good day, Lord Westix.' She smiled. 'Welcome back to London.'

He examined a bunch of violets—a symbol of faithfulness. Their blue-purple petals were brilliant even in the dismal grey light of yet another rainy day. Perhaps they might be ideal for Lottie upon his return. Nearly losing his mother had taught him there was not a moment in life to waste when one knew what one wanted.

And, above all else, he wanted Lottie as his wife.

'Thank you, Miss Flemming,' he said to the shop girl, who had worked there since his first visit to the establishment, two years past. 'I trust you're well.'

'I've told you to call me Bess.'

Perhaps water lilies for purity of heart, so that Lottie would know he would never waver. 'Thank you,' he replied distractedly.

'Another bouquet for Miss Rossington?' Miss Flemming asked.

Miss Rossington. Even her name made Evander's chest go tight. 'Yes.'

'You've been sending them to the lady for two years now, my lord.'

A cluster of myrtle caught his attention. Once upon a time he'd been so bold as to add a few of those delicate white flowers to a bunch he'd intended to give Lottie. That first time he'd called on her, just after they'd first met.

'Forgive my boldness, my lord, as I mean no disrespect,

but perhaps the lady doesn't return your regard.' Miss Flemming stepped closer.

A purple flower caught his attention. Hyacinth. Sorrow. Forgiveness. There was a darkness in him that longed to send Lottie a vase filled with them, so that she might know the extent of the hurt he still suffered over losing her.

'There are no doubt any number of women who find you extraordinarily attractive. Women who would welcome your esteem and who aren't averse to a mere dalliance.' Miss Flemming touched his gloved hand.

Evander was startled, and regarded her wide brown eyes as she gazed up at him expectantly.

'Red roses, I think,' he said. While not especially imaginative, how could a chap go wrong with flowers that spoke of passionate love?

Miss Flemming lowered her head. 'We recently received some china roses. For eternal beauty and grace.'

Ah, now, there was a rare and enchanting flower—much like his recipient.

'Yes, perfect.' He glanced at his pocket watch, noting it was nearly three—almost time for his meeting with several investors regarding a silver mining operation, for which he was the prime contributor. Another venture that would guarantee an impressive return. 'Preferably red.'

'Of course.' Miss Flemming looked up.

The smile on her face somewhat diminished for some reason, he thought, although he could not hazard a guess as to why.

'And hyacinths.'

She faltered. 'With red china roses? Perhaps white roses instead?'

Purity. Evander immediately shook his head. He would not remind Lottie of the absence of her innocence, of what he had cost her. 'You will make it look pleasing. You always do.'

The smile was back on Miss Flemming's face. 'Is there anything else I can do for you, my lord?' She moved closer to him once more. 'Anything at all?'

He frowned at her curious action. 'The flowers will do well enough. Thank you, Miss Flemming.' He would have just enough time to make it to the meeting. 'Do forgive me, but I must go.'

Miss Flemming nodded. 'I'll see you next week, for another bouquet for Miss Rossington.'

And that was why he appreciated Miss Flemming. She could craft a fine bunch of flowers and she always anticipated what he would need.

The bouquets would not make things right with Lottie, he knew. He was not so daft as to anticipate such paltry things would win her heart. But they were a symbol—not only of his ever-present sentiments towards her, but of his loyalty to her. The flowers were delivered each week without fail—a reminder to her that he was not that foolish young man any more. That he was steadfast in his determination to win her back. That he would spend his entire life trying to make up for his egregious behaviour and find a way back into her heart.

'Indeed,' he replied. 'Good day, Miss Flemming.'

With that, he left the shop and rushed towards his appointment.

In the years that had passed since he'd first arrived back in England, he'd sold the spices, fabrics and other treasures acquired on his travels for even more than anticipated.

It should have been enough.

Yet somehow no amount of fortune ever seemed as if it was. There was always another investment to be had, another pocket of wealth to unearth.

What's more, he was damn good at it. It was something tangible. Something he could control. All his efforts yielded reward.

He climbed into his carriage and leaned his head back as it lurched onward. If only his efforts with Lottie would prove as successful.

Lottie made her way down to the drawing room to meet with her first and only male student: Viscount Rawley. Ironically, Lady Caroline, the object of his affection, was another student of hers. The young lady was a black-haired beauty whose dark eyes shone with infatuation every time she mentioned Lord Rawley.

It should have worked out impeccably, and yet attempting to put the two together was about as easy as blending oil and water.

The issue was due in large part to the Viscount's misgivings which Lottie knew would require the most work.

He lurched to his feet as soon as she entered the room. 'Thank you for seeing me with such expediency, Miss Rossington.'

His normally immaculate attire appeared a bit dishevelled. His cravat somewhat crooked and his brown hair a mite ruffled.

To anyone else, these minor disruptions would be easily dismissed. But Lottie had come to know Lord Rawley well after the months she'd met with him. Those small changes indicated a catastrophe of monumental proportions.

'Of course.' She smiled affectionately, so he knew she was not mocking him. 'Has something happened with Lady Caroline?'

'Yes.' Lord Rawley rubbed the back of his head, leaving a tuft of hair jutting out. 'No. I confess, I am entirely unsure. But then, I do have a keen skill for bumbling everything.'

'Truly, what is the worst that could happen?' Lottie asked. 'Especially when you know she wants you with her?'

He huffed a heavy sigh. 'The usual things, I suppose.

Unknowingly ingesting something that contains shrimp and being violently ill before her. Tripping down a set of stairs and accidentally pulling her down with me. Saying something ridiculous. It's foolish, I know, but she's always so very witty and pleasant. I'm such a dullard by comparison.'

'You are certainly no dullard, and I imagine the occurrence of any of those events to be highly unlikely,' she said encouragingly. 'Lady Caroline is important to you, is she not?'

Lord Rawley regarded her with an open look of sheer desperation. 'She is the most important thing in all my life.'

Lottie liked the Viscount very much. He didn't regard her in a libidinous fashion, as did so many men of the ton. He respected her as much as he would the daughter of a duke. And he would do anything for the woman he loved.

Perhaps in that way he reminded her somewhat of Evander. His loyalty to the woman of his choice was unwavering, his purpose steadfast. Lottie's heart flinched at the recollection of Evander. He had yet to return to London after his years in the country, where he tended to his ill mother.

Perhaps that was for the best. Seeing him never became easier.

'I would suggest that if Lady Caroline is truly important, you treat her as such,' Lottie said. 'Make her know what she means to you. From what you've told me of her, I believe she will be overjoyed at your affection.'

Of course Lottie could not reveal that Lady Caroline too was one of her students. Identities must be kept confidential, no matter the circumstance.

Lord Rawley nodded to himself, lost in deep thought, as though already formulating a plan. And truly Lottie hoped he was. Poor Lady Caroline was besotted with the

Viscount, and wanted nothing more than for Lord Rawley to open himself to her.

Speaking of the lovely Lady Caroline, her session with Lottie was next—but thankfully she would have a bit of time to herself before the lady was due to arrive.

It was in that respite that Lottie studied her drawing room, revelling in a spell of silence before she once more assumed her role as tutor to the ton. She ran her fingertips over the strings of the harp sitting in the corner and a gradient melody rippled from the instrument. She didn't play, but her mother had. It was for that reason Lottie had gone to the expense of purchasing the item and keeping it in her drawing room. Likewise, the diamond-patterned Brussels weave carpet had been bought with her father in mind. As though pieces of them still followed her, even in a world they wouldn't approve of.

A knock came from the double doors and Lottie's maid, Sarah, breezed in. Of all Lottie's staff, Sarah was the most trusted. Not only did she see to the running of the house, but also to the hiring of staff—all of whom were selected with great care, as Lottie required the utmost discretion from her servants.

'More flowers from the Earl of Westix,' Sarah said in a bright chirp.

Lottie shot her an exasperated look. 'I don't want them.'

'You never do, lovey.' Sarah set them on the smooth marble surface of the side table, turning the bouquet this way and that as she assessed each angle with a careful eye.

'Yet you always insist I keep them.' Lottie grudgingly looked upon the flowers as the familiar constriction tightened in her chest.

They *were* lovely. They always were. But flowers could not mend old hurts. They could not bring back trust. Nor could they make a lady out of a courtesan.

'That man loves you.' Sarah handed her a small note.

'Perhaps I harbour hopes you'll find happiness with him again.'

Lottie scoffed, but still accepted the note. 'Perhaps?'

Sarah shrugged with a cheeky grin and disappeared out through the doors, closing them behind her as she left.

Lottie fingered the small note as she studied the deep red and purple arrangement. The roses were extraordinary, with rippled petals, in a red as brilliant as a geranium. No doubt the card would explain it.

She lifted the small flap and found the same familiar neat script which always accompanied the flowers.

China roses for everlasting grace and beauty. Hyacinth for sorrow and forgiveness.

If only forgiveness could come so easily.

'Excuse the intrusion,' Sarah said.

Lottie startled, not having heard another knock or the doors opening again.

'You have a guest.'

Sarah looked like a cat that had swallowed a canary. Which meant the guest was not Lady Caroline arriving early—a fact confirmed by a glance at the gilded bracket clock, which revealed there was still a half-hour before Lady Caroline's appointment.

'Your visitor is not Lady Caroline.' Sarah raised her brows. 'It's Lord Westix.'

'Tell him—'

'He knows you're at home.' Sarah batted her long-lashed green eyes innocently at Lottie.

The older woman was impudent, but she knew Lottie would never put her out. Perhaps that was why she was so bold. Though if Lottie were being grudgingly honest, she knew it was because Sarah was her friend.

They had known each other for years, having met at

the opera. Sarah was just ending her career as Lottie was beginning hers. Sarah had been in despair as to where life might cast her, with her youth having faded, and Lottie, who well understood what it felt like to be lost, took her on as a lady's maid once she obtained her first protector. They had been together ever since, and Sarah had proved herself invaluable time and again.

'So there's no hope for it, then.'

Lottie's pulse spiked, the way it always did when he came to call. Their conversations were always the same— him begging for another chance and her declining before asking him to leave.

She shot Sarah a peevish look. 'Are you pleased?'

'Delightfully so.' Sarah didn't bother to suppress her smile. 'And, anyway, if you put him off, he'll only come back in an hour.'

Lottie sighed.

'You know I'm right.'

'You're very outspoken for a maid.'

'You mean I'm the only one who will not mollycoddle you.' Sarah nodded her head once, as if confirming the accuracy of her own statement. 'I tell you what is what when you need to hear it. Like now.'

Lottie eyed her maid warily. 'Out with it, then.'

Sarah inspected the new bouquet with exaggerated interest. 'You get hothouse flowers once a week. I've never had them once in my whole life.' She lifted her gaze to Lottie. 'That man loves you the way every woman wishes she could be loved. Give him a chance.'

Lottie frowned. 'You don't understand.'

Sarah approached her and put a hand on her shoulder. 'I took care of you, remember? I don't understand like you do, but I know better than most.' She lowered her hand and strode back to the doorway. 'Some day he may stop sending flowers. Or worse…'

Lottie waited for her to finish the warning.

'He may send them to someone else.'

Much as Lottie hated to admit it, the words made something in chest twist at the thought. Not that she would allow Sarah to know her words had affected her so deeply. The maid would truly be incorrigible if that happened.

Instead, Lottie feigned a lack of concern and waved to her maid. 'Please have Andrews see him in.'

Chapter Ten

Lottie smoothed her hair down so many times she reminded herself of Lord Rawley. But even as she told herself to stop fidgeting, she swept her hand over her dark blue satin gown.

Confronting Evander never ceased to rattle her.

The door swung open and her heart caught in her throat as he strode in with his usual confidence. His broad shoulders were squared, his attire pristine, and he had a regal air only nobility could possess. Though he had written and sent flowers, she hadn't seen him since the end of the season the year before last, when he'd told her he would be returning to the country with his mother.

His gaze locked on hers now, his jaw set with determination. This was the season when he'd reclaim her affection—or so he'd said in the letters he'd sent throughout his absence from London.

He stood before her for a moment, studying her with a reverence that took her breath. She remained frozen beneath those jade-green eyes, locked in the power of his observation.

'Lottie.' He said on an exhale, as if saying her name caused him to hurt.

And perhaps it did.

Hyacinths. Sorrow. Forgiveness. Pain.

'Lord Westix,' she replied.

He flinched, as though wounded. 'Are we back to that?'

It was good to maintain the formality. For Lottie. She needed the reminder of their stations in life. He was an earl—one whose family counted on his good name. And she was a woman whose reputation would always remain tarnished. A woman whose trust had once been shattered into so many pieces that it could never again be fitted together.

He lowered himself onto the sofa and she took the chair opposite him, with the tea table between them. She needed him to feel the space between them—to realise they could never rekindle what they'd once shared. Her heart could not bear it.

But then, her heart could not bear this either—having him before her, but not having him with her. Seeing him and not being able to go to him.

He spun her emotions about until she didn't know which side was which, and all she could remember in the end was a tangle of love and hurt and loss.

'Did you get my letters?' Evander asked.

'I did.' There had been one a week while he'd been in the country. As he'd promised.

'Did you read them?' He jostled his leg, bouncing his knee momentarily before he caught himself.

She had. Every one. Multiple times.

She knew of his mother's slow recovery, and how she was well enough now for him to return to London. He'd told her of the garden he strode through, and how it reminded him so much of the walks they'd taken in Binsey all those years ago. And she knew how much he regretted what he had done to her.

The door to the drawing room opened and Sarah brought in a tea tray.

'Would you like some tea, Lord Westix?' Lottie asked, hoping he would decline.

'Please.'

She went about steeping the tea and pouring it into his cup, the stream wavering as her fingers shook with the nerves that never ceased to tremble in his presence. His focus went to her hands. He knew his effect on her.

'If you have read my letters, then you know why I am set this year on making you my wife.' He accepted the tea-cup from her and promptly took a sip.

She winced, hating it that his mother had been so very near her end. She knew it had frightened him—not only with the realisation that his time with her was not unlimited, but that all time was not so. It was a reminder to him of what he had lost with Lottie, and had sharpened his need to have it back.

'You know why I cannot,' she replied softly.

'I'm the wealthiest man in London.' He set his teacup down hard. 'That was by design. So I could bloody well do what I want without caring about anyone else's opinions.'

He had fallen back on the easier excuse rather than confront the real issue—the one that prodded at a deeper wound.

Trust.

Or rather its absence.

'You're well aware the ton doesn't work that way.' She took a sip of tea. 'I don't understand why you continue to persist with this.'

There was no need to elaborate on what she meant by 'this'. It was his ardent pursuit of her, his insistence that they be together.

He edged forward in his seat, closer to her, bringing with him that achingly familiar sandalwood scent.

'Because I love you.'

That man loves you the way every woman wishes she could be loved.

But that wasn't the case.

She shook her head. 'You love the memory of the woman I was six years ago. There's nothing left of her in me any more.' Grief tugged at her, and the loss of who she had been. 'You can't love me when you don't even know me.'

He tilted his head and several strands of silver at his temples caught the light. 'Give me a chance. Allow me the opportunity to get to know who you are now.'

He reached out with his large hands and folded them over hers. His palms were warm, his fingers strong.

She longed to close her eyes and bask in the familiarity of his touch. Even after all these years, he felt like the closest thing to home that was left.

'You hurt me,' she said in a quiet voice. 'I don't know that I can allow my heart to open to you as it did once before.'

His face collapsed, and she knew he was well aware of what she spoke of. The true issue that lay before them. The impenetrable wall that had formed the toughest callus around her heart. One she was not yet ready to slough off—not when it would leave her too pink and tender, raw enough to flinch at even the slightest of touches.

She pulled her hand from his grip and pushed to her feet, fully prepared to ask him to leave. He rose alongside her and closed the distance between them, filling her space with his familiar scent, triggering memories that made her heart ache.

Tears blurred her vision unexpectedly. This was why she so often tried to put off seeing him. Her heart could not bear the closeness of him any more than she could stand the futility of their meetings.

'Why will you not leave me alone?' she asked, transferring her hurt into anger. 'It's been two years and I've repeatedly rebuffed your attentions.'

Those green eyes searched hers with gentle affection. She did not look away, yielding to the part of her that wished it was possible to peer down deep into his soul, to know the truth of his words, to glean more of his character. Time and circumstance had shaped them both, and she did not know him now any more than he knew her.

The skin around Evander's eyes tightened in a way that suggested he was doing the same as she: trying desperately to see what was inside.

'You love me.'

'I don't love you,' she protested weakly.

'You're lying.'

He lifted a brow and eased even closer, near enough to kiss.

Her pulse tapped an erratic rhythm. How she wished she could close her eyes and wait for the softness of his mouth on hers once more. Could give in to the desire burning in her veins and the yawning, aching need in her empty chest.

'Why would you think such a thing?' Her voice was far too breathless, but she could no sooner control it than she could her rapid pulse.

'I saw how your hands trembled when you poured the tea, how your cheeks reddened when I entered the room.'

He spoke low, but his mouth was near enough to her ear that she heard every word, felt every one of them with the brush of his warm breath against her neck.

'Even now you are still flushed, as if you know how tempted I am to kiss you.'

She drew in a soft breath.

He was not wrong. And they both knew it.

Some day he might stop sending flowers. Or worse... He might send them to someone else.

He hovered near her for a long moment, her pulse frozen in a maelstrom of wanting him to kiss her and wishing he would leave.

At last, he straightened. 'My mother has insisted on having a ball for my thirtieth birthday. I think she feels she must show her gratitude for my staying with her through her illness, though I've told her it's entirely unnecessary.'

'How wonderful,' she replied, sensing immediately why he had mentioned his birthday ball.

'I want you there.'

He lightly touched her face, a mere brush of his fingertips over her jaw. Her breath locked in her chest, unwilling to budge in or out.

Give him a chance.

Attending his birthday ball was no more prudent than hoping he would kiss her. Yet as she became lost once more in his handsome green eyes she could not bring herself to say no.

Blast Sarah for planting such foolish notions inside her head.

'Send the details.' Lottie stepped back, giving herself room to breathe. To think. 'I may be there, but that is not a yes.'

'Nor is it a no.'

He broke out a smile that took six years off his face and twisted at a tender place she wished would remain buried.

'You'll have what you need in the morning,' he said. 'Please truly consider it.'

As he left the drawing room to exit the townhouse she found herself warring with the idea of attending the ball. She was grateful she had not said yes. Yet also grateful she had not said no.

She wasn't certain if she could ever allow herself to open herself to him again as she'd done before, but perhaps it was time to at least become acquainted with Evander once more, to give them both a second chance.

* * *

The birthday celebration was larger than anticipated, with Evander's guests pouring into Westix Place. It was good to see some familiar faces in the crowd: the Marquess of Kentworth, Viscount Rawley, the Earl of Dalton and his lovely new Countess.

Eleanor had been the first to arrive with Charles—a match that filled Evander's chest with pride. To see his sister a duchess, and more than that happy, was all he wanted for her.

There was one guest, however, who had not yet arrived. The most important one of all.

Lottie.

Evander checked his pocket watch. She was only a few minutes late, and dancing had not yet started. He considered the chalked dancefloor, the pine boards artfully covered in a whirling design of brilliant colours. The art had been costly, and would be ruined once the dancing began, but Lottie would love it.

Except if she did not arrive soon she would never have the opportunity to see the colourful work before its destruction.

'Miss Charlotte Rossington,' the caller bellowed from the entrance of the ballroom.

Evander's attention snapped to the open doorway as Lottie entered.

Her sapphire-blue velvet gown had a white silk sash just beneath her bosom, where the fabric flared out over her waist, and white silk gloves ran up her slender arms, stopping an inch above her elbows. What appeared to be diamonds sparkled and winked in her dark hair as she moved through the room.

Towards him.

His breath caught and the entire world faded away as she strode towards him with the grace of a queen. She was dressed more grandly than the finest duchess, and her modest neckline, he noted, was at least an inch or two above that of most women in the room.

Her gaze was fixed on him, and it did not waver as she approached.

'Lottie,' he whispered.

'Happy Birthday, Lord Westix,' she said formally, her chin elevated to an almost haughty angle.

It was a reminder of their need for refrain from familiarity with one another. While he didn't relish the idea of once more having to revert to titles and all that, he understood the need. He would take Lottie any way he could get her—even if it was as Miss Rossington, beneath the ever-present judgment of the watching ton.

Though he suspected the formality was also for her. Another layer of protection. He had hurt her—he knew that. God, how he knew that.

But now he might finally have a chance to prove to her he was a trustworthy man. One worthy of her heart.

He tried to dim his smile, but doubted his success. In truth, it was most likely impossible, when he was filled with such elation at knowing she'd accepted his invitation. And at what it might mean.

'I didn't think you'd come,' he said.

She discreetly glanced around the room. 'Everyone is staring.'

'Of course they are.' He lifted her hand and kissed the smooth white silk of her glove. 'You're the most beautiful woman in the room.'

'Flatterer,' she accused, with a pleased smile.

He straightened and gave her a coy look. 'Whatever is necessary to ensure I see more of you.'

She lifted a brow.

'And you've arrived just in time,' he said quickly, be-

fore he could chase her off. 'The dancing is about to begin.
Will you do me the honour?'

She hesitated.

'It is my birthday,' he reminded her with a grin. 'And I
have a surprise I want to show you.'

Before she could protest, he indicated the dance floor.
Her attention wandered to the chalked artwork and her
eyes widened.

'Do you like it?' he asked, already knowing her answer
and glad of having gone to the expense and effort.

'It's a marvel.' She turned from him and walked towards the whorls of blue and green set over the yellow
background of the polished pine. 'Oh, but it will be ruined
once the dancing begins.'

'As it is supposed to be.' He held out his hand to her.
'Dance with me.'

Her lips parted in protest as she looked once more to
the chalked art.

'We'll be very careful,' he promised.

Not that it mattered, of course. Once everyone joined
them the colours would be smeared together. But he would
not lose this opportunity to dance with Lottie before the
ton and make it known how he felt about her.

They took their positions for the cotillion and, as anticipated, all eyes were fixed on Evander and Lottie.

'It's been half an age since I've danced,' she admitted,
when the music brought them together.

'Yet you are still as graceful now as you were the first
time I danced with you,' Evander replied.

And she was, her steps light, intentionally delicate over
the artwork, so only her toes moved across the chalk and
left the smallest of scuffs in the design.

As other couples moved around them the chalk smeared,
as expected. No one took the care that Lottie did.

'The first time we danced,' she said wistfully. 'That was a lifetime ago, wasn't it?'

Evander took her hands in the dance and led her to the left. 'That was when I was my happiest.'

He hadn't acknowledged such a truth until that very moment. But it was true, when he was with Lottie, he was happier than he'd ever been. Nothing else had brought him similar joy since. Not travelling, nor food, nor even wealth.

She skipped away from him, as per the steps of the co-tillion, her feet moving lightly enough that they almost did not mar the chalk, and he found himself grinning. While she claimed to be a different woman now, there were still traces of the girl she once was, even if she didn't see it.

But he did.

'Do you still enjoy painting watercolours?' he asked, when the music brought them together again, recalling how spots of paint had always found their way to her gowns, especially her long sleeves. He ran his thumb over her wrist in memory.

She chuckled, obviously understanding. 'I do, but I've become much more careful in what I wear when I paint now.'

All too soon the music drew to a close and they were forced to bow and curtsey to one another. Formality would draw them apart for the better part of the night now, but Evander was loath to leave her side. Not when he had waited so long for this moment.

'Thank you for the dance,' Lottie said. 'And the memories.'

'Miss Rossington.' Kentworth appeared beside them and offered a bow. 'May I have this dance?'

Evander gritted his teeth and only partially masked his irritation at the Marquess's interruption. It would not be the last, Evander knew. Lottie had always attracted attention. But when she was younger she hadn't noticed.

She was well aware of her ability now.

Without any right to lay claim to her, as he would like, Evander relinquished Lottie into the waiting hand of Kentworth and departed the dance floor.

Charles found Evander in the crowd not long after. The Duke's eyes followed Lottie as she moved across the dance floor, her steps still as careful as they were graceful, despite the chalk having been already scuffed beyond repair by others.

'You look well,' Evander said, complimenting his brother-in-law.

'You're going to hurt her,' Charles said. 'You do realise that.'

'I beg your pardon?' Evander turned to his sister's husband.

The Duke frowned at him. 'Society will never accept her, no matter how much you wish they would. You know the people of our set. They are as unforgiving as they are cruel.'

'Bollocks,' Evander said under his breath. 'You know as well as I do that most of these people can be bought.'

'Not all.' Charles pulled his attention from Lottie and settled his bright blue eyes pointedly on Evander. 'And the ones who cannot are the most brutal, the ones with the most influence.'

He was right, of course—damn him. Evander didn't want to admit it, but his statement was undeniable.

'She's fragile.' The Duke returned his focus to the dancefloor, where Lottie danced with her undeserving partner. 'She may not seem it, but it's a hard exterior built over a woman who is tender beneath.'

This claim Evander did not protest, though he wished he could, for it was the truest of all.

'I suggest you consider the consequences before acting on your own whims.'

Charles turned from Evander then, and walked away. Had the man not made his sister so blissfully content, Evander would have had the sod removed from his party. And as for the warning...

Evander pushed it aside, certain that everything would be set to rights.

Indeed, he found himself to be far more hopeful than he had been in the past six years.

Chapter Eleven

It had been far too long since Lottie had enjoyed herself as much as she did at Evander's birthday ball. He was exactly the way she remembered him: charming, handsome, aristocratic. And his eyes remained fixed on her whenever she was near, a besotted grin pulling at his lips.

Being in close proximity to him once more recalled a plethora of feelings she'd worked hard to push away. Warmth filled her chest, and a nervous energy radiated from within: unmistakably love.

It was too alluring to imagine how it could be between them, easy and intoxicating, the way it had been when they were young. Except even the idea of letting her barriers unfurl had her muscles tensing with wounded fear. It was too soon. Even after all these years, it was far too soon to consider allowing herself to be that vulnerable.

'Lottie,' a familiar voice called.

She turned to find Eleanor waving towards her.

'Lottie.' Eleanor took her hand and squeezed it. 'It is good to see you. I trust you are well?'

'Better than I've been in a long time,' Lottie answered earnestly. 'I'm so grateful to you and your mother for the opportunity you've allowed me to pursue.'

'And I assumed that glow on your face had something to do with my brother.' Eleanor winked at Lottie.

Heat washed over her cheeks in a blush. An actual blush. Goodness! How long had it been since her blushes had been genuine? Not since she was a young woman in the company of Evander, before he'd left. When it was just the two of them in the country and a whole future stretched before them like a sunlit field.

'Have you been finding your travels pleasant?' Lottie asked, referencing the many trips the Duke and Duchess took together through the foreign locations written about in the journals of the adventure club.

Eleanor clasped her hands over heart and sighed with elation. 'I never knew life could be like this. That love could be like this. I cannot imagine the world I would have lived in had I never had our meetings.' She inclined her head. 'Thank you. Truly.'

'You needn't—'

'But I must.' Eleanor's green eyes glinted. 'And I have someone to introduce you to. Shall I have her come to-morrow evening?'

Ah... A new student. 'By all means,' Lottie replied grate-fully. 'Thank you.'

'I assure you it is the least I could do.'

And while they were on the topic of students, Lottie noted that Lord Rawley was on one side of the room and Lady Caroline, rather unfortunately, was on the other.

'Do excuse me,' Lottie said to Eleanor, who waved off the request and made her way towards Lady Westix.

Lottie approached Lord Rawley, who regarded her the way a child might a snarling beast creeping out from under the bed.

'Good evening, Lord Rawley.'

Though she tried to say it as kindly as possible, his eyes grew large in his face. She almost felt bad for him. Almost.

'Lady Caroline doesn't appear to have any dance partners.' Lottie looked to where the young lady lingered, near the wallflowers.

'Yes, but…' Rawley looked at his palm, frowned, and then opened it to her. A smear of ink was visible at the centre of his white glove.

Not understanding, Lottie gave him a quizzical look.

'My steps,' he whispered. 'For the dance.'

'Oh, come, now. You can't be that bad.' She held out her hand to him. 'Practise on me.'

The offer was made in earnest, and hesitantly accepted. But it proved to be to Lottie's detriment, in the end, for she was incorrect: Lord Rawley truly could be that bad.

They ran into several dancers, he stepped on her toes half a dozen times, and once managed to crack his forehead against hers. Whatever hopes Lady Caroline had harboured for a dance appeared to have dissolved into horror as she watched Lottie return from the dance floor with Lord Rawley.

Not that it mattered. The poor Viscount was so thoroughly humiliated by his performance that he scuttled away, dragging Lottie with him. If nothing else, he hadn't forgotten his manners in never leaving a woman unattended after a dance.

However, a fine idea lodged in Lottie's mind, on how to help him overcome his fear of dancing. She glanced down at her blue silk slippers. The tops were now muddied with a blend of blue, green and yellow-brown from the chalk. Though she'd squelched her discomfort at the time of impact, her toes ached from the abuse Lord Rawley had unintentionally administered.

'Miss Rossington.' A portly man stopped before her, his beady eyes bright as they skimmed over her dress. 'I'd hoped our paths might cross.'

Though Lottie tried to step back, she bumped into a

woman in a purple frock. She cast an annoyed look at Lottie and did not move. Nor did the women on either side of her.

Lottie was trapped.

Lord Devonington's eyes moved over her like hands.

'Would you care to dance?' He held out his hand in invitation.

God, how she wished she could flee.

Lottie suppressed a shudder of revulsion. It was a trick necessary for a courtesan. And although the three protectors she'd had in her short career had been kind, the skill was one she'd had to implement on several occasions.

Only now she had a new means of employment. One in which she did not have to spend time in the company of men she did not favour. Chiefly, men like Lord Devonington.

'Forgive me, but I'm taking a bit of a respite.' She gave him a false smile.

'For the entire evening?' he queried.

Lottie maintained her pleasant expression. 'Perhaps. It's been some time since I've danced.'

He smirked. 'Surely your other activities keep your constitution in good order.'

She gritted her teeth at the blatancy of his crass remark. 'And what, pray tell, do you mean by that?' she asked, determined to make him say it aloud, so that she might counter it with the truth.

'Activities I'm inclined to discuss with you in private, activities that we might pursue and enjoy together.' His stare oozed over her and settled on her bosom. 'I was hoping for something lower cut. You do have such fine breasts.'

Her mouth fell open in outrage. 'You've never seen... How could you possibly...?'

His mouth curved into a slow smile. 'That gown you

wore with Lord Astly. Do you not remember the masquerade?'

The masquerade?

Her stomach dropped. *That* gown.

Lord Astly had been her protector at the time—a wealthy earl who had never bothered with marriage. He had once been invited to a ball meant for peers and their mistresses—the sort of event where a lady would never be seen. Mistresses were put on display at parties such as these like baubles, wearing sheer fabrics and brazen gowns.

Lottie was no different. The gown was of thin white silk, opaque enough to keep the shape of her legs unseen, but cut extraordinarily low, with the pink of her nipples visible where they just peeked above the fabric of her risqué neckline.

She'd hated that dress almost as much as she had hated being paraded around like something to be owned.

What she hated even more, though, was the fact that she could not erase such memories from the minds of others. While Evander would always see her as a fresh-faced vicar's daughter, with her country innocence, others would always remember her for the men who'd paid for her company and for what she'd done in her time of employment.

No matter how Evander tried to appease her fears, Lottie knew she would always be no better than a courtesan.

'Now you remember.' Lord Devonington licked his lips. 'I assure you I have not forgotten.'

The urge to be sick pressed at the back of Lottie's throat. She didn't bother to excuse herself from the conversation, not caring for manners with someone so rude. She rushed away to the retiring room, where she slid behind a curtain for a moment of privacy.

Coming to the ball had been a mistake. She hadn't realised how many would be in attendance. Evander's explanation had made it sound small. Once she realised it was anything but, she ought to have left. Except she'd already gone to the expense of her dress, spent time putting her hair just so and indulging in that terrible thing called hope that now felt as though it were strangling her.

'Did you see her?'

A woman's voice came to her.

'Dancing with all the men. No doubt propositioning them.'

Lottie closed her eyes, knowing full well they referred to her.

'Perhaps that is her angle, then,' another woman replied. 'To rub elbows with her betters in an attempt to acquire several more. And I thought a man of the Earl of Westix's wealth would be enough to sate her avarice.'

Lottie pressed a hand to her mouth to squelch her sob, but it did nothing to keep the hot tears from coursing down her cheeks. She wished the carpet beneath her would part and swallow her whole. Or, better yet, that she might sprout wings like a bird and fly out of this awful place, never to return to London or anywhere anyone had ever heard of her transgressions.

'Lady Norrick and Lady Cotsworth—how lovely to see you.'

Lottie recognised the woman speaking as Violet, the new Countess of Dalton. The lovely young woman had once been the secret author of the scandal sheet the *Lady Observer.*

The women acknowledged Violet with murmured greetings.

'I'm quite certain both your daughters are under Lottie's tutelage—unless I'm mistaken,' Violet said in a conversational tone. '*Am* I mistaken?'

The two women stammered.

Violet tsked. 'Shame on you both. Yes, Lottie is beautiful enough to make any woman jealous, but it's only in the truly awful that such hateful spite arises.'

There was a gasp of outrage, followed by the bustle of hasty departure.

Lottie leaned her head back against the wall and remained where she stood. She was grateful to Violet, but by no means eager to return to the ballroom.

After a bit of time had passed, and Lottie was certain Lady Cotsworth and Lady Norrick wouldn't be lingering beyond the door, she removed herself from the retiring room and, after retrieving her cloak, from Westix Place.

Rather than endure the interminable wait for her own carriage, she took her chances in the open night air, in the hope of securing a hack. After all, not worrying after one's reputation did have its benefits, though they were indeed few and far between.

As the cool night air rushed across her blazing cheeks, Lottie reconciled herself to what she'd known all this time and what she had been trying to make Evander understand: it didn't matter how much he longed to be with her. People would never forget who she was or what she had done to survive.

She wished he had never left her, that she had never had to degrade herself. Hurt and anger flashed like sparks. Not that they did any good. There was no going back over the bridge she had burned.

She pushed through the door of her townhouse, startling Sarah into a scream. The maid had been walking past the door when Lottie made her abrupt arrival, and now held her chest with open hands, as though keeping her heart from spilling out.

'You gave me a fright,' Sarah exclaimed. Her shock blinked into confusion. 'Why are you home so early?'

'Come, now,' Lottie's butler swept past Sarah and came to take her cloak. 'Is that any way to care for our mistress?'

'Thank you, Andrews,' Lottie whispered.

He folded the heavy velvet in his arms and regarded her with concern, furrowing his brow into a new series of wrinkles. 'Is something amiss? Has someone hurt you?'

Yes.

She swallowed back her answer and shook her head. 'I'd simply like to be left alone. You may have the remainder of the night off.'

He hesitated, his thin lips arcing downward in a frown.

'I'll take it from here, if you don't mind,' Sarah gloated as she bumped past him.

'I'd prefer to stay.' Andrews lifted his chin with the haughtiness all butlers seemed to bring to their profession.

Lottie had kept her composure in the privacy of the hack she'd been able to acquire. But now, in the sanctuary of her own home, that resolve began to crumble. Rather than argue with the stoic butler, she nodded and allowed Sarah to guide her upstairs.

'Did you see him?' Sarah asked.

Lottie nodded.

'Was he cruel to you?' There was a sharpness to Sarah's tone.

Lottie shook her head, and a sob escaped her as Sarah swiftly opened the door to Lottie's bedchamber.

'What happened?' Sarah pressed.

Lottie shook her head, not wanting to speak of it.

'Tell me,' the maid insisted as she removed the pins from Lottie's hair and helped her undress.

Blast Sarah for her inability to be put off.

The shame of it rushed at Lottie in a hot wave. 'It will never be the same. Not with the ton, who will never accept me, and not with Evander, who I don't know if I can allow myself to open my heart to again.'

Sarah helped Lottie into a warm nightrail and guided

her towards the bed. 'Come, love, get into bed while I fetch you some tea.'

In truth, tea did sound lovely. She crawled into the large bed, with its sheets that felt like cool silk, where there were no witnesses to her humiliation, no one to judge her. There she gave way to the torrent of tears she'd managed to dam. Tears for the innocence she had sacrificed, for the life she had lived, for her terrible, terrible loss.

A cold, wet nose nudged her after a while, and her grey tabby, Silky, butted her furry head against Lottie's. Sarah had found the cat three years ago, when Lottie was near her own wits' end. The thing was nearly starved to death and scarcely weighed anything at all. She had bonded with Lottie immediately—two broken souls finding one another— and a sense of comfort formed between them as a result.

The door creaked open and the sweet scent of tea followed the quiet whisper of footsteps. Finally Lottie explained what had happened, her fingers idly stroking through Silky's thick fur while Sarah listened

Only when Lottie was done did the maid speak up. 'Lady Norrick's husband has a new mistress. One he holds in high regard, if the time and wealth he spends on her are any indication. From what I understand, Lady Norrick has been quite miserable.' Sarah gave a sad smile. 'She loves her husband, you see.'

Lottie regarded her maid with appreciation, seeing Lady Norrick in a new light in the understanding of her suffering. 'It's rather disconcerting, isn't it?' she said. 'How freely servants speak?'

'Not me.' Sarah winked. 'But I do like to listen.' She eyed Lottie's empty teacup. 'More tea?'

'No, thank you.' The hour was truly late now, and Lottie's eyes were gritty from her tears. Heavens, how she hated crying.

'And regarding Lord Westix,' Sarah said hesitantly.

'You have not given yourself the chance to recover from what happened, and you'll never be open to him if you don't.'

Lottie shook her head, not wanting to talk about the topic. It was still far too tender.

'Feel better?' Sarah asked.

'Yes.' Lottie smiled at the woman who had become so dear to her over the years. Bless Sarah for her inability to be put off.

'If I may…?' the maid hedged.

'When has my lack of permission ever stopped you before?' Lottie scratched under Silky's chin and the cat's low, lazy purr intensified.

Sarah's grin answered that question. 'Don't let anyone ruin your chance at happiness. Even yourself.'

Lottie nodded, but said nothing. Because it wasn't simply about how Devonington and those awful women had made her feel, it was also the delicate topic of allowing herself to heal, which would mean facing her hurt head-on.

It was far too great a thing to do. Perhaps even greater than she could manage.

Evander had long since abandoned discretion in his search for Lottie. The last time he'd seen her, she'd been dancing with Rawley.

Kentworth, having no one to entertain him now Rawley was preoccupied, had fastened onto Evander, regaling him with tales from a house party he'd attended over the Parliamentary break. The Marquess was in his cups, as was typical of him, and he went on at length about the various games he'd won.

'Have you seen Lottie?' Evander asked abruptly, as Rawley finally joined them.

Kentworth stopped midsentence and regarded Evander with a curious look, as if he couldn't quite deduce whether or not he ought to be offended by being cut off in the middle of his story—or epic saga, as it was turning out to be.

'I haven't,' he finally replied, appearing nonplussed. A sloppy smile sloshed over his face. 'But I've been meaning to ask you about her. Are you finally luring her out from under her rock after all this time?'

'Kentworth,' Rawley spoke in a warning tone from beside his friend.

The Marquess pulled back and regarded his more austere acquaintance. 'I daresay you are trying to prevent me from being punched.'

'Again?' Rawley slid his small silver watch from the pocket in his waistcoat.

Kentworth snorted a laugh and elbowed Rawley. But the nudge wasn't what pulled the shorter, more studious man from studying the time. No, it was the lady walking towards him.

Lady Caroline's face lit up like a candelabra at his besotted expression.

Irritation surged through Evander. He was fed up with Kentworth's antics, and he wanted nothing more than to find Lottie. After finally succeeding in encouraging her to join him at the ball, he was not going to see it all go to waste.

He turned to go when Kentworth caught him by the elbow. 'We'll find her.'

'Find who?' Lady Dalton asked, arriving with Lady Caroline.

'Miss Rossington,' Rawley said, staring shyly at Lady Caroline. 'She appears to be missing.'

'Lottie is missing?' Lady Dalton turned, looking over her shoulder in thought. 'I wonder...'

'Did you see her?' Evander pressed.

Lady Dalton frowned. 'No, but I overheard several women speaking ill of her.'

Rage flashed through Evander. 'I do beg your pardon.'

'I had words with them.' The Countess gave a haughty toss of her head. 'Wretched gossips. I'd seen Lottie enter the retiring room before me, and wondered at the time if she had somehow overheard.'

'What did they say?' Evander demanded.

'Nothing polite.' Lady Dalton sighed and gave him a pointed look. 'Exactly what you would expect.'

Evander's stomach dropped. He knew how upsetting that would have been for Lottie. He uttered a soft curse and strode away, ignoring Kentworth's calls for him to return.

Evander found his butler and immediately asked after Lottie.

'She's taken her leave, my lord,' Edmonds replied.

'You're certain she's gone?' Evander asked.

Edmonds lifted an austere brow. 'I'm familiar with Miss Rossington. I assure you it was she who left the ball, perhaps an hour ago. She didn't request her carriage.'

Evander frowned. She hadn't bade him farewell, which was suspicious enough when she'd seemed to be so happy dancing with him previously. But to leave her carriage?

'Fetch me my carriage,' he said. 'At once. And inform her driver she has left so he may return to Bloomsbury.'

Edmonds rushed off to comply with Evander's request. Within moments his carriage pulled to the front of Westix Place and Evander was on the cushioned seat, on his way to Russell Square in Bloomsbury.

On his way to Lottie.

But when he arrived her townhouse stood dark and forbidding, and his footman's knocks went unanswered. He pushed out of the carriage himself, foregoing decorum, and rapped hard on the door.

When no one opened it, he stepped back to regard the darkened windows and called out for Lottie.

Still there was no response.

At last he had no choice but to return home, where his birthday celebration had concluded and carriages were departing the townhouse in a steady line.

This had been his first real opportunity with Lottie since he had returned from his travels, and he had been careless. He should have stayed at her side the entire night.

He had failed her yet again.

A hard knot of despair twisted in his gut, along with the understanding that he might not be given another opportunity.

Dejected, he exited the carriage and trudged into the townhouse. The multitude of candles had all burned out, and only a few remained lit for the servants to clear away glasses and tables, casting the room into an atmosphere as dark as his mood. The floors were streaked with muddied chalk, which would be quite a feat to clean the following day. Evander would ensure the staff received a generous bonus to compensate for the effort.

'There you are.'

Lady Westix rushed towards him, the soft light catching at the beads on her silver dress and making them shimmer. When she stopped before him, he could make out the worry creasing his mother's face.

'Where did you go?' she asked.

'Lottie left.' He glanced back towards the doorway, as if it would be possible to see her departing.

Lady Westix sighed. 'I know you long to be with her, my son. However...' She pursed her lips.

'However?' Wariness simmered beneath the word. Surely his own mother understood how he felt, Surely she—of all people—would not castigate Lottie as the rest of the ton did.

'When it comes to women, some wounds take a considerable amount of time to heal. Especially those that run deep.'

'But it doesn't mean they'll never heal.'

'No,' she replied slowly, 'it doesn't. But it might take an extraordinary amount of patience on your part. As well as tenderness and consideration.'

'I'm willing to do anything it takes,' he said with finality, then softened his tone. 'The hour is late. Come, I'll walk you to your room.'

She gave him a grateful smile and allowed him to lead her from the empty ballroom. Their footsteps echoed around them, amid the clinking of glassware being neatly stacked.

'Do you truly love her?' she asked suddenly. 'Or is this insistent need to be with her derived from guilt?'

'It's love,' he answered without hesitation.

His mother stopped just before they began climbing the stairs. 'It is not me who requires the answer, Evander. I simply want *you* to know for certain. Here.' She lightly settled her hand over his heart. 'If you love her—truly love her—I suggest you never stop trying to win her affection. For if anything can heal deep wounds, it's love.'

A soft smile touched her lips, a new expression he'd seen her implement since his return.

Evander led his mother up the stairs, which she took one careful step at a time. She was the second person to warn him about Lottie that night. But Evander knew the extent of the love that existed between him and Lottie. They didn't know how deep his determination that she should be his wife ran. They didn't appreciate how far he was willing to go.

That he would stop at nothing to win Lottie back.

Chapter Twelve

The following morning Evander made his way to Lottie's townhouse once more. This time her butler appeared at the door and showed him in.

She was waiting for him in the drawing room, wearing a white muslin gown with dark blue ribbon woven through the lace at her neckline, hem and high waistline. A similar ribbon adorned her neck, with a small cameo hanging from its centre, just under the sensual hollow of her throat.

The effect of these small notes of blue and how they made her eyes appear all the more brilliant was stunning. *She* was stunning.

But then she always had been.

Her hair was bound up in coils, with a single large curl that rolled over her right shoulder. Evander was struck suddenly by the urge to brush aside that curl and run his lips over the smoothness of her graceful neck, not stopping until he had kissed that delectable hollow and even lower still.

In that moment he was entirely certain that his resolve to win her back had nothing to do with the weight of his guilt at having left her for so many years. Though he did indeed feel guilty. For as he looked at her now, he knew beyond the shadow of a doubt that his love for her superseded anything that could be tossed their way. Prejudice, vitriol, being cast out from society. None of it mattered more to him than this woman.

Now he need only prove to her that he would not hurt her as he had before.

'Good morning, Evander.' Lottie's attempt at a smile was not entirely successful. 'Forgive me for leaving your ball without bidding you farewell. I'm afraid I felt rather ill and didn't wish to ruin your enjoyment.'

He settled on the settee beside her. She smelled of a sweet perfume, something floral with a musk to it that he found appealing. Again, the urge to nuzzle her neck teased at him, to brush his lips over the warmth of her skin and breathe in that wonderful scent.

Her gaze slid towards the teapot. 'Would you like some tea?'

'I want to speak with you.'

He reached out tentatively and took her hand in his. She didn't pull away from his touch, and for the first time in six years her smooth skin lay against his.

As if realising the poignancy of it, she glanced at where their fingers were locked together before returning her attention to him once more.

He had meant to say he understood why she had been upset, that he didn't care and she need not allow it to trouble her. But now that he was in such proximity to her, cradling her slender hand in his, those were not the words that came from his mouth.

'I'm grateful for the time you were there,' he replied. 'And I do regret my inability to spend more time with you. I'm afraid there were more guests than I had anticipated when I extended the invitation to you.'

She looked down again to watch their linked hands and said nothing.

'Seeing you there was a dream,' he continued. 'Holding you so close to me, dancing with you, hearing your laugh, seeing your smile. God, you looked so beautiful.'

A flush of colour washed over her cheeks.

'I wish I could have spent the entire night with only you.'

He reached up, tentative, expecting her to pull away. When she did not, he ran the back of his forefinger down her petal-soft cheek. Her lashes fluttered closed on the look of someone savouring a caress.

'It can't work,' she whispered.

'It can.' He leaned closer to her.

Her lips were red and full. Sensual. His fingertips gently lifted her chin, angling her face towards his. The beat of his heart slammed in his chest like a drum. He lowered his mouth to hers and their lips met in a tender brush. Her lips were smoother than he remembered, sweeter. Sheer heaven.

She lifted her hands to his face, but rather than kiss him, she rested her forehead against his. 'I can't.'

When she drew back there were tears shining in her blue eyes, making them all the more brilliant. He pulled the handkerchief from his pocket and offered it to her. She accepted it with both hands and kept it crumpled between her palms.

'Because of what others say?' he asked.

She pinned on a false smile. 'Are you sure you don't want tea?'

'I don't want tea.' He kept his gaze locked on her. 'I want you.'

'The world you want me in will never accept me.' She turned away from him.

'You overheard those women being malicious towards you?' he said.

She bowed her head slightly forward and exhaled slowly.

'I don't care about them, Lottie.' He carefully drew her

attention back to him with his fingertips. 'I don't give a fig about anyone's opinion. I only care that I love you.'

'And what of your family? Your friends? They too will be cast aside because of who I am. What I've done.' She shook her head and the curl tumbled across the shoulder of her gown.

'None of them care.' He reached for her hand once more, and she did not pull it away. 'You shouldn't either.'

She didn't reply.

'Do you know what will improve your spirits?' he asked.

She glanced up at him, her expression wary.

'A ride through Hyde Park.'

Her brows rose and she pulled her hand away.

'At the fashionable hour.' He grinned. 'With me.'

'I don't think that will make things better,' she said quietly.

'It will be the perfect opportunity for us to see one another again.' He softened his voice. 'And I do so enjoy seeing you, getting to know you again.'

She twisted her fingers against one another, the gesture one from their days in Oxfordshire. Clearly it was still a habit.

'Evander, I—'

He put up his hand to stop the rejection before it could be spoken. 'Please at least consider it. I'll have a carriage sent tomorrow. If you should find the idea agreeable, the carriage will bring you to me. Should you not, I will enter the park alone on horseback.'

Breath held, he waited for her response. It had been so good the night before to see her, to hear her laugh, and not only to learn who she had become, but to allow her to see who he had become. Hopefully one day she would deem him worthy of her trust once more. He only needed time. With her.

If she would grant it.

At last, she nodded. 'I will consider it.'

It was as close to a yes as he might get. Now he only needed to wait to see if she showed. And he hoped to God she would.

No sooner had darkness fallen than Sarah entered Lottie's room to inform her that her newest student had arrived. Lottie tugged off the dark fitted smock she wore, that protected her gown from being spattered by paint.

The watercolour was almost done. Lottie stepped back, mindful to avoid Silky, who often settled just behind her heels, and regarded the painting. It was a small cottage set in a field, with dots of trees in the distance and a small garden at the front.

'It's lovely,' Sarah said. 'But you always paint that cottage. Shouldn't you try something different?'

Lottie stared at the small house and a hollow ache rang in her chest. 'It's where I was happiest.'

She took a strip of linen, washed the paint from her fingers, and stroked a hand over Silky before making her way down the stairs to where her new student awaited her first lesson.

As soon as Lottie entered the drawing room and spied the pretty blonde, she recognised her. It was Lady Alice, a young woman who had once been the most sought-after lady of the ton and had disappeared suddenly after a terrible scandal involving her then betrothed.

'Lady Alice.' Lottie smiled at her. 'It's a pleasure to see you once more in London.'

'Thank you,' Lady Alice replied, with a flicker of a smile in return. 'I confess my mother bade me return. I did not wish to.' She shifted her focus towards the Brussels weave carpet. 'People can be cruel.'

'I understand that well,' Lottie said, with more bitterness than intended.

Her new pupil lifted her head and regarded her with renewed appreciation. 'I don't even know if it's possible for me to find a new suitor after what Lord Ledsey did.'

Lottie indicated the settee.

It was fascinating, how certain personalities required different approaches—something she had learned in her days as a courtesan that served her well now, as an instructor. With Lady Alice, Lottie knew, things would need to be handled gently. After all, it was not every lady who had to overcome the scandal of having had a betrothed who had attempted murder.

'Do you want to take instruction with me?' Lottie asked, as she did all her students. It was important to understand their intention in being there. Pupils who were forced into her tutelage weren't inclined to succeed.

'I do.' Lady Alice smoothed her pink silk dress in an anxious fashion Lottie herself was familiar with. 'But not because of my mother. Though she does agree with these lessons,' she added quickly. 'She hopes I'll find another suitor.' Her smile was brittle. 'I believe she has pinned hopes upon me I may not be able to fulfil.'

Lottie remained silent while she spoke, allowing Lady Alice to fill the space with her thoughts.

'Eleanor, the Duchess of Somersville, is the one who suggested I come.' Alice pursed her lips. 'You see, I feel rather outside of myself, and have for some time. I don't know how to find who I used to be, and Her Grace said you might help guide the way.'

Ah, now it was making sense. There had been some hurt in her life, which left her bereft. That was something Lottie understood far too well.

'Since Lord Ledsey?' she asked, referencing the young woman's former betrothed.

'Since…before,' Lady Alice replied slowly.

Lottie lifted an eyebrow in silent query and Lady Alice's lovely face took on a pained expression.

'I was in love with a baron's son—George.' She smiled wistfully as she said his name. 'He was a fourth son, and determined to pave his own way in this world. That is how he came to be a soldier. His mother received a letter stating he was missing after a battle.' She drew in a shuddering breath. 'My mother let me grieve for a year, as long as any widow, even though we'd never wed. She thought herself generous for the consideration and then we came to London.'

'And Lord Ledsey was an earl,' Lottie supplied.

'Precisely.' Lady Alice toyed with a small rosette on her gown. 'I played the part of dutiful daughter and tried to be happy. But I simply…wasn't. Not without my George. I never have been and I'm not sure I ever can be.'

Her admission struck a deep chord in Lottie's chest. How often had she wondered that same thing about herself? If she could ever be truly happy again?

Lady Alice's eyes filled with tears and Lottie produced a handkerchief from her pocket. Experience had taught her never to begin a lesson without several handy.

The young woman accepted it gratefully and wiped at her eyes. 'Mother allowed me to return to the country after Lord Ledsey, to recuperate from my melancholy. Except it has not improved.'

Indeed, the poor young woman did appear rather miserable.

Lottie sat on the settee beside her and put a gentle hand to Lady Alice's shoulder. 'We'll see what we can do to make you feel better. Whether it be with a suitor, or even on your own.'

Alice gave her a sad smile. 'I'm not hopeful, I confess.' The handkerchief in her hands drew her focus. 'Do you ever think that perhaps it isn't a place or a status that makes you happy, but a person?'

Lottie sat back at that revelation. 'I'd never considered it.'

'I don't think I can be happy—truly happy—without my George,' Lady Alice said. 'No matter how much I pretend otherwise.'

The young woman's words clung to Lottie for the rest of the evening and into the next day, like a burr lodged in her mind. Perhaps it was for that reason that when Evander's carriage came at half-past four she was dressed in a gown she'd recently had sewn by her modiste and promptly climbed into the carriage to meet him at Hyde Park.

As an adult, she'd had two happy times in her tumultuous life. One could never be reclaimed. And the other was with Evander. Perhaps there was hope for her yet?

Chapter Thirteen

Evander hadn't expected Lottie to come to the ball for his birthday, and was even less inclined to believe she'd show at Hyde Park. At least at the celebration she'd expected some control over the guest list, however wildly off-course it had veered. But at Hyde Park, everyone who was anyone appeared. Meaning she would be seen by the collective ton. While she was still licking her wounds over their spiteful gossip.

However, just because he did not expect her, did not mean he didn't continue to watch the entrance to the park, in the hopes of seeing his carriage arrive. His horse remained stoic beneath him as he waited by a tree, amid the flecks of sunlight that streamed through the leaves overhead.

A parade of carriages entered the path and rolled past, their occupants well-dressed and gazing out through the windows to observe the other attendees. And, of course, to be seen.

Evander was very nearly ready to give up when he caught sight of his own carriage with a single occupant inside.

Lottie.

He nudged his horse to trot towards the carriage, where

he disembarked and handed the reins to his footman, who would tie the steed to the rear of the carriage so he could join Lottie inside.

She smiled as he took the seat opposite her. The cabin smelled of her sweetly floral, sensual perfume, and he found himself hoping the scent might linger within, so that every time he took his carriage somewhere he would be enveloped in her perfume.

'This time I truly did not think you'd come,' he admitted.

'Then I mustn't make this a habit, lest you expect me regularly.' She spoke as she looked out of the window, overly casual—except for the flirtatious wink she tossed in his direction.

'If only I were so lucky.' He put a hand to his heart and she laughed.

'I came because... Well, because while the vipers are out there—' she nodded towards the window '—I knew I would be in here. With you.'

Trust. It was a crumb, a mere sample of it, to whet his appetite for more, but by God it was a start.

A grin tugged at his lips, enjoying her play as he parried, 'And you wanted to be with me?'

'Should I even answer that?' she asked, as a smile teased at her lush mouth.

'You don't really need to.' He gave a small shrug, feigning a lack of care. 'I already know.'

'Do you?'

She was so beautiful staring at him, pouting with mock indignation, her skin creamy in the golden sunlight. He wanted to kiss her again, as he'd done the day before. Except this time he didn't want to stop.

Bit by bit, piece by piece, he was learning more about her—not through what she said or shared, but by her reaction. At present, he found himself longing to know if she still made those little humming sounds of pleasure as their kisses deepened.

An image of her being kissed by another man flashed in his mind, sharp as a dagger. Evander jerked his attention to the path, where a couple strode together, concentrating his gaze on their attire, which bordered on matching in similar pale shades of green. It was a better detail to fix his thoughts upon than where they were leading.

'Pray tell what do you mean?' asked Lottie flirtatiously.

Damn. What had they been speaking about?

Whatever it was had made him think of kissing her, and then wonder how she had reacted when other men had kissed her.

Had she loved any of those men?

He shook his head to clear those thoughts. After all, she wouldn't have had to do any of it if he'd remained in England. Or, better yet, remained in contact with her, had been there to help her. Returned when he was supposed to.

But he had abandoned her. And she'd had to forge her own way in life. As a woman, she'd done that the only way she could. And it was no one's fault but his own.

'Forgive me, I was wool-gathering,' he admitted. 'What do I mean about what?'

'Why do you think I wanted to be with you this afternoon?' She leaned forward and slowly lifted her eyes to meet his in such a way it struck him dead in the centre of the chest. The look was sensual. Confident.

Practised.

Damn it.

'I've always known you enjoyed my company,' he said. His tone was light and playful. Not at all indicative of the heaviness bearing down on him.

'Do you think you make me happy?' she asked.

It was a teasing question, but one that he considered

more deeply than the query warranted in light of his turbulent mood. 'I think I did at one time.'

The silence that settled between them seemed to grow thick, the smoothness of their conversation congealing with his honesty.

Lottie tilted her head, turning the pointed white brim of her hat just so, to obscure only one eye. 'Do you think you will make me happy again?'

Now there was an answer he knew well.

He leaned forward, taking her gloved hands in his, and answered with the utmost certainty. 'I know I will.'

Lottie had always been attracted to Evander's sense of confidence. When she was younger she could not imagine possessing such self-assuredness. And even now, as a woman who stood on her own two feet, the way he carried himself held great appeal.

The manner with which he claimed to know she would be happy with him again did wonders to soothe that place in her chest where he had wounded her before. Part of her was still calling his words a mere fantasy. And yet there was another part of her, desperate to revel in life again, that wanted to believe that fantasy was reality. She wanted to be the woman in the story, rescued by the man who loved her.

But how did she open a wounded heart that was so wrapped in on itself?

'What are you thinking?' he asked.

She felt her lips curl up in spite of herself. 'You used to ask me that all the time.'

He settled back in his seat, his pose relaxed, in an almost arrogant manner. 'I still want to know.'

'I'm thinking that I want to be happy.' She toyed with the fingertips of her gloves in an attempt to fight the urge to twist her fingers.

The motion gave her away regardless, and he raised his brow with suspicion. 'There's more.'

She shook her head and returned her gaze to outside the window, where couples strode by arm in arm, their unions seeming so simple, so natural. 'I'm wondering if it's even possible. If I can…'

There was so much between herself and Evander. So much pain. Such a breach of trust that had cost far too much.

His hands closed over hers. She startled from her thoughts.

'I know,' he said gently, and the hurt in his green eyes told her he truly did. 'Will you try?'

Without realising what she was doing, she nodded.

His expression brightened. 'You will?'

'I'm here now, aren't I?' she asked, suddenly breathless with the boldness of her decision, the risk she was taking. She was balancing on the razor-sharp blade of a knife— one whose cut she could not withstand a second time.

'Yes.' He gave a relieved chuckle. 'I will do everything I can to prove to you I am worthy of a second chance for us.'

'Us.' Warmth glowed inside her as she repeated the word. 'I like the way that sounds.'

'I do too.'

Somehow the space between them in the carriage seemed far more intimate. All at once she recalled how he'd kissed her the day before, his mouth so tender on hers, his affection so apparent.

'I've been invited to a ball at Dalton Place in two days' time,' Evander said. 'Will you be in attendance?'

Lottie considered her correspondence over the prior few weeks. Social events were not things she agreed to attend, but that didn't mean she never received invitations. Generally they were from pupils who had found happiness and now considered her a friend. Violet, Countess of Dalton, was one such lady. It would not surprise Lottie if she did have an invitation to the Dalton ball and had either declined or not yet responded.

'I may be,' Lottie finally replied.

'I should like to see you there.' Evander glanced towards the townhouse on the other side of the narrow windowpane.

Her townhouse.

When had they wound their way back to her home?

How had their time together come to such a swift end?

Perhaps it was a whisper of happiness, a promise of better things to come.

Lottie nodded. 'I too should like that very much. Thank you for a lovely afternoon.'

'I assure you the pleasure was all mine.' He gazed at her, besotted, as he exited the carriage, helped her down with tenderness, and walked her to her front door.

She wanted him to linger there for ever. Except they were in full view of everyone. With a bow, he left, taking her heart with him.

Once inside, she located Sarah and informed her she must find the invitation to Dalton Place, which was easily done, and reply saying she would be delighted to attend.

The ball would be filled with many friends, and there was no hiding from the ton now that Lottie and Evander had been seen in Hyde Park. Whether she was ready or not, Lottie had plunged herself into the opportunity of a second chance with Evander. A possibility that some day she might actually allow herself to be with him again, trust him again. In whatever form that might take.

And, while the idea of the ton's reaction filled her with trepidation, there was also an unmistakable excitement for a future with Evander—an excitement that could only be rivalled by Sarah's enthusiasm.

And so it was that Lottie found herself counting the hours until she next saw Evander, and wondering about the happiness they might once more find with one another.

Chapter Fourteen

Whatever nerves had plagued Lottie on her previous outings among the ton with Evander were non-existent the night of the ball at Dalton Place.

She wore a lavender gown with a layer of white tulle over it that glittered with brilliants as they caught the candlelight. Sarah had done a simple, elegant arrangement of Lottie's hair, one not requiring the aid of curling tongs or ribbons or jewelled combs. The mirror reflected Lottie as a woman who knew the power of her own beauty, with a confidence unlike any she ever thought to possess when she'd been a naive vicar's daughter.

With such self-assurance, surely it was possible to rise above people's opinions.

Her stubbornly tilted chin was reflected in the glass with matched determination.

She could do this. She *would* do this.

But behind her determination there was melancholy hovering about her awareness—the same way it did every year around this time, and had done for the last three years. A memory she could never forget.

She embraced the pain of it, cupping it against her heart, and left for Dalton Place with a steeled spine.

She arrived in a flood of other guests and donned her

confidence like a cloak, sweeping into the ballroom when she was announced.

Lady Dalton rushed towards her as soon as she entered. Her pink silk dress and the lovely flush to her cheeks, placed there no doubt by the recent birth of her daughter, accentuated her creamy skin.

'Oh, Lottie, it's so wonderful to see you.'

Violet had been miserable when she'd first begun seeing Lottie the previous year. There was no evidence of any sorrow on her glowing face now. Marriage suited her well.

'I apologise for my late acceptance of your gracious invitation.' Lottie reached for Violet's hand and squeezed it affectionately.

'You needn't apologise at all.' Violet smiled. 'We're just so happy you're here.'

Lord Dalton joined his wife and nodded to Lottie in greeting. 'Thank you for coming. Violet was delighted when you agreed to attend. And I'm thrilled to see my sister so happy.' He glanced over his shoulder across the room, to where Lord Rawley was speaking with Lady Caroline.

'I do so hope things work out for them,' Violet clasped her hands to her chest. 'Caroline truly cares for him.'

'I think we can at least hope for a dance this evening,' Lottie said, thinking back to the shirt she had gifted him on their last session—a shirt with cuffs that were embroidered with the steps of the cotillion. There would be no lost scraps of paper or smeared ink on his palms this time.

Lord Dalton lifted his brows. 'Do you know something we don't?'

Lottie simply gave a little shrug.

Someone else caught her eye in the crowd of guests, several paces from Lord Rawley.

Evander.

Violet gave a little laugh. 'I think you have your own dance waiting. We won't detain you.'

Lottie inclined her head graciously to them and slipped into the crowd.

'Miss Rossington.' Evander, handsome as ever in a green waistcoat and dark jacket, bowed and kissed her hand. 'Is that lovely smile for me?'

She laughed. 'You are incorrigible.'

Several people shifted around them to make room on the dance floor.

Evander offered her his hand. 'May I claim your first dance this evening?'

'I would love nothing more.'

Lottie allowed him to lead her to the dance floor, where they were several couples away from Lord Rawley and Lady Caroline.

Lottie stole a quick glance in their direction just as Rawley peeked at the cuff of his shirt beneath his jacket sleeve. As the music filled the air his steps were as they should be, and he gave only occasional glimpses downward.

'It feels like heaven to dance with you once more, Lottie,' Evander said, drawing her focus back to him. 'You're even more graceful than I remember.'

His flattery warmed Lottie with pleasure. He always had been complimentary of her. She still remembered when she'd shyly shown him her watercolours. She'd thought them simple things, of no great import other than to bring her peace when she painted. But he'd gone on about her skill and made her feel as though her painting was more than just dabbling to fill her time.

Through the dance they laughed and talked as they had in old times whenever the music brought them together, watching one another in eager anticipation as the dance pulled them apart. All too soon, it came to an end.

'You appear flushed, Miss Rossington,' Evander said with a wink.

She immediately caught on to what he implied. 'Mercy me, I am feeling rather warm. Do excuse me. I require a moment on the terrace.'

'Of course.' He stepped back to allow her to pass through the double doors at the rear of the ballroom.

Lottie stepped out into the cool summer night. It was colder than previous summers, but at least the rain had taken a respite. Overhead, in a cloudless sky, stars winked like diamonds, and all around her the quiet of a still evening cast a reprieve over her ears after the volume inside.

The door opened and Evander exited the ballroom on a wave of raucous music and humming conversation. It faded to a light background murmur as the door closed behind him.

He strode to where she stood in the shadows. 'I won't keep you, but I was not yet ready to let you go.'

'Nor was I ready to be released.' She rested her hands on the cold stone railing. 'I wish it was possible for my every dance to be with you.'

'It could be,' he answered slowly. 'If we were to wed.'

The suggestion hit her with a mix of excitement and fear. She didn't respond, unable to summon any sort of proper thought as his words hung between them. It was one thing to see him again, to allow her walls to crack. But marriage. It was so large, so permanent.

Too much.

She had said yes to his proposal of marriage before and then he had wounded her deeply. It was impossible not to think of that now. Just as it was hard to push aside the rise of melancholy inside her.

Coming out this night had been a poor decision.

He cleared his throat. 'It's too soon.'

'Yes.'

'But not for me.' He put his large, warm hand over hers. 'I've wanted this for six years. I've wanted you that long.'

She swallowed and looked out into the garden. Her heart was pounding hard in her chest, its beat whooshing in her ears. Memory pressed on her once more, of an anniversary she would never forget—one that loomed in her mind, in her heart, and twisted through her, bringing agony.

'I'm not ready,' she whispered.

Evander studied her, his expression tender, patient. 'I understand.'

But he didn't. Not really. And he probably never would. Not when she couldn't bring herself to be wholly honest with him about what had happened in his absence.

He reached for her then, his touch a gentle, loving caress down her cheek. 'I would wait a lifetime for you, Lottie.'

She wanted to say she didn't need a lifetime, to laugh it off and kiss him. But she wasn't at all sure when she would be ready. *If* she would be ready.

She truly wished to give him a second chance, but she needed to move slowly, day by day, and not with any immediate promise of a future together.

But, after everything they had been through, was it even possible to open her heart completely again?

Evander eased away from Lottie. Not only to offer a respectable distance between them, should someone else escape to the terrace, but also to allow her the space she needed.

Her hair was styled simply—it was something he'd noticed earlier, as well as the delicate necklace at her throat, that made his eyes wander towards the graceful line of her neck rather than to the jewellery. She always had been most beautiful to him when she was simply adorned.

Though they had spent more time together in this season than the previous two years, he sensed in her a nervousness, like a skittish deer teetering on the edge of bolting. The anxiety which had all but disappeared these last few days, suddenly resurfaced at the mere mention of marriage.

While disappointing, it did not mean she would never be ready. He had hurt her—he knew that. He knew that and he hated it. But she could not seem to move past what she had become in life.

A courtesan.

It had changed her in some ways. She was sure of herself, more flirtatious, confident. But this new woman made Evander less certain—as if one wrong word or action might make her run from him for ever. As if she was always holding something back from him.

This was the woman she had become—what she had salvaged from the ashes of his betrayal, rising with armour intact.

'We should return before we're missed,' he said.

She glanced back towards the doors and he saw a flicker of trepidation.

'I can go first if you'd rather,' he offered.

She shook her head. 'I'd prefer not to give them fodder for gossip if I'm gone too long.'

Though she smiled when she said it, he knew that despite her resolve she truly was worried about the backlash of opinion.

'However, I do appreciate your consideration.' She rose up on her toes and pressed her mouth to his in a quick kiss.

As his lips still tingled with the warmth of her affection she strode towards the door and disappeared inside. He passed the next several minutes thinking of her, staring out at the darkened garden with memories of her heavy on his mind. Those from the past and those in the present. And, if he was being entirely honest, he hoped for some more in the future.

Once a sufficient amount of time had elapsed after her

departure, he followed her into the ballroom. The light
and sound were a veritable assault after the cool quiet of
the night outside. His gaze swept the area, seeking out the
delicate lavender gown.

He almost missed her on the first pass, given the bulk
of Lord Devonington's body blocking her. Clearly she had
not made it farther than a dozen steps into the ballroom
before being detained in conversation. Which meant they
had been speaking together for some time.

He ought to leave her to her privacy. Except that Lord
Devonington was a foul sort—one who said what was on
his mind. And that was seldom a good thing.

Evander edged closer, using the crowd to mask his actions, in an attempt to get within earshot. Unfortunately
the Earl was speaking so quietly Evander was practically
behind the man before he could make out what was being
said.

'…it's why I offered to become your protector before,'
Lord Devonington said in a low voice.

Evander's blood went cold.

Good God. Had Lottie been Devonington's mistress
in the past?

'I've declined you twice in the past and I am doing so
again now,' Lottie replied firmly. 'Good evening, Lord
Devonington.'

'I have not finished speaking with you,' the Earl hissed.
'I'm willing to pay good money for your favours—'

Evander flew into action, grabbing Devonington by the
shoulder, spinning the man round and slamming his fist
into that fleshy jaw.

But that wasn't enough.

He grabbed the Earl as the man blinked in surprise, too
stunned by the suddenness of the attack even to put up his
arms to block his face. Evander hit him again, smashing

his fist into the cur's face with a force so hard pain shot through his fingers and up his arm.

Devonington fell back as blood spurted from his nose. He held his dimpled hands to his face, eyes wide. Somewhere nearby a woman screamed.

Perhaps that was what recalled Evander to his senses. Or perhaps it was the heavy way Devonington sat back, the floor around him spattered with blood.

Lottie.

Evander caught her horrified expression and immediately went to her.

'Lottie.' He said her name softly.

She didn't move. And then her gloved hand wrapped around his, her touch like a caress, as concern showed in her eyes. 'Are you hurt?'

He shook his head rather than lie. His hand hurt something fierce, but she didn't need to know that. 'Come, I'll see you to your carriage.'

She nodded and allowed him to lead her from the ballroom as every set of eyes remained fixed on them.

The night had a chill to it he hadn't noticed when they were outside previously. Lottie seemed to be suddenly aware of it as well, for she shivered. He removed his jacket and placed it over her shoulders.

'I heard what he said to you,' Evander said softly.

Lottie closed her eyes slowly. 'I wish you hadn't. It's humiliating, this life I have lived. And everyone knows it.'

'I'd like to come to you tomorrow.' Hidden by the bulk of his jacket, his hand slid into hers.

'Please don't,' she whispered.

His heart fell. So they were back to that again.

He ran his thumb over the back of her hand. 'I want to help—'

She spun on him, ripping her hand from his. 'You can

never undo the past. No matter how much you wish to. I can't do this, Evander.'

Her carriage pulled up then, and the footman rushed to open the door. She climbed in, her frame small as she huddled beneath his jacket, appearing very much like the fragile woman Charles had claimed her to be the night of Evander's birthday ball.

Except Evander hadn't listened to him. And, damn it, he still wouldn't.

He would go to her tomorrow, when she was in a better frame of mind. She might be faltering in her hope of their future together, but he had enough faith for both of them, and he would never, never lose hope.

Chapter Fifteen

The following day did not work out as Evander had hoped. Lottie did not appear to be recovered and his footman was turned away from her door almost as soon as it had opened.

The man came back, dejected, with the news that not only was he told to leave, but that the very austere butler had informed him no one was interested in hearing him plead Evander's case.

Evander was not so easily put off. He directed his coach to Aphrodite & Cupid, where Miss Flemming gave him a smile tinged with some confusion.

'Isn't it Wednesday?' she asked. 'I cannot say I've seen you here any other day of the week except Saturday.'

'It is Wednesday,' he confirmed. 'And I need a new bouquet—perhaps the most exquisite you've ever done.'

Her brows lifted, as though she was surprised by his request. 'Not for Miss Rossington?'

'Oh, yes, for Miss Rossington.' His gaze passed over the flowers and settled on some brilliant purple blooms. 'Irises.'

'Hope?'

He nodded. 'And white tulips.'

'Forgiveness?'

'She'll understand.'

Or at least Evander hoped she would. His dream had felt so attainable up until the moment Devonington had propositioned her in the corner of a ballroom, the foul beast of a man.

Deep down, he knew that if it wasn't Devonington it might have been some other cad. And Evander was to blame for all of it. If he hadn't gone—if he hadn't left Lottie for so long—she would never have had to turn to such a profession to survive. It was Evander's fault and they both knew it.

'I'll have the bouquet delivered this afternoon,' Miss Flemming said with a smile, polite and courteous as always.

Evander's hand ached from punching that cur. He flexed and clenched his fingers now, so his bruised skin stretched over sore knuckles. 'I'll wait for it, please. I'd prefer to deliver them in person.'

'Oh.' Miss Flemming flushed, momentarily taken aback, but recovered with an over-bright smile. 'I hope this means all is working in your favour? I've never seen a man so devoted.' She flushed. 'I'll prepare these for you straight away.'

True to her word, she had a magnificent bouquet put together in less than half an hour. Most likely her most beautiful one yet. The bundle was made up of irises, and peeking between the purple petals were strategically placed white tulips. She had bound it together with silver ribbons that formed a bow comprised of several intricate loops.

'It's perfect,' Evander said appreciatively.

'Best of luck to you, my lord.'

'I'll need all the luck I can get,' he muttered.

Then he tipped his hat to her and departed the small shop, returning to Lottie's with the weighty flowers clutched in his hand.

This time he didn't bother sending his footman up the path, but went himself instead. He marched up to the door and rapped the brass knocker.

There was no answer.

Surely she hadn't dismissed her butler? Where the devil was the old man?

Evander knocked again. And again. And again.

A window next door opened and a scowling face glowered down at him. 'Enough of that racket.'

'I daresay I will continue to knock until this door opens,' Evander said loudly.

Over the past two years since they had been reunited Lottie had turned him away often. Time and time again he had given her the space she requested, waiting sometimes months before returning. But this was different. He'd never before been this close to a chance with her again, and he'd be damned if he lost it now.

Truth be told, he was worried about her. And he wanted to console her after the way she'd been treated. No one deserved to be spoken to as Devonington had to her. Least of all Lottie, whose heart was as golden as they came.

The repetitive metallic bang of the knocker echoed in his mind, pounding into his brain. His forefinger had begun to go numb, but still he continued. Suddenly the knocker was ripped out of his hand as the door flew open, revealing Lottie's maid.

Her gaze fell on him first, studied him, then went to the flowers in his hand.

'Good God,' he said, affronted. 'Where is the butler? Has something happened?'

'The servants have all been given the day off.' She glanced to the carriage. 'I imagine the butler would have told your footman as much, prior to leaving for the day.'

The information had not been conveyed, apparently.

Evander tried to glance past her into the empty hall, in

the hope of seeing something that might offer a clue as to what was going on. 'Lottie—'

'She's as well as can be expected.' The woman spoke with a considerable amount of sympathy.

'I'm sorry to hear she has been affected so badly.'

The maid's brow furrowed. 'I imagine it would affect most.'

'Last night was indeed upsetting. I swear, if I could have another five minutes alone with Devonington...'

The older woman frowned and tilted her head, studying him. 'Do you know what today is?'

'It's Wednesday.'

She tsked softly.

Taken aback, he went over the days in this head. Yes, he was correct. It was indeed Wednesday.

'May I see her?'

The maid hesitated. 'She wouldn't like that. Forgive me, my lord, but I must say no.'

'Please.' Desperation edged into his voice. 'I'm worried about her.'

The maid's chin jutted outward in a stubborn fashion she had most likely implemented her entire life. 'I'm worried about her too, truth be told. This may be the act that finally has me thrown out, but...' She opened the door. 'I believe Lottie needs you right now.'

He didn't bother to stop and question why her maid referred to her so informally, or to feel the incredulity that a servant had allowed him in when her mistress had clearly given instructions to be left alone. All he cared about was Lottie and the opportunity to see her once more.

The maid led him swiftly up the stairs and rapped upon a door on the left.

'Leave me be, Sarah,' Lottie replied, her voice thick with tears.

Evander's heart crumpled in his chest at the sound. He was aching to do what he could to offer her comfort.

'Forgive me, lovey…' Sarah moved back from the door and allowed Evander to go in.

He turned the handle, pushing aside the small voice in his head screaming at him that this was a bad idea.

The curtains were drawn, shading the room in heavy shadows. Lottie stood off to one side of the room in a plain white muslin gown, her long, dark hair unbound. Her arm hovered in front of an easel; a brush was poised in her hand. A small candle flickered on the table beside her, illuminating the painting as well as part of her face.

'What are you doing here?' She stiffened. 'Sarah.'

'Forgive me, love, but I don't think you've told him,' the maid said. 'And pardon my saying so, but you need to.'

The door clicked closed behind Evander with the maid on the other side, leaving him alone with Lottie.

Evander whispered her name and set the flowers aside on a small table near the door. His vision adjusted to the partial light as he approached her. Her eyes were red-rimmed and puffy—further evidence she'd been crying.

'Please leave.'

'I'm worried about you.'

'You're worried about me?' She gave a mirthless chuckle as she exhaled. 'I told you I didn't want to see you. Not today of all days.'

'Because of what happened last night? Forgive me, but I couldn't stand by and allow Lord Devonington to speak to you in such a way.'

His blood simmered with rage even as he thought of it. Were the man in front of him now, Evander would punch him all over again. Except this time he wouldn't stop.

Her brow furrowed.

'It isn't that, is it?' Evander asked slowly. 'It's something your maid mentioned…something that you need to tell me.'

Lottie sagged backwards, her gaze distant and listless 'You shouldn't be here,' she said sadly. 'I asked you to leave me be.'

'Whatever it is, however difficult you think it to be, I want to know so that we can face it together.'

He glanced at the painting to find an image of a cottage with a cluster of trees behind it, and the beginnings of a small garden boxed in front with a simple fence.

'This isn't Binsey,' he said. 'Where is this?'

'Evander.' Her eyes sparkled with tears in the candle-light. She shook her head. 'Please.'

There were more paintings on the floor—all of that same small cottage from various different angles. Close-up views of a garden filled with pink geraniums and daffodils, another of vegetables climbing up stakes thrust into rich, dark soil, still others of a view of the forest from a window presumably inside the cottage.

He bent and lifted one that appeared to have been painted from inside the home. 'Where is this?' A knot formed low in the pit of his stomach. 'What are you not telling me?'

She drew in a shuddering breath as a tear fell from her eye and left a wet trail glistening on her cheek in the candlelight. Her hand pressed to her heart and she began to sob. The sound was soft, as if she had previously exhausted herself of tears but her hurt was still just as intense.

He went to her and put his arm over her shoulders. 'Please, Lottie.'

'That was the last place I was truly happy,' she said, in a hoarse, tired voice.

Truly happy? He frowned. 'After I departed?'

She nodded; her gaze fixed on the image of the cottage. 'It's located just outside London, close enough that I could visit as often as was possible.'

Was this where she'd met one of her protectors, perhaps? 'I don't understand.'

Lottie sucked in air hard, as if it hurt even to breathe. 'That's where she was born.'

Evander's heart caught in his chest. 'Where who was born?'

'Our daughter.'

His arm fell away from Lottie as the shock of her words sank in.

They had a daughter?

Emotions slammed into him with enough force to make his knees go weak. Elation at the idea of having a child, guilt at having abandoned her for all those years, at having never met her, and anger at having never been told until this moment.

Six years.

She would be five.

His little girl.

'Good God, Lottie,' he said in awed shock. 'How could you have kept this from me? All this time I've been back I could have seen her, got to know her, let her see how much I love her.'

He stepped back from Lottie as she began to cry harder.

'We had a daughter.' Lottie covered her face with her hands, her words muffled but not indistinguishable. 'Three years ago she died.'

The ache splitting Lottie's chest was great enough to make her wish for her own death as she spoke the words she had put off saying for far too long.

Sarah, insubordinate though she may have been, was correct: Evander did need to know.

'I don't...' He regarded his empty hands as if they might somehow hold the answers. 'That is, I... When...?' His face crumpled, mirroring the hurt radiating through her, and he shook his head. 'Please. Tell me everything.'

Lottie sank into the ladderback chair near her easel and he pulled over the silk padded stool from before her vanity, his actions loose with the effects of his shock. As he gathered the small seat she did what she could to collect herself. As much as she could, given the circumstances and the magnitude of such loss.

But she had to do this.

A light clatter sounded from outside the door. 'I've brought tea, if you want it.'

Tea. Lottie swallowed, not realising how parched she was until that moment.

Evander lifted his brows in question and Lottie nodded. He stood swiftly, as though grateful to have purpose, and went to the door. He returned with a tray bearing tea, along with several rough sandwiches—clearly made by Sarah, as the cook had been given the day off with everyone else.

Lottie thanked him as he prepared a cup of tea for her with hands that trembled. When he poured a second cup for himself, she took a sip, letting the wet heat of the tea soothe her dry throat.

'I told you my father died soon after you left.'

She set her cup into the saucer perched on her knee. It would be best to explain it all from the beginning. Not only so Evander could learn about Lily, but also so he would understand why Lottie had taken the path she did.

'I didn't realise I was with child at the time.' She looked into her teacup and shook her head at her own youthful ignorance. 'I was overcome with grief at my father's death, and assumed that food being so disagreeable to me was due to my mourning. By the time the new vicar arrived, however, I had deduced the reality of my situation. I was with child.'

Her free hand went to her stomach as she recalled the

wonder of realising a baby was in her womb—Evander's baby. That their love had created something so magnificent.

'My father had always provided me with a comfortable life,' she continued. 'His death was so sudden there was little left for me to live on. Enough for a year or so.'

'And you expected I would return home to you by then,' Evander murmured.

Lottie did not reply. He already knew the answer. Her confirmation would only shove the dagger of guilt deeper into his chest. This tale needed no further pain. It captured enough on its own.

'I couldn't stay in Binsey, of course.' She tried to breathe around the ache in her chest. 'I couldn't sully my father's memory with my delicate state any more than I could bring shame to the home of anyone who tried to help me. I found lodging near London, where jobs would be more plentiful. I left my new address at Huntly Manor for you and waited out my pregnancy at this cottage.'

She indicated the painting with her eyes, and lingered on memories that tugged her back. 'I could wear my ring there, since no one in that small village knew me as anything more than a wife in a delicate condition.'

She smiled, recalling her pride at being referred to as 'Mrs Murray'.

'And when she was born...' Lottie's voice caught. The teacup rattled on its saucer, threatening to topple. She withdrew it from her knee and set it on the floor. 'Oh, Evander. She was so lovely.'

Tears welled afresh in Lottie's eyes as the night of Lily's birth pushed to the forefront of her thoughts. The hearty wail of a healthy baby girl. 'She had a tuft of auburn hair, like her father. And blue eyes.'

Evander watched her as she spoke, transfixed as he drew in every detail. 'Like her mother.'

'She was equal parts both of us—a beautiful child conceived in such love.' Lottie wiped at the tears on her cheek. 'I was with her for nearly four months, before my money ran out, but they were some of the happiest days of my life. Every coo, hiccup, smile, I revelled in it all, in our incredible child.'

'What did you call her?' Evander asked.

His voice was thick, and she realised then that he was barely containing his own sorrow.

'Lily,' she replied. 'Lily Rose Murray. Our own little flower.'

Emotion shimmered in his eyes.

She swallowed and looked away from him. It would be hard to meet his gaze for the remainder of her tale.

'I knew I had to work to support her, and was fortunate enough to find a woman willing to help in return for room and board until I had the means to pay her. It had been my intention to be a governess, as you know.'

'You don't need to explain yourself.'

'I do.' She gave him a hard look. 'You have to understand why I—' She squared her shoulders to steel herself for telling him this part of her past. 'The clerk at the employment agency wouldn't even consider me for the position of governess, as no wife would be willing to hire me without a reference. He suggested that with my 'pretty face' I would earn more coin working at the opera.'

Lottie pressed her lips together. The day she'd gone to the opera house had been overcast, with drizzling rain and air so cold her breath fogged. She had remained outside the doors so long, until someone finally came out to her, to see what it was she required.

She had been hired immediately.

'The pay was inadequate at best.' Lottie frowned at the memory of how the cost of her soul had yielded so little. She hadn't known then how truly low she would fall. 'But it allowed me to return to the cottage from time to time, to be with Lily. Those days were precious. She was such a good babe. She smiled with her whole body when she saw me, flapping her arms and squealing with delight.' Lottie laughed at the recollection. 'Then, as she grew, I saw her first teeth, watched as she learned to crawl. I was even there for her first steps.' Lottie's smile faded. 'And when she first began to wheeze.'

Lottie could still hear the whistling of Lily's breath as she struggled to breathe after playing too hard one afternoon.

'She needed a physician, but my meagre pay was not enough to cover a doctor's fee. The midwife I asked to look at her said a bit of honey would help, but the wheezing only seemed to get worse. I needed funds and there was nowhere to get them. Aside from the men who offered them to me. One in particular was persistent.' Emotion tingled at her swollen eyes and drew a familiar knot in her throat. She paused a moment before whispering, 'I had no choice.'

Her eyes wandered unbidden her hand, locating the back of her ring finger where the small diamond chip had once sat. 'I took off my ring before I went to him. I couldn't —' Her voice broke.

'My mother…?' Evander asked.

Lottie gave a mirthless laugh 'I considered it, but I had no proof you were truly my fiancé. Imagine it—a country woman knocking on her door, dressed in a simple day dress that had been darned so many times over I could have made a pattern from the stitchwork. I wasn't your wife. I was just a pauper claiming my babe was yours. I wasn't even sure if I'd been mentioned…'

A quick glance at Evander revealed him to be regarding the floor, his mouth pressed in a flat line.

It was as she'd thought, then. His father's funeral had

doubtless consumed his time in London and she hadn't been mentioned. As a vicar's daughter she was educated in all societal matters, and knew she would never be accepted into Westix House to plead her case.

'Once I had the funds,' Lottie continued, 'I paid a physician to go to the cottage and see Lily. He said she had a weakness in her lungs and I was to rub a paste on her chest at night.'

Sometimes Lottie still woke in the middle of the night, imagining that awful odour of mint and camphor permeating the air. On those particular instances she found herself straining to listen in the darkness for the soft, even wheezing of Lily's breathing as she slept. A sound so familiar for so long. One that Lottie would never hear again.

'Did the paste help?' Evander asked.

Lottie startled, having lost herself in her thoughts. 'No. I tried another physician, who recommended mercury, but every time I managed to force her to drink it she became ill.' The burden of the past pressed at Lottie, crushing her. 'Evander, I felt so helpless. I spent none of the money I earned aside from what was necessary. The rest I saved in the hope she would soon recover and I would be able to stop being a...a courtesan. That we could be together in that cottage again, just the two of us, and some day...'

Though her words died in her throat, she slowly glanced at Evander. He wiped at his eyes and sniffed.

A swallow revealed Lottie's throat had gone dry as parchment once more. She took a sip of tea. It had gone cold in the time she'd been speaking, but it was still wet and steeled her for what came next.

'Lily continued to live with her ailment for the next two years. Springtime was often the worst, especially when she played too vigorously and her breathing suffered. And oftentimes during the winter, when it was cold. But she grew into such a sweet girl. She sang these little songs to herself, and twirled in the sunshine as she plucked flowers from the garden. As though the world she lived in wasn't a place where breathing hurt her, but it was all magic instead. *She* was magic.'

Lottie stared into the cup clasped between her fingers. 'One day while I was in London I received an urgent post that she was poorly. I went as soon as I could, with her most recent physician in tow. When we arrived she could only lie on her bed, gasping for air. She looked at me as if I could help.' Emotion clogged her throat. 'There was nothing I could do. Even the physician was at a loss. He returned to London, to meet with some colleagues, but he didn't return in time. And even if he had there was nothing he could have done.'

'No,' Evander whispered.

A tear splashed on the back of Lottie's hand as all the memories she'd pushed away for so long came rushing back to her. That awful moment when she had lost her little girl for ever, the empty days following that had blurred together in a torrent of pain.

'I returned to London because I could not bear to remain there without her,' Lottie said. 'My third protector and I had parted ways by then, and I used the funds I had saved to support myself for a spell. Thankfully, before I needed to secure another protector, your mother approached me to instruct Eleanor. I was grateful for the distraction, and for the opportunity to find employment of a different means.'

Evander ran a hand through his hair. His head was tucked down. When he looked up, his cheeks were wet with tears, his eyes filled with true understanding of the loss she had endured all these years.

Chapter Sixteen

Evander had never fully realised the extent of his selfishness until that moment. It wasn't just that she had to become an opera dancer to put food on the table for herself and then could not find a respectable husband. The truth was so, so much worse.

She had been trying to save their daughter's life.

He had been amassing a fortune while Lottie had simply needed enough to cover a doctor's fees. More than that, she had needed him.

Lily.

His daughter.

God.

He had left her with child. To fend for herself.

He wanted to say something, but his throat ached with grief. Tears blurred his vision and he ground the heels of his hands into his eyes. He was the worst kind of monster for what he had done. No wonder she could not forgive him.

He would never be able to forgive himself.

'She sounds like the most amazing child,' he said softly. It seemed surreal, the idea of having had a little girl, of having never had the opportunity to meet her. To love her.

'She was.' Lottie gave a sad smile.

He would never have the chance to know their daughter the way Lottie had. And it was his fault.

Realisation dawned on Evander. 'When you saw me at Comlongon it was nearly the one-year mark of when she…'

Lottie nodded.

He held out his hands, palms up, helpless. 'Why didn't you tell me?'

'Because I was so lost in my own grief,' she said. 'Because I couldn't bring myself to actually say the words aloud. And because I was angry. That's why I slapped you. Seeing you standing there amid your towering fortune when I had struggled, had been forced to endure such pain on my own.'

Regret crushed in on him 'It was my fault that she——' The thick ache in his throat cut off his words.

'No, Evander. Even if you had been with us, you couldn't have helped her live.' Lottie stared at the painting of the cottage and slowly closed her eyes. 'Nothing would have helped.'

'But I could have been there for you.' He pushed off the small stool and came to her, longing with a powerful poignancy to reach for her. 'You wouldn't have had to endure it on your own.'

'Sarah was with me after…' Lottie opened her eyes and looked up at him. 'She's been with me since the opera house.'

Evander nodded, stepping back. His mind was still spinning at what she had confessed, and what had originally felt surreal now sank in with horrifying clarity.

Emotions lashed at him—a soul-deep sorrow at losing the daughter he would never know and an ugly, bitter rage with himself.

Lottie had begged him all those years ago not to leave. Wealth had never mattered to her—not as it had to him. And while he had been dreaming of grand manors with gilded place-settings, and fine jewels sparkling at her throat, she had been living in hell, doing whatever it took to get by.

'It should have been me,' Evander said through gritted teeth. 'I should have been the one who was with you.'

She looked away.

'Say it, Lottie,' he demanded.

'There's already been enough hurt, Evander.' She kept her gaze averted. 'Now you understand why it is so hard for me to open my heart. I fear there is little left of it after our Lily died.'

He strode around her to face her. 'Rage at me the way I should be raged at. Let out the hurt you've kept so neatly tucked behind a facade for so long.'

'I can't.' Her face crumpled as she began to sob.

'You must.' Evander cried out, in a mix of anger and pain, unable to bear what he had forced her to endure. He wanted her to yell at him, to throw every hard-edged thought he had earned at him. 'Hurt me the way I hurt you—the way I deserve.'

'I can't,' she said vehemently. 'I can't because I love you.'

He choked in a breath at those words he had no right to hear.

'I can't say those things to you because I cannot bear to cause you pain.'

She reached out with a trembling hand and touched his cheek. Her fingers were cold. It made him want to press them between his palms to warm them.

'I've caused you so much agony.' His voice had gone hoarse with anguish.

'You have.' She gazed up at him through red-rimmed eyes. 'And now you see why it's so difficult. Our love was simple once. Our love now...' she exhaled slowly '...is entirely too complicated. Who I am and what I've done. Why I had to do it. My shattered heart. It all stands between us.'

'I'm so sorry.' He reached for her, and when she did not pull away he drew her towards him, wrapping his arms around her. 'By God, I'm so sorry.'

She curled into him and her shoulders began to tremble with the force of her weeping. 'I miss her every day,' she said between gasps.

Evander bent his head towards Lottie's and let his tears flow with hers. His tears were for the child he would never know, while hers were for the memories she would always cherish.

They remained like that, unmoving from one another's embrace, long after their anguish had quieted. There was a silent comfort in the shared warmth of their bodies, in the steady rise and fall of each other's breathing.

Her head lay on his chest and he couldn't resist the urge to press a tender kiss to her hair. She looked up at him, her expression calm, almost languid.

In that moment he wanted to be closer, needed to be as near her as possible to ease the intense ache of grief within them both. He lowered his face as she lifted hers and their lips met somewhere in between.

That kiss was like coming home. It was comfort and love in its truest form. And it made him crave more.

He caught the back of her head in his palm and deepened the kiss. She moaned, making the same little noise in the back of her throat that he remembered. Lust slammed into him at the familiar sound. All the nights of missing her, of yearning for her, now combined with the desire to comfort and be comforted. His hands moved over her face, her neck, her shoulders and back, her waist.

He couldn't touch enough of her, insistent on having all of her at once, and her reaction matched his. The roaming of her hands was just as restless and eager. Her kisses became frenzied, rushed, with the extent of their need.

Lottie's fingernails raked through his short hair, lightly

grazing his scalp and sending tingles of pleasure racing down his spine. He groaned at the sensation and tightened his grip on her so their hips met one another.

They weren't young and innocent any more. Neither one of them hesitated as the intensity of their lust flared beyond their control.

Regardless of what happened going forward, they had each other in that moment. For comfort. For lust. For the love that once was.

And for the hope it could some day be once more.

How Lottie had dreamt of this moment. Evander's body strong against her own, a rock of support she had been too stubborn to admit needing for a long time.

Part of her wanted to collapse against him and borrow his fortitude. A greater part, however, was starved for affection, too long put off from emotion and feeling to be denied.

That greater part was the one she gave in to now. She touched him everywhere, with a rapacious longing to confirm this was truly happening, that he was before her, in her room, his mouth tender and yet insistent as he kissed her with a matching hunger.

'I love you, Lottie,' he said against her mouth, the declaration vehement.

She pressed her lips to his to silence him. She couldn't bear to hear it. Not when they still could never be.

He didn't care what people thought of her now when he wanted her so desperately. But once he had her and the flames of lust were doused, he might think differently. The way everyone else did.

She kissed him harder, in an effort to scorch those thoughts from her mind. But still they lingered, bitter, simmering with her residual anger at Evander for having left her.

No, she did not want to cause him pain for what he'd done, but it didn't mean she still did not feel the sting of it. Perhaps she always would. And perhaps that would be the downfall for any chance of their shared happiness.

His hands cupped her breasts, his fingers finding her nipples. She cried out, and her thoughts finally went blank.

Quickly, before anything could resurface in the dark expanse of her mind, she worked at the buttons on his jacket. They slid free easily and she shoved the garment from his shoulders.

He retaliated in the most delicious way, by popping free the small buttons at the back of her gown. Their mouths remained locked with one another as they tore at each other's clothing. The shoulders of her gown loosened and it was dragged down her body to pool at her feet.

Her fingers navigated blindly, unravelling his cravat and impatiently casting it to the floor. Next she pulled his shirt from where it was tucked into his trousers, even as he undid the small bow under her bosom, holding her chemise closed.

With a growl, he bent and kissed the area just over her breasts, delicately flicking his tongue along the low neckline. Lottie gasped with pleasure and tugged his shirt over his head. His lips shifted from her skin for only a brief moment, to allow the muslin to pass over his face, before he resumed kissing her.

His powerful back rippled with muscles that shifted and flexed as he wrapped one arm around her to draw her closer to him and his free hand loosened the ribbon on her petticoat at her waist. It quickly joined her gown on the floor. Her stays came next, leaving only her shift, which she divested herself of.

In the six years since they had last been intimate, her body had changed. She'd become softer after her pregnancy, her curves more ample, and delicate silver lines traced over her lower stomach.

Before self-consciousness could whisper its poison into her mind, Evander stepped back and regarded her as though she were a work of art. He issued a low curse under his breath.

'My God, you are beautiful, Lottie.' He wrapped his arms around her and his hands glided over her skin. 'Even lovelier than I remember.'

She pushed up on her toes and kissed him. Their bodies stretched against one another, her nakedness against his bare chest, where the sprinkling of auburn hair rasped against her nipples. Being this close to him, being held, being cared for by someone who truly loved her, brought a peace to her she hadn't known since before Lily's death.

Lottie's body burned for him—not only for his closeness and his intimacy, but to have him possess her totally and completely. She reached for the fall of his trousers and a muscle worked in his jaw.

The last time they'd been together had been too fast, and she had been too innocent. She hadn't looked at him. Now she was a different woman, and as the placket of his trousers fell open her gaze slid down his body to where his arousal jutted from a thatch of copper hair.

She moaned as she reached for him, stroking the thickness of his arousal, revelling in the silky heat of his skin. Her fingers curled around him and glided from base to head. Evander groaned and closed his eyes. He was so hard, like steel. For her.

'I want you,' she whispered.

He opened her eyes and reached for her, lifting her into his arms before carrying her to the large bed. Gently, he laid her on the mattress and covered her with his body. He fitted over her perfectly, his weight comfortable, the press of his arousal against her stomach almost more than she could bear.

His gaze locked on hers. He was saying with his eyes what she couldn't bear him to say aloud.

I love you.

He ran his hand down her cheek, her neck, to her breasts, where he swept his fingertips over her nipples and then further past her navel.

Her breath came faster as his touch found the aching spot between her thighs. Pleasure shot through her and she cried out.

Most men would take her then and there. But not Evander. He eased a finger inside her while his thumb worked over the sensitive bud at the top of her sex. She gasped in delight, moving her hips in time with his ministrations, until release caught her in the most delicious grip.

Her hands fisted in the bedsheets beneath her, as though somehow they might keep her grounded even though she felt as if she was floating away.

Evander removed his hand and shifted over the top of her, the tip of his arousal nudging against her. She nodded, eager for them to be completely together, united in their desperation for comfort, in the love they'd once shared. Regardless of what happened afterwards, she needed this. In this moment, she needed him.

Chapter Seventeen

Never had Evander wanted something more than he wanted Lottie at that moment. It wasn't simply a physical desire, it went far deeper. Powerfully poignant.

He watched her as he pushed inside her, noting how her lashes lowered with pleasure, her soft exhale. Her core gripped him as he shifted back and thrust into her once more. A groan tore from his throat and he pushed the fist supporting his weight into the mattress, in an effort to rein in his control.

It had been six years since he'd been with a woman—when he'd last lain with Lottie. There hadn't been anyone else he wanted. Not like her.

Her arms slid up his back and she pulled him down to her.

He resisted. 'I don't want to crush you.'

She shook her head. 'You won't.'

Finally he acquiesced and lay against her, skin on skin, hot with desire. Sensual.

Lottie moaned in his ear as she clung to him, shifting her hips in time with the flex of his pelvis. He slowed his pace, savouring the feel of her under him, around him, their bodies moving in perfect tandem. It was a marvel how each subtle shift brought the most exquisite pleasure.

Her breath was warm against the crook of his neck, her exhalations near his ear as her sweet, floral scent embraced him with an intoxicating decadence. She lifted her face and he kissed her as their bodies joined together, again and again. When her breathing changed, becoming faster, he quickened his thrusts, pumping into her.

Fire scorched his veins and they both panted with their effort until at last their bodies exploded with the force of their mutual release. They clung to one another as their climax took them. They didn't let go, not even as their heartbeats calmed and their breathing evened.

Holding her was a heaven he'd dreamed of for far too long to relinquish her with any haste. No, he wanted to stay like this for ever, his blood humming with the lingering effects of their mutual pleasure, cradling her against him like something precious. His chest ached with the wish to have her this way always.

She gazed up at him, studying him with an expression he couldn't read. He wanted to tell her he loved her again, that he would always love her. But even though they'd shared the depth of such intimacy, she seemed almost more skittish to him now than she had before.

Maybe it was being this close to her that made the force of his hope too powerful. To be rejected by her again after what they'd shared would be devastating.

He withdrew from her and rolled onto his side next to her. Neither spoke as he curled his arms around her protectively and held her. They remained thus until their body heat and emotional exhaustion had them drifting towards a quiet slumber.

It was some time before Evander woke. Light still peeked in through the bottoms of the drawn curtains, indicating night had not yet fallen. Lottie remained in his arms. At some point she'd turned in her slumber, so her head lay on his chest.

He stroked a lock of hair away from her face and studied her profile. Though six years had passed, she remained untouched by age. Her skin was still smooth as cream, her dark lashes long where they rested against her cheeks. But there was another element to her now.

When she'd been young, she hadn't known of her own beauty. Now, as a woman, she was well aware of it—and of its power. It made her seem untouchable.

Except that she was there, next to him, having given herself wholly to him.

What she'd told him earlier that day sat like a stone in his chest. Their daughter, Lily. How hard it must have been for Lottie to endure what she'd gone through without him there. She had sacrificed every part of herself to ensure the safety of their child.

Evander had never faulted her for what she'd done to survive in his prolonged absence. Now, knowing all he did, he admired her for it. Her strength was unlike any other he'd known.

He ran the back of his hand down her cheek and she tilted her face towards the caress. A slow smile lifted the corners of her mouth. She blinked her eyes open and he was once more struck by the lovely, brilliant blue of her eyes.

'It would appear we both fell asleep.' She gave a lazy, indulgent chuckle, and put her hand under her chin to look up at him. 'Thank you for being here today.'

'For forcing my way in?' He lifted a brow. 'I hope Sarah won't be judged too harshly.'

Lottie sighed. 'Sarah knows exactly how much she can do without a reprimand. She takes advantage of how very dear she is to me.'

'I'm grateful you have her.' Evander swallowed. 'That she was there for you when I wasn't. I owe her an enormous debt of gratitude.'

'You couldn't possibly have known what had happened in your absence,' Lottie said softly.

But not knowing didn't excuse him from what he'd missed in Lottie's life. And in Lily's. Not when it was his own fault for not sending more than two letters that somehow never made their way to English soil.

'I wish I could reverse time,' he said. 'To be there for you. And to meet her. I would give up anything to go back.'

But such wishes were impossible. All the money in the world couldn't buy back time.

It was a hard-won lesson. And one whose effects would be felt for the rest of his life.

He looked across the room to where the painting of the cottage still stood on the easel, half finished. All around it, discarded on the floor, were other paintings. If he put them together he would know what the cottage looked like from all angles. And yet there were none of the little girl Lottie had described. There were none of Lily.

Suddenly he wanted the experience of going there. Of seeing where they'd lived— how they'd lived. And, if Lily had been buried there, of seeing her small grave.

'Lottie,' he said gently.

She followed his gaze. 'Yes?'

'Will you take me to the cottage?'

She stiffened. The movement would have been imperceptible had they not been so close to one another.

'I beg your pardon?' She pushed up and off him and rose on her elbows to regard him, the sheets tucked over her breasts.

'The cottage.' Evander indicated the painting. 'Will you take me?'

Lottie's thoughts raced at Evander's request. It was simple enough. And it made sense. Of course he would want to see where Lily had lived. No doubt he would also want to visit her grave.

Except his enquiry made her freeze. She hadn't been back to the cottage since Sarah had finally prised her away from the grave. And as insistent as Lottie had been then, on remaining there day and night, in vigil for her lost daughter, she was just as insistent now on not going back.

Her heart could not bear it.

The comfort she'd drawn from Evander ebbed and was replaced with a restless agitation. She rose from the bed and went to the ewer to freshen up.

'Lottie,' Evander said. 'What is it?'

She shook her head, not quite certain exactly what it was herself. But the ache of it split open like a void within her.

'Why do you want to go?' she asked.

It was a stupid question. The reason was obvious. Anyone in Evander's position would want to go. She was simply postponing having to give him an answer.

He rose from bed, his lean body all sharp angles and cut muscle. Her hands tingled with the memory of how such strength had felt beneath her touch.

'I want to see where you lived,' he answered, with more patience than the question deserved. 'It's the closest thing I can have to being near Lily.' He hesitated before adding, 'Is she buried there?'

Lottie nodded, unable to answer the question out loud. She'd lain over that small grave for three days before Sarah had finally convinced her to leave. It had been more than Lottie could bear, imagining her sweet girl all alone in the small wooden coffin, surrounded by cold, dark earth.

'Please, Lottie.' He strode towards her, unabashed in his nakedness, and reached for her shoulder.

But Lottie stepped back.

Hurt flashed in his eyes for the briefest of moments,

but he hid it with a glance downward as he dragged a hand through his hair.

'You could go without me,' she suggested.

He looked back at her with a frown. 'Why don't you want to go?'

The answer sat heavy in her mind, her tongue suddenly too thick to put her reply into words.

'What is it?' he asked.

'I'm afraid,' she answered at last.

His brow furrowed with apparent confusion. 'I don't understand.'

And how could he? He hadn't lived through what she had. Yes, he knew what she had told him, but it wasn't the same as experiencing it. Words could never properly convey the level of her despair, the precise anguish of her grief. And there was more…

There was the fear that she would relive the emotions she had felt when she resided in that cottage. When she had received no letters from him. How many times had she sat in the small rocker, considering the diamond on her finger and wondering how worthless his promises had been?

There had been no news of him in all those years. If there had been she would have known, as she'd made it a point to be in the proper circles to gain such information.

Some nights she'd presumed him dead and wept. Others she'd berated herself for a fool who had been played by a rake. She had wept then too, bitter tears for her own naivety and for what such carelessness had brought upon her sweet, innocent child.

And when she had seen Evander at Comlongon all those nights had rushed back to her, along with the pain of the struggles she'd endured. That rage that had burned within her flickered to life once more. He'd been right earlier. She should be angry with him for what he'd done.

Except she'd been too tender after having just told him about Lily. She'd been too desperate for comfort.

'I haven't been back there since...since she was buried,' Lottie said slowly. 'I haven't been able to bring myself to.'

Evander was quiet for a long moment, and when he finally spoke his voice was thick with emotion. 'Perhaps it might help us both heal if we go together.'

Lottie gritted her teeth. 'There's more. I... I fear that I might never be able to forgive you if we go back.'

A muscle flexed in his jaw, but he did not lash out at her. Instead, he offered a stiff nod, eyes blazing with a pain he could not mask. 'I understand.'

They said nothing as they both gathered their clothes and put themselves to rights once more. Evander helped tie her undergarments into place and buttoned the back of her gown.

'If you don't forgive me, I would not blame you.' He cleared his throat. 'I am sure I will never be able to forgive myself. I was never able to meet our daughter. I've never seen where she lived, heard stories about her life. My heart is aching for a connection with Lily.' He rubbed a hand over his face. 'I would never ask you to go through something that causes you pain except in this. Lottie, I want to know about our little girl. Even if it is the final wedge between us, I cannot stand the idea of not knowing about her.'

He was right, she knew. He needed to find a connection with Lily in any way he could. Only Lottie did not know if she was brave enough to agree.

She wrapped her arms around herself, though it did not bring comfort. Not as Evander's embrace had done. How could she say no to such a request?

'I'll consider it,' she said at last.

He nodded. 'Thank you.'

He reached for her, but again she stepped back.

'I'm sorry,' she said softly.

He nodded. 'Good day, Lottie.'

She pressed her lips together, saying nothing in reply as he left the room. Only when the door clicked closed did she sag to the floor and give in to utter despondency.

How could she deny him? And yet how could she possibly bring herself to go back there?

She knew what she ought to do, but she did not know if she was brave enough to face those incredible fears.

Above all else, she did not want to hate him.

And going back to the cottage, reliving such suffering, might well make her do that.

Chapter Eighteen

Nothing made the press of heartache greater than witnessing new young love.

The next day Lottie sat opposite Lady Caroline, whose dark eyes glowed with joy.

'He had this ingenious shirt with the steps of the dance. Not only did he not miss a single step, he asked me to dance the next cotillion set with him.'

'I'm so pleased to hear it,' Lottie said. And truly she was. It warmed her to know her gift yielded such impact.

She had been like Lady Caroline once—innocent and hopeful, her entire self given to the idea of love. And, happy for the young woman, she could not help but remember when she too had gloried in the throes of first love. The world had seemed so perfect then, as if all the pieces had fallen perfectly into place.

'He's already asked when my next ball is,' Lady Caroline said. 'I believe he actually enjoyed himself.' She shifted forward on the settee and her dark curls bounced with the movement. 'I want your counsel on an idea.'

'An idea?' Lottie gave her a curious look.

Lady Caroline's suggestions were often subtle, yet clear enough to determine. By most people, that was. Seldom by Lord Rawley, unfortunately. It wasn't that he was a stupid man. Quite the opposite. He was extraordinarily intelligent. But Lord Rawley was the sensitive sort—not so much in how he took other's remarks, but in regard to his consideration towards others.

His father had passed away when he was barely out of the nursery, and as a result his mother doted on him. Perhaps that was why he was so perceptive in reading others, and overly careful in how he treated them—women, especially.

The Viscount was a man who took his responsibility seriously and had a care not to give in to the same vices as most of his peers. There was no excessive drinking or gambling or whoring for him. And, while it made him the ideal husband, it made for a frustrating man in the courting game.

Which was how poor Lady Caroline had ended up on Lottie's settee. She was beautiful, with dark eyes and hair like her brother, Lord Dalton. Any man would have been all too eager to wed her. But she didn't want any of them. Her heart was set on Lord Rawley.

'I want to encourage him to kiss me,' Lady Caroline said with a gleeful lift of her shoulders. 'Perhaps if I invite him onto the veranda when no one else is there…' A shrewd expression replaced her delight and she appeared to gauge Lottie's reaction.

Lottie lifted a brow, preferring Lady Caroline to admit the unlikelihood of her scheme actually working rather than having to say it herself.

Lady Caroline sighed. 'I know he won't do it. But what if I kiss him?' The gleam was back in her eyes.

'Have a care for your reputation,' Lottie cautioned. 'It would be preferable if he was courting you first.'

At that, Lady Caroline beamed.

Lottie gasped. 'Do you mean…?'

Lady Caroline squealed in a very unladylike manner.

'He spoke with my brother this very afternoon. Seth told me he was practically melting with sweat, the poor dear.' An endearing smile widened on her face. 'He said Lord Rawley asked if he might court me. When I asked Seth what he said in reply...' She giggled behind her hand. 'He told me he replied, "It's about bloody time. Please do, by all means."'

Lottie laughed along with Lady Caroline, and went to the sweet young woman to embrace her. 'I'm so very happy for you. Perhaps that kiss isn't too far off, then. But mind you are still careful.'

'Most certainly,' Lady Caroline vowed with seriousness. 'And what of you?'

The question took Lottie aback. 'Me?'

'You and your handsome hero,' Lady Caroline prompted. 'We all saw Lord Westix punch Lord Devonington at the ball. I wager most men have wanted to put their fist in that man's face a time or two. And he did. For you. If that isn't romantic, I dare say I don't know what is.'

'I... I...' Lottie stammered.

'And I hear he sends you flowers once a week.' Lady Caroline glanced at the irises and white tulips, sitting beside a bundle of pink roses. 'Eleanor told me.'

'It isn't like that between us.' Lottie shook her head. 'It can't be. I would never be accepted among the ton.' Her cheeks went hot as the familiar blanket of humiliation fell over her.

'You already have been. By me, Violet, Eleanor—and all the other ladies you have taken the time to instruct. Fie to the rest of them, I say.'

'We thought to wed once,' Lottie admitted. 'But we were young. I was...different.'

'A second chance at love, then?' Lady Caroline pressed her hands to the crimson velvet bodice of her gown and gave a wistful sigh. 'Now, that is terribly romantic. Like Lady Alice.'

'You don't mean with Lord Ledsey, do you?' Lottie tried to keep the scowl from her face. The Earl really was terribly despicable.

Lady Caroline recoiled in horror. 'Heavens, no. I mean her soldier—George.'

Lottie had received notice from Lady Alice earlier that day, begging off her lessons with a message that she would explain later. Perhaps a miracle had happened.

'Is he home?' Lottie asked in disbelief.

'Yes,' Lady Caroline breathed. 'Isn't it a marvel?'

Indeed, it was. And Lottie was overjoyed that her student would be able to recapture her lost love. The topic of the returned soldier was also a fortunate way for Lottie to brush aside any of Lady Caroline's concern for herself and put the focus back on encouraging Lord Rawley's affections. Hopefully their courtship would soon turn to marriage and a lifetime of happiness.

Following Lady Caroline's lesson, Lottie retired early, sitting before the vanity as she readied herself for bed.

Silky bumped her head against Lottie's ankles. Just as she bent to stroke her cat, Sarah approached, regarding her through the reflection in the mirror.

'I wasn't listening in, but I did overhear what Lady Caroline said as I was passing by about taking a second chance at love. You know how I feel.'

'I do,' Lottie replied. 'And I'm still cross with you.'

Sarah folded her arms over her chest in the stubborn way she exhibited from time to time. 'Better you be cross with me and find happiness rather than be merely content and remain sad and lonely.'

Lottie straightened and turned to look at the maid. 'He wants to go to the cottage.'

'Of course he does.' Sarah gently shifted Lottie's shoulders forward and dislodged the jewelled comb from Lottie's hair. 'He's seeking a connection with Lily, and the cottage is the best way he can find it.'

Lottie, of course, knew this already. She remained quiet in contemplation as Sarah slid free her hairpins and Lottie's dark hair tumbled down over her shoulders.

'Think of it this way.' Slowly Sarah began to brush out Lottie's long tresses. 'If he had been there with Lily and you hadn't, how would you feel?'

Lottie pulled in breath.

Sarah smirked. 'Precisely.'

'I fear returning will recall all my previous anger,' Lottie said, twisting her hands in her lap. 'If that rage should resurface, I don't know that my heart could ever open again.'

'You owe it to yourself to find out.' Sarah swept the brush down the full length of Lottie's hair. 'And you owe it to him. That man has been loyal to you for six years. He has returned time and again, no matter how many times you push him away.'

Lottie exhaled on a long, deep sigh. 'You're meddlesome—do you know that?'

'You're welcome, lovey.' Sarah grinned at her in the mirror.

Lottie glanced at her maid over her shoulder. 'Please bring me some stationery.'

Sarah set the brush down with a smidgen too much delight. 'With pleasure.'

Despite Sarah's happiness at her decision, Lottie's pen still hesitated over the parchment. Whatever happened at the cottage stood either to fully unite them or tear them apart for ever. There would be nothing in between.

The wealth in Evander's accounts had grown exponentially. His investment with the mine had been sound.

Granted, he shouldn't care about money at this point. But that was the thing about having once been without a fortune—one was always in terrible fear of losing it again.

The return gained from the mines, and all his other investments, was security. It would ensure his mother was always well cared for and that he would never have to leave Lottie again. Not that he would ever make such an error.

Lily.

The little name had become something of a chant in his mind, like a sorrowful cry, or even a prayer of sorts. He leaned back in his seat and sipped his brandy, though the liquor did scant good to ease the burden in his chest.

Going to the cottage had been a recurring thought as well. He'd come to the conclusion that if Lottie would not accompany him, he would go alone. If nothing else, he owed it to Lily.

He downed another swallow of brandy.

'Evander, you wished to see me?'

His mother entered the room, elegant in an emerald silk gown that made her eyes look as bright as the gem. Her hair, once gold and now more silver, was twisted back from her regal face. She was thinner, after having been ill, but just as strong as ever.

Her gaze skimmed his open account book. 'Am I correct in presuming you haven't called me in here to discuss your investments?'

'You are.'

'Thank heavens.' Using her gold-topped cane—a new device, following her ailment—she lowered herself to a chair.

'Shall I send for some tea?'

'I also presumed your refreshments would be limited to libations no woman ought to consume, and took the liberty of ordering myself a tray.' A knock sounded at the door and she turned with a smile. 'Ah, there it is now.'

After they each had a cup of tea in front of them, his unadulterated and hers with two fat lumps of sugar, they could finally settle to the matter at hand.

'When I returned home for Father's funeral, did I mention my engagement to Lottie?' He lifted the cup of piping hot liquid to his lips. That was how he liked it best—while it was only tolerably sippable.

'You did not,' Lady Westix said with certainty. 'I know this because I was shocked when you mentioned it upon your return from travelling abroad.'

He deflated somewhat, at this confirmation of how terribly he had fallen short on his commitment to Lottie…

His mother took a sip of her tea, swallowed it and set the cup back in its saucer with a delicate clink. 'Surely that was not all you wished to ask me?'

This was the most difficult part. But he had to know that there wouldn't have been any alternative available.

He shifted in his seat. 'If a woman of little means were to have come to you while I was away on my travels, stating that she was my fiancée and required assistance, would you have aided her?'

'I would like to say that I would.' Lady Westix stirred her tea thoughtfully. 'But, cold-hearted as it may be, I would more likely have turned her out.'

'Even if…' He hesitated. His mother did not need to know all of this.

'Even if?' She gave a soft sigh. 'Truly, please stop treating me as though I'm some fragile, breakable thing. I'm far stronger than I seem.'

Except she looked scarcely strong enough to withstand a stiff breeze.

'Even if she'd had a child with her?' Evander finished.

Lady Westix straightened, her face lighting up.

Evander shook his head swiftly and she wilted with understanding.

Lady Westix looked down at her tea, her lips pursed. 'I'm afraid I would have considered it a ruse to get at our assumed wealth. It wouldn't be the first time fortune-hunters had set upon nobility. And during that time I was particularly shrewd.'

Evander nodded in understanding. Lottie had known his own mother better than he.

Lady Westix reached a hand across the desk towards Evander. 'Losing a child is one of the hardest fates a woman can suffer.'

He stretched towards her, taking it, her fingers cool and dry in his, blue veins evident beneath her translucent skin.

'If what you say has merit, Evander,' she said, 'I too owe a debt to Lottie.'

'You may well have the opportunity to make good on that debt. I mean to marry her, and most of the ton will not approve.'

His mother's hand tightened around his. 'I've played by their rules long enough. I told you before—if you love her, you should not stop fighting for her. And I meant it. I stand by your side, son. I stand with Lottie.'

Evander gave his mother a grateful smile.

A knock sounded at the door. 'Forgive me, my lord,' said Edmonds. 'But a missive has arrived for you.'

'Enter.' Evander released his mother's hand and straightened.

Edmonds crossed the room with a salver and extended it to Evander. He immediately recognised Lottie's looping handwriting, which addressed the envelope to him.

'Excuse me,' he said to his mother, accepting the letter and cracking its seal.

He unfolded it, revealing the single line that made his heart leap.

I will accompany you to the cottage.

Chapter Nineteen

In the past, her carriage rides from London to the cottage had always seemed interminable. Today, however, Lottie found the trip from town passed with an alarming swiftness.

Evander sat opposite her, his elbows on his knees, his brows furrowed, appearing as anxious as she. And she was indeed dreading their arrival as she imagined the little house tucked in the woods.

It had been three years since she had last been there. She'd purchased the building outright from the owner, who had rented it to her when Lily was still alive. The house was small, yes, but its proximity to London, while still remaining remote, could not be matched.

Lottie had considered the possibility of bringing Lily to London, but with heavy smoke from the factories clogging the air, and the bustle and filth of so many people, it had not seemed prudent for her daughter's health.

Truth be told, Lottie wished now she had contacted the former owners and asked them to care for the cottage—perhaps find new tenants who would have cleared out her belongings or put them to a new purpose. If that were the case, they would not be able to enter, and all the memories contained within could be held at bay forever. Except she hadn't contacted the former owners and now she had to face what was left of her previous life.

The feeling of being watched pulled Lottie from her musing. Her gaze met Evander's, which was fixed worriedly on her.

Saying nothing, he reached for her hands and took them in his as the buildings of London sped away behind them and they turned on to the empty forest road that would eventually lead to the cottage.

Lottie's heart slammed hard against her ribs. Everything in her wanted to rear back in stubborn objection. She did not want to go. But even as her muscles tensed, and her mind prepared to voice her displeasure, the trees cleared away and revealed the lone cottage in the distance.

Perhaps she ought to have looked away, to prevent the pain as much as was possible. But she couldn't.

She pulled her hands from Evander's and shifted on the blue velvet bench, edging closer to the window. There it was, the thatched roof gone grey with age and lack of upkeep, the whitewashed walls, and the simple locked wooden door whose key sat like an anvil in her reticule.

The fence surrounding the cottage had begun to sag, as if sighing towards the garden, which was in sore need of tending. Lily had always loved that garden, delighting at each new thing that began to grow. But at that time she'd been delighted at everything in life.

Something stirred on the ground. For a brief moment Lottie's heart leapt with the hope that it might be Lily, lying among the flowers as she once had, her fingers outstretched towards the sun as she sang a song she'd spun in her head.

Lottie touched the glass. The chill of it against her fingertips surprised her, and pulled her to her senses once more. She blinked, and a fat brown rabbit hopped from the former flowerbed into the surrounding forest.

Her shuddering exhale fogged the glass.

'Lottie…?' Evander said in a tender voice.

She shook her head to brush him off. 'This day is certain to be one of the most difficult I have endured.'

'I understand.' He shifted from his seat to hers and took her hand. 'I am fully aware of how difficult today will be.' His thumb ran over the back of her fingers. 'Thank you for this.'

'You have a right to know as much of her life as you can.' She swallowed thickly, but it did little to clear the lump in her throat.

When she looked out of the window again the cottage was directly in front of them and the carriage pulled to a stop. She didn't want to exit the cabin, but could not stop her feet from moving down the single step and onto the dry, crackling grass underfoot.

The familiar scent of damp, rich soil mingled with the sweet hay of the thatched roof and the perfume of the various flowers that had managed to survive among the weeds in their garden. The air held notes of a perfect summer's day, with the sun shining down and bringing the earth's aromas to life. It smelled like picnics and laughter and a beautiful little girl with auburn curls chasing butterflies while being cautioned not to over-exert herself.

Lottie's ribs constricted her heart and made breathing nearly impossible. This was where the laughter had stopped, where those gasping wheezes had gone quiet, where her Lily had died.

The weight of it was too great.

Lottie's knees buckled. She couldn't do this. She couldn't be here, remembering these painful memories, subjecting herself to the greatest emotional agony of her life.

A firm grip caught her shoulders, strong and true, comfort when she needed it most.

'I'm here with you,' Evander said in her ear.

Lottie lifted her head to find him staring earnestly down at her, his face set with a fierce determination.

'You are not alone, Lottie. Not this time. I'm here.'

She nodded and withdrew the key from her reticule. Her fingers shook so badly she could not close the clasp. Evander took the bag from her, clicked it closed and handed it to his coachman.

He held out his hand. 'Would you like me to do it?'

She considered his offer, but in the end declined. If she was to do this, she needed to maintain as much control as was possible.

They made their way up the small front path, now overgrown with weeds that crawled over the stonework. From their new vantage point the fence was in even worse condition, bowing low enough to the ground at the far end that it actually lay on a ratty bed of snarled plants that had once grown peas and beans on slender wooden sticks. The flower garden was likewise a tangle of growth, some alive, most dead, with an errant bloom peeking through here and there.

Lottie stopped in front of the door and slid the key into the thick metal lock.

She stopped.

On the other side of that door would be pain.

Evander said nothing as she stood there, steeling herself to confront the power of those memories. He remained with his arm around her shoulders, his patience as solid as his strength, waiting for her.

She drew in a hard breath and let it hiss out between her teeth. In a swift move, before she succumbed to her dwindling courage, she turned the key with a click and pushed at the heavy oak.

The door groaned open on ungreased hinges and revealed the place that had once been home. The place where she had once been truly happy.

She couldn't move to cross the threshold. Her feet were rooted in place as she took it all in. The wooden kitchen table where Lily would 'help' shell peas. The slender glass vase still at its centre, filled with wilted wildflowers bent over at their slender necks, their stalks now dry, dusty husks.

There were three chairs by the fireplace. One for Lottie and one for Dina, the kind woman who had cared for Lily in Lottie's absence, and a small one for Lily. Lottie's gaze fixed on the tiny chair, recalling how her daughter would always stretch her bare toes towards the fire on cold nights. Her feet were so tiny, soft and pink, not yet callused by life.

She had been too young.

Far too young.

The room blurred and the arm around her shoulders squeezed her slightly. 'Lottie? Do you need—?'

She swallowed a sob and shook her head. 'I can do this.' But could she?

She strode forward on limbs that felt as old and rusty as the door's hinges. The room inside was musty, with the sharp odour of dust and disuse. For that she was grateful. If it had smelled like life being lived, and the little girl she had loved, Lottie was certain she would have broken.

Once inside, the rest of the room became visible. In the corner was the desk Lottie had used for correspondence and managing her meagre funds. It was incredible now to think she had made twenty pounds last a year.

Evander remained at her side, silent and still, an awkward guest in a home where he hadn't truly been welcomed. She swallowed around her dry throat, wishing for a bit of tea. 'It's small.'

'I imagine it was perfect,' Evander replied after a pause,

as though he was filling the silence rather than speaking in earnest.

'It was.' Lottie nodded as she regarded the three-room cottage.

The two bedchambers were still cut off by their closed doors. She would have to rebuild her courage to open them. Or at least the one on the left, where she and Lily had slept.

Evander looked around with interest, but Lottie knew that to him the whole of it was little more than a blank page. It would be up to her to paint upon it, to show him the scenes of her life so he could truly know Lily.

She owed it to him to share her memories, so that through them he might know his daughter.

And she owed it to Lily.

Evander kept his face impassive as he looked around the cottage. In truth, it was little more than a hut. Dust coated the surfaces, casting a dull finish over a home that no longer served its purpose. He could fit the entire cottage inside the ballroom at Westix Place, the space was so small.

This was where Lottie had lived while he'd been travelling through the world imagining her dripping with diamonds and sleeping on satin.

His chest squeezed.

As destitute as he had thought his own estate, it would have afforded Lottie a life a hundred times better than life in the place where he now stood.

Suddenly, he regretted having come. She was right. There was only pain to be had in these dingy walls. And even if she didn't hate him as she feared she might, he was beginning to hate himself.

What he had subjected her to—it was unforgivable.

'Over here is the kitchen.'

Lottie eased out from the hold he had on her shoulders and slid her hand into his. He let his fingers fold around hers, grateful for the connection as he was suddenly finding he needed comfort as much as she.

She led him to the left side of the open room, where an old stove and a basin were set near the wall, with a few shelves that housed a teapot and some dusty teacups. A cupboard sat near the corner, with a porcelain ewer settled in a basin with a chipped rim.

'Lily would set the table for every meal,' Lottie said softly, her voice unsteady. 'At least she pretended to. She took the self-assigned task very seriously, and would touch each of the napkins in turn after she'd set them.'

They strode to the table next.

'I always sat here when I was able to be at home.' Lottie indicated the chair nearest the cupboard.

Home.

She said it with a familiarity he felt in his soul. For this *had* been her home. With Lily.

Suddenly he felt a flash of self-castigation for having judged the cottage so harshly, the way any arrogant earl would—one who had never known a life that did not consist of wealth. Even when he thought himself sorely without.

'That was where Dina sat.' Lottie indicated the seat opposite her. 'She was always so kind to Lily in my absence. She moved to Hastings to be with her parents after...' Lottie faltered, losing some of her zeal for a moment and clearing her throat. 'And this is where Lily sat.'

Her fingers trailed over the table in front of the chair that sat between the other two. The gentle touch left streaks in the dust, but Lottie didn't seem to notice.

'Dina said when I was in London Lily would drag her chair to the window by the door to watch for me.' Lottie looked at the window and smiled through the tears glittering in her eyes. 'I tried to come as often as I could.'

'She clearly enjoyed your company.' Evander swept his thumb over her cheek, where one tear had escaped.

Lottie took him to the hearth next, and shared how they would sing songs before the fire as Lily prepared for bed.

On and on the stories went, their details filling Evander's mind with the little girl he would never know.

What was more, they filled his heart.

They stopped near the far corner of the room, where a desktop had been secured to a frame, boxing the piece of furniture in on itself. Lottie hesitated in front of it for a long moment. Then, lips pressed together and back stiff, she undid the latch and slowly lowered the top of the writing desk. Inside there was a pile of paper.

'Do you...?' She drew in a shaking breath. 'Do you want to see what she looked like?'

Lottie placed her hands on the stack with a reverence that caught at his chest.

'More than anything,' he answered with his whole heart.

She took another breath, long and deep, which she slowly let out. 'I haven't been able to paint her again since. I left them here because...because I couldn't bring myself to look at them.'

Even as she spoke she averted her gaze and passed the stack to Evander. The pages crackled in his hand, the watercolour paint having left them stiff. Though he knew they weren't as fragile as they felt, he used the greatest care as he turned each one over and froze.

There was a little girl with laughing blue eyes gazing up at him, her mouth in a smile that reminded him of Lottie, auburn curls blowing against her cheek on an unseen breeze.

All at once those stories Lottie had shared solidified in his mind. The child who had been blank now had a face. It was her sweet likeness singing songs she'd made up, begging to let a rabbit from the forest live with them, and sticking her tongue out with concentration as she organised flowers in the vase before dinner.

Suddenly it was real.

She was real.

They were no longer stories, no longer something he couldn't imagine. Now there was depth. Heart.

That happy girl in the paintings had once been alive. She had been his daughter.

And she was gone for ever.

Emotion swelled in him with a force he couldn't control. He set aside the papers swiftly, so they wouldn't be damaged, and covered his eyes as the tears began to fall.

Lottie's arms folded around him as he gave in to a grief he could not control. They held one another while he pulled at a strength buried deep and mustered his wits.

'She was beautiful,' he said hoarsely.

Lottie gave a sad, tender smile. 'She was.'

'I'd like to see the rest.' He reached for the stack once more, but Lottie set her hand atop it.

'I would like to look at them with you,' she said slowly.

'I'd like that too.'

She leaned back against his chest. Her head came to just beneath his chin, which worked for them now as she lifted the pages and together they studied the first image Evander had come across.

Lottie had always had an amazing talent, possessing the ability to bring anything to life with a pallet of watercolour paints, some ink and a few brushes. What she had captured of their daughter, he knew, would be as accurate as any portrait that could be commissioned.

One by one they looked through all the paintings Lottie had left tucked away in the protection of that little writing nook. She shared the inspiration behind each one with tales that had him smiling and laughing. In each one Lily's likeness had been captured to perfection, from infancy until midway through her second year of life.

Getting to the bottom of the stack was like turning to the final page of a captivating book and wishing to have more. Evander wanted the paintings to go on for ever— to show their daughter meeting him upon his return from his arduous travels, then later having her coming out ball, and later still marrying the man who won her heart, having children of her own.

Lottie looked back towards the door near the table.

'Was that her room?' Evander asked.

'Hers and mine.' Lottie's gaze didn't move from the door. 'The other room was where Dina slept.'

Evander gently set the pictures back on the desk and led the way. The floorboards creaked under their feet as they walked, and Lottie's hand tightened on his.

He waited for her to turn the knob, but she shook her head. 'You. Please.'

He put his hand on the cool metal latch and pushed the door into the bedchamber.

The odour of camphor hung in the air, too sharp a scent to be dulled completely even by time. A small trundle bed lay beside a larger one.

'I wanted to be there for her.'

The pinch of Lottie brows showed the pain she felt being in that room. Such memories were perhaps best left in her heart, and he would not intrude. He pulled the door closed and Lottie released a long exhale as though she had been holding her breath.

'There is one final thing I would like to see...' He didn't finish his request aloud, but there was a resignation in Lottie's eyes that told him she knew.

She led him back towards the front door, but before she opened it he asked her to wait and retrieved the paintings she'd done of Lily.

He hesitated. 'If I may?'

Lottie nodded, and he returned to her side with the most precious treasure he'd ever held cradled in his palms. He left those beautiful portraits in the carriage, tucked in a small drawer beneath his seat for safekeeping, and then Lottie guided him towards the woods.

They walked for several minutes in silence, their hands clasped together as the clicks and pops of nature mingled with the chirping song of various birds.

Evander considered Lottie as they walked, seeing her in a new light. Not only as a confident, sure woman who had done what was needed to survive in his absence, but as a mother—a woman who had gone through great sacrifice for the wellbeing of her child.

What was more, despite what he had subjected Lottie to, she did not hate him. Even now, even with everything she'd been through, her heart was so pure that she could not hate him.

Tears pricked his eyes and he was filled with revered awe at this woman Lottie had become, and at the beautiful little girl she had raised with love despite her dire circumstances.

The forest opened up into a small clearing with a stream flowing beside it. There, at the top of a small hill, was a statue of an angel, the words on the marker indistinguishable from their distance.

But Evander didn't need to read them to know that the grave belonged to their Lily.

Chapter Twenty

Evander led the way to the marble statue. Initially he'd thought it a likeness of their daughter, but up close he saw that the angel was older, with longer hair. With proximity, he could make out the words on the marker.

Lily Rose Murray
January 19th 1811—June 16th 1813

Lottie clung to him—not only to his hand, but also his arm, as if he was all that kept her upright. They stayed there for a long while, not saying anything, each lost in their own thoughts for the child that had been ripped away from them. Lottie with her old memories and Evander with the memories she'd given him by way of her words and the pictures she'd painted.

Behind the grave, the sun began to set. It was a ball of glowing orange, sinking into a pillow of clouds and casting rays of purple, orange and pink through the sky.

'I've never seen the statue before.' Lottie looked up, studying the marble angel with obvious consideration.

'You haven't?'

She shook her head. 'I couldn't bear to. I had Sarah

come and oversee its placement.' Her gaze lowered to grass. 'I never said my farewells to Lily either.'

Evander put his arm around her shoulders again and her weight sagged against him.

'I was here, yes. But I was...' She shook her head, as though she couldn't find the words she was looking for. 'I... I was in such a state. My heart had been ripped from my chest and my mind stopped without its familiar beat. Perhaps that's why I didn't come here. Because if I didn't face it, I didn't have to accept it.' Her voice caught.

Evander hugged Lottie to him, wishing he could go back to that day and be the one to help her through such grief.

'Are you ready to say farewell now?' Evander asked.

Lottie pulled in a deep breath and tears filled her eyes.

'I want to thank you,' Evander said. 'You've given me the greatest gift today in letting me know Lily. You were both parents when she had only one.'

He pulled her into his arms, and she allowed herself to be folded in his embrace against him.

'Thank you for coming here, for wanting to know her.' Lottie looked up, her lashes spiked with tears. 'She would have adored you. As I do.'

Evander stroked a hand down Lottie's cheek. 'I love you, Lottie. I always will.'

She pulled in a soft breath.

Something in his chest constricted as he recalled her fears about coming to the cottage: that she might relive all her anger and resentment towards him for having left her.

He would never fault her for such feelings. Most especially after learning about what had transpired in his absence.

'I understand why you have been hesitant to trust me, why it's so difficult for you to open your heart to me.' He lowered his head to hers and spoke gently.

She sniffled and looked down at the grave.

'I would give every last shilling I have to undo the past,' he said. 'To have been here with you.'

She returned her attention to him. 'You didn't know I was with child.'

'My God, Lottie, I'm so sorry.' His heart felt as though a fist were squeezing it, forcing out every drop of hurt. 'You told me not to go and I did anyway. I left you alone to face all this with no one. I'm so, so sorry.'

Emotion choked off his apology. It didn't matter. Words could never undo his horrible error of judgment.

She caught his hands in hers. 'I forgive you for leaving. You left because you wanted me to have a good life. You didn't know about Lily. You didn't know what I was going through.'

'I should have written more, ensured my letters got through—'

Lottie reached up and touched his cheek. 'You couldn't have known. This is not your fault.' Her eyes searched his, clear and honest and filled with affection. 'Evander, I forgive you. And I...' She swallowed hard. 'I love you.'

At the admission, she pressed herself against him in an embrace once more.

She loved him.

She forgave him.

Two magnanimous gifts he didn't deserve. Yet those two things above all else were what he craved most in this world. He held her tight until a chill touched the air as the light of day began to fade.

Lottie shivered in his arms.

'Shall we return to London?' Evander asked.

Lottie nodded against his chest and allowed him to guide her in the opposite direction, towards the cottage. After only several steps, Lottie stopped and turned back.

This time when she approached the grave he held back,

remaining where he stood for several minutes as Lottie knelt in the grass before the statue and bent towards it.

No doubt finally saying her farewells.

When she returned, tears shone on her cheeks. She brushed them away and took his arm to be led to the waiting carriage. They shared a bench the entire way back to London, taking comfort in the closeness of one another.

Finally, they arrived at her townhouse. She turned to him before the footman opened the door and parted her lips in preparation to speak. He hoped she might invite him inside, that the quiet peace of being with her didn't have to come to an end.

The door opened and she twisted her hands—that old habit she'd never quite lost. She looked behind her at the rising townhouse, then back at him. 'Good evening,' she said softly, and gracefully exited the carriage.

He watched as she strode up the path to her home and thought of all the things that stretched between them. There was still so much left to say, to discuss, but the events at the cottage had been taxing on them both.

She loved him.

That affirmation at their daughter's grave had been something of a balm on his wounded soul.

He waited until the carriage pulled away from her home before he slid the drawer under his seat open and withdrew the paintings. Though it was dark, light flickered in through the window from the gas lamps, allowing Evander to look again at the images of their daughter.

He ought to have married Lottie before he left on his quest to save the Westix estate. At the time he'd been too foolishly hung up on the notion that only a grand wedding in the opulence of St George's would do. If only he'd known then what he did now.

Upon arrival at Westix Place, he removed himself from the carriage and trudged up the two short steps into his home, before wending his way to the study. He sank into the fine leather chair behind his desk and opened the bottom drawer, intending to put the paintings of Lily inside for safekeeping.

The small diamond chip ring Lottie had thrown at him at Comlongon sat there, atop the deeds to Huntly Manor. He'd purchased the property some time ago, fully intending to give it to her as a gift. Except there had never been an appropriate time to do so.

The same with the ring. He'd kept it with the hope of asking her to marry him again. He reached into the drawer and retrieved it. It was such a diminutive thing—hardly the sort of tribute an earl would give to his future Countess. And yet he knew Lottie better than anyone else. This would still be the ring she would want above all others.

Perhaps it was finally time to offer it to her once more.

A cold, empty house greeted Lottie upon her return. While she'd been at the cottage she had craved the familiarity of her townhouse and all the fine furnishings she'd used there, to try to fill the empty space Lily had left behind.

But seeing the comparison between the homes—*feeling* the comparison—made her realise how much more she had preferred that small cottage full of love to this townhouse full of wealth.

Her footsteps rang out on the tiles and echoed off the walls around her, and suddenly she missed Evander's presence with a visceral pang.

When she had been at the cottage when Lily was alive Lottie had had to be a pillar of strength. There was no one strong to lend her support, no one like Evander.

She recalled how he had put his hands to her shoulders to brace her against the worst of the agony wrought upon her by seeing the cottage again. How he had fortified her as she leaned against him. Even as he suffered.

A fire had been lit in the drawing room, and Lottie followed the warm glow like a beacon. The fire had clearly been lit some time ago, its logs now little more than crumbling embers awash in the grey powder of ash. She lifted another log from the ornamental metal bin by the hearth and set it atop the dwindling flames, sending glowing sparks scattering upward.

Heat blossomed from the hearth once more, and she held her hands to the invisible wall. Memories from the cottage overtook her exhausted mind. A little girl, giggling and pushing her cold toes towards the fire. Evander cradling Lottie's hands between his own.

Evander.

She exhaled deeply and the fire licking over the fresh log wavered at the movement of air.

She recalled how he'd gently put aside Lily's pictures before bowing his head into the large palm of his hand and weeping. For their daughter.

Her heart flinched.

He had never met Lily, yet he loved her. It had been evident not just in his tears, but in the flash of pain in his eyes when he opened the door to the room Lottie had shared with their daughter, with that terrible unmistakable odour of camphor.

It made her hurt for him to have understood fatherhood and loss on the same stark day. At least she'd had two and a half years to revel in the joy of parenthood before losing Lily.

Lottie's initial fear of hating him again after their time at the cottage was unfounded. Rather, it had been quite the opposite. Seeing his love for their daughter only endeared him to Lottie more. Still, she should not have told him she loved him. Not the day before, when she mourned their daughter on the anniversary of her death, nor at her grave. Not after all this time of having been so successful at keeping him an arm's length away.

Now he knew she loved him he would never stop his pursuit of her.

But she did love him. She always had. Even when she'd been enraged to find he had returned home, she had been relieved to see him alive after so long, fearing he might be dead.

No, she had never stopped caring for him.

And that was exactly why she could never be with him.

'Gracious,' Sarah exclaimed behind her.

Lottie spun round to find Sarah with her hand pressed to her chest and her face red.

'You gave me quite a start,' she said. 'Forgive me, love. I didn't hear you come in.' Her face softened at once. 'You were gone for quite a while. I hope that implies it went well? Or at least as well as it could, I suppose.'

Lottie nodded. 'Yes, thank you, Sarah.'

'The servants are able to return to their usual duties tomorrow?' she asked hesitantly.

Lottie had given them all the day off again today, knowing she wouldn't want anyone hovering about. Aside from Sarah, who had declined to leave—as she did on all the days off Lottie tried to offer her.

'Yes, thank you,' Lottie said.

'Lady Alice sent you a message.' Sarah approached the fireplace and slid a heavy card onto the table.

Lottie regarded the envelope with her name written on it in neat, careful script. She hoped it wasn't an invitation to a soiree or a ball. The last thing she wanted was to attend a social event.

'Her maid said she's in quite a state and wants to see you as soon as you're free.' Sarah indicated the message.

Lottie lifted the envelope and opened it to read the contents within, which reiterated what Sarah had relayed. 'I'll see her tomorrow, whenever she is free to come.'

Sarah remained stubbornly where she stood. 'How did Lord Westix do with seeing the cottage?'

An image flashed in Lottie's mind of him holding his face in his hand as he wept for their lost Lily.

'Appropriately,' Lottie said softly.

'I knew he would.' Sarah nodded with a sad smile. 'He's a good man, your Lord Westix.'

Lottie turned back to the fire and let her gaze become lost in the flickering orange and red flames. 'He is.' She mustered a weak smile. 'You did well on the statue. Thank you.'

'It was the least I could do for you, lovey.' Sarah approached where Lottie still stood by the fire. 'Has something else happened?'

Lottie swallowed. 'I told him I loved him.'

Sarah remained silent.

'I know you're smiling.' Lottie turned to regard her maid and discovered the woman was indeed grinning like a fool.

Sarah propped a hand on her hip. 'Is it really so bad that he knows, love?'

Lottie returned her gaze to the flames once more. 'Only time will tell, but I am almost certain it is.'

Chapter Twenty-One

Red roses, this time. As deep a red as could be found. A dozen of them. Or maybe three dozen?

No, that was too much.

Evander didn't want to be ridiculous.

His nerves jangled like church bells in his ears. Two years he had been waiting for this moment. Everything had to be perfect.

He scarcely heard anything Miss Flemming said, aside from her wish to bid him good luck.

The pace of the carriage seemed to be a slow crawl all the way to Bloomsbury. His leg bounced with the force of his anxious energy, as though somehow that might hasten them to Lottie's townhouse.

Doubt crossed his mind like a shadow, but he cast it in the light of assurance. Yes, Lottie did love him.

Evander removed himself from the carriage and Lottie's butler settled him in the drawing room.

Though he'd been in her home countless times before, it all felt different on this particular visit. The path to the drawing room seemed longer, his steps over the carpet running along the polished wood floors louder.

The butler indicated the settee, which he sat on despite his restless agitation.

His gaze wandered towards the iris and white tulip bouquet he'd purchased for Lottie following the night when he'd punched Devonington. Though it had only been a few days ago, it felt as if an age had passed since then.

He regarded the roses in his hand as the double doors opened and Lottie walked in. He swiftly got to his feet, roses offered in presentation.

She smiled and accepted the flowers. 'You'll run all of London out of hothouse flowers if you keep this pace.' She leaned over the bunch of perfect roses, closed her eyes and breathed in. 'They do smell lovely. Thank you.'

Her gown was a butter-yellow that made him think of those sunny summer days Lottie had described at the cottage. Though she was as lovely as ever, the effects of the emotional day before had left the delicate skin under her eyes slightly bruised. He wanted to hold her as he'd done the day before, to gently kiss her sweet lips and whisper words of undying affection in her ear.

The maid, Sarah, came in with a tea tray and took the flowers from Lottie to put them in a vase. Evander did not miss the way Sarah's brows rose with enthusiasm as she passed Lottie.

'Would you care for some tea?' Lottie asked, when the door had closed and she'd taken a seat.

Evander shook his head and settled on the settee. 'I wanted to see you today.'

She pursed her lips. 'And you see me and have my attention.'

'That's the thing of it,' he continued. 'I want you always.'

'Always?'

There was a sudden remoteness to her expression, making her entirely unreadable.

Damn it.

He'd come with purpose and he would not be swayed.

Not when she was what he wanted. When she was all he'd ever wanted.

He drew the ring box out of his pocket. Not the original one, of course—he didn't know where that might be. But a finer one, with a bed of black silk as glossy as Lottie's luxurious hair.

'Charlotte Rossington, I have loved you since the moment I met you at that dance in Bedfordshire, when you struck me with your beauty and won me over with your wit.'

The small muscles in her neck stood out, but still her face reflected not a hint of emotion.

'I have never stopped loving you,' he continued, as one was wont to do when one was proposing and unsure of how things were progressing with the opposite party. In for a penny, in for a pound, and all that. 'You will receive hothouse flowers for as long I'm living and I vow to be unwavering in my loyalty to you.'

His thoughts at her blank expression became like frenzied ants after their hill had been kicked. She looked as if she did not want him to be doing this, but did not wish to be so cruel as to tell him to stop.

'I will always love you,' he said.

And on that pathetically clichéd note he concluded what was perhaps the worst proposal of all time to the most important woman of his life.

He knelt before her and presented the box, with the little ring of their youth nestling beneath the lid. She looked down at it, not taking it.

'I have wanted to do this since I returned to London,' he said. 'I never wanted you to feel I was forcing your hand. However, now that I know you feel the same way...'

Her brows pinched together.

'Lottie, will you do me the honour of becoming my wife?'

'Evander.'

She said his name slowly and his stomach began the long, awful slide to his toes.

'You're an earl,' she said softly.

He got to his feet. 'And you'll be my Countess.'

'You know I will never be accepted among the ton.' She swallowed. 'Not after what I've done.'

'You did that to survive. For—'

'They don't care about the reason.' Her tone was flat, resigned.

'Why should their opinion of you matter?' he demanded.

'Because you're right—I do love you.' Lottie looked helplessly out the window to the garden, where rain pattered over the heavy rose blossoms. 'I can't bear the thought of your good family name being ruined because of my tarnished reputation.'

'Lottie, please.' He reached for her hand, setting the box against her palm. 'I love you. I've loved you since—'

'Since the Bedfordshire ball—I know.' She glanced down at the box in her hand, toying lightly at one corner with her thumbnail. 'But I'm not that young woman any more. There's nothing of her left in me.'

In a slow motion that threatened to tear his heart from his chest, she extended the ring box back towards him. Returning it.

Rejection.

He stepped back, refusing to accept it. 'Tomorrow,' he said. 'Think on it and give me your answer tomorrow.'

'It won't change,' Lottie said sadly.

'Think on it,' he said again. 'At least promise me that.'

She pulled the box back towards her and folded it in her hand. At last, she nodded. 'I will think on it.'

Evander breathed a sigh of relief. For now. Tomorrow might truly bring the same answer again. If that were to happen…

He gritted his teeth, resolved not even to think it. She had to say yes. It would be foolish not to when two people loved each other as they did.

Now all he needed was a miracle to convince her.

Chapter Twenty-Two

June 1816

Lottie stared down at the small diamond ring, her heart hammering in her chest. Evander would be back tomorrow for her answer.

But how could she say anything but no?

The door to the drawing room opened.

'All red roses,' Sarah said wistfully.

Lottie's head snapped up as her maid entered the drawing room with the large bouquet of red roses in a crystal vase.

Sarah's perceptive gaze settled on the ring. 'I've seen that before.'

Of course she recognised it. She had been the one to keep it safe while Lottie was with her protectors. Never had she allowed herself to wear that ring around any other man. At least not in any intimate setting. And when her time was her own, it had hung on the chain or been on her finger.

'You are not glowing with delight.' Sarah frowned. 'Please tell me you did not refuse him.'

'I didn't.' Lottie folded the ring in her hand. The metal was cool against her palm. 'Or at least he wouldn't allow me to. He asked me to think on it and I promised him that I would.'

'And will you?' Sarah set the roses on the table beside the irises and white tulips, her head tilted in assessment.

'How can I marry him?' Lottie demanded. 'How can I let him destroy his family's good name by being with me? I've told you how I've been spoken to. Evander will be treated thus as well. His mother too. I cannot do that. Not when...'

'Not when you love him so much,' Sarah finished for her. 'I know, lovey. I know... But you would be happy with him.'

'But would he be happy with me?' Lottie asked bitterly. 'When his friends turn on him and his associates no longer want to do business with him? When his mother is ostracised by her friends? When he...' her voice grew husky '...when he hears stories of the men I shared company with?'

Sarah moved the red roses from the table and placed them on the mantel. 'I can't answer those questions—but I can tell you that I've never seen a man care for a woman as much as Lord Westix does for you.' Sarah nodded to herself, content with the relocation of the roses. 'Now, I hate to pull you from your contemplation of his offer—which I do think you ought to truly consider, if my opinion is needed. But, mercy me, the time has slipped away. Forgive me, lovey, but Lady Alice will be here soon.'

It was very rare that Lottie saw her students during the day, but Lady Alice had insisted on coming as soon as possible.

'I'll go prepare a fresh pot of tea.' Sarah glanced again at the ring. 'You know my opinion.'

'I do.' Lottie gave her a pointed look. 'Though I don't recall having asked.'

Sarah simply grinned and exited the drawing room.

Once she was gone, Lottie tucked the ring back into its small box, knowing for certain her answer would not change. No matter how vocal Sarah might be on the subject.

There could be no second chance—not with everything that stood between her and Evander.

Her butler arrived in the drawing room, his uniform as crisp as his demeanour. 'Forgive me, mistress, but Lady Alice is here to see you.'

Lottie opened the drawer in the table and slid the ring box inside before swiftly closing it. 'Please show her in.'

Lady Alice practically charged into the room, her eyes red-rimmed, her bonnet still secured under her chin after her carriage ride.

'Thank you so much for agreeing to see me so quickly.'

She yanked unceremoniously at the pink bow of her bonnet, tugging it off so her blonde hair became mussed, a long way from its usual neat coiffure, and offered it to the butler with a nod of thanks.

He accepted the hat, gave a little bow and quit the room, closing the double doors behind him as he did so.

Lottie helpfully smoothed Lady Alice's hair for her. 'Please have a seat and tell me what's happened to have you so upset. I thought George had made his way back to you?'

Lady Alice promptly slumped onto the settee and gave a miserable sniffle. 'He has—except that now he feels he's unworthy of me.'

'Tell me what happened,' Lottie said. 'First by explaining where he has been.'

Lady Alice took a deep breath and nodded. 'He was in Spain, but he was injured and knocked unconscious in a battle near the end of the Peninsular War. When he woke, he had no recollection of who he was. He's only recently recovered his memory and made his way home.'

Sarah entered with a fresh pot of tea and then bustled out swiftly.

Lottie poured some tea into a delicate china cup for Lady Alice while she continued.

'I was overjoyed to see him again. Though my mother wasn't, as she's now convinced I should marry an earl after my engagement to Lord Ledsey.'

'So she's stepping between you?' Lottie poured herself a cup of tea and settled back to let it cool. 'I presume she's not aware you're here.'

Lady Alice lifted her shoulders in a guilty shrug. 'I told her I was taking tea with a friend. I wasn't lying.' She lifted her cup and took a delicate sip. 'My mother knows I love him. I believe she'll allow me to marry him.'

'Then the problem…?'

'George.' Lady Alice folded her hands in the lap of her pink sprigged day dress and looked down at them. 'He feels he's not worthy of me.'

'Because he was gone so long?' Lottie asked, before she could stop herself.

She immediately chastised herself for the assumption. This was Lady Alice's life. Not her own. Discussing matters with Evander had lodged them into the forefront of Lottie's mind and was now impacting how she handled her students.

'No,' Lady Alice scuffed the toe of her slipper against the carpet. 'He lost an arm due to the injuries he sustained in battle, and he fears it's made him less of a man than he was before the war. Of course I don't feel that way, but he won't listen. Men are so terribly stubborn, aren't they?'

'Oh, I'm so sorry.' Lottie moved over to the settee to sit beside the young woman and embraced her. 'Yes, men can be terribly stubborn,' she agreed.

'Well, I can be stubborn too.' Lady Alice raised her chin with determination. 'I love him with all my heart and I told him as much. He told me he loves me too, and that's why he's doing this—which is all foolishness.' Lady Alice sighed. 'For me, there will never be anyone else. I've been given a second chance with him and I refuse to lose it.'

Lottie smiled at the younger woman's determined spirit. 'That is exactly as it should be, then, if you truly love him.'

'I do.' Lady Alice nodded firmly. 'Now, how do I go about convincing him?'

Lottie settled back in contemplation. Except all she could picture in her mind was Evander, fighting for her with that same resolve. What would she want him to tell her? What *could* Evander tell her that would change her mind?

And then she knew exactly what answer to give—though Lady Alice would not like it.

'I think,' Lottie said gently, 'he will need to come to that conclusion on his own.'

Lady Alice's pretty face fell. 'There's nothing I can do to help?'

'Perhaps let him know what it is you love about him, but he must realise it on his own.' Lottie recalled how Evander had punched Devonington for her. 'And stand up for him if someone speaks ill of him.'

Lady Alice nodded firmly. 'I can do that.'

'I pray he comes around quickly.' Lottie held the younger woman's hand in her own and gave it an affectionate squeeze.

As Lady Alice left, Lottie could not stop thinking once more about Evander and how eerily similar their situation was. Except that a missing arm would not destroy a family's name. A missing arm could not have a sordid past that might shake a husband's stoicism.

While the sentiments might be reminiscent, their situations were entirely different. However, it did give Lottie an idea for a way they could still be together without her blemishing the Westix name.

Evander had blundered in his first attempt with Lottie. He would not do so again. This time he anticipated that she would reject his proposal. And this time he knew exactly what to say.

Once more, he stopped by Aphrodite & Cupid.

Miss Flemming greeted him with her usual smile. 'Another grand bouquet, Lord Westix?'

'Not quite.' Evander glanced around the shop. 'I should like a bunch of flowers, nothing grand. Daffodils and pink carnations, please. However, I should like you to choose the shoddiest flowers you can find.'

Miss Flemming blinked. 'I do beg your pardon, my lord, but we only have fine flowers here. We wouldn't have any that aren't beautiful.'

Evander frowned. 'I see. I suppose whatever daffodils and carnations you have will suffice.'

Miss Flemming sucked in a quick breath. 'It suddenly occurs to me we have daffodils in the small garden we tend at the back. Would you... Would you like some of those?'

'Please. And charge me for the cost of replacing them in the garden.'

'That isn't necessary—'

'Of course it is.'

Miss Flemming flushed. 'You're a good man, Lord Westix. Thank you.' She gave him a quick smile. 'Do forgive me a moment, while I step out.'

Evander nodded, and waited while she assembled the flowers. When she returned, the daffodils were already beginning to wilt where they were bunched against the sturdier stems of the quality carnations.

She cast him an apologetic look. 'I'm afraid they will not last long.'

He assessed the pathetic flowers. 'They're precisely what I was hoping for. I need only one last thing.'

'Of course.'

He took a long, deep breath. 'A lily.'

'Only one?'

He nodded. 'The smallest you have.'

She disappeared, and returned with a flower held between her fingers. 'Will this do?'

The delicate curling white petals appeared healthy and beautiful, and it was indeed the tiniest lily he'd ever seen.

His throat tightened. 'It's perfect.'

Once more he made his way back to Lottie's townhouse, noting how, upon his arrival, the butler regarded the daffodils with apparent disdain.

She was waiting for him in the drawing room when he arrived, wearing a simple blue day dress with her hair in a quick knot.

The ring box sat on the table and his heart went to it.

He kept the flowers hidden behind his back as the double doors were closed behind him.

'I have my decision.'

She drew in a quick breath, and in that span of time Evander rushed to speak, saying, 'Before you give me your answer...'

At that same moment, she continued, 'I will be your mistress.'

From outside the door someone gave a choke, followed by a feigned cough.

Evander paid them no mind. Instead he stared in horror at Lottie, the woman he had spent six years wanting to have as his wife. 'What did you say?'

'I'll be your mistress.' Her gaze slid to the ring box. 'But I cannot marry you.'

'Lottie...'

'Let me say my piece.' She looked down at her hands

and twisted them against one another. 'I love you. I'll never deny it again. But it is my love for you that makes me unable to be your wife.'

Evander shook his head vehemently. 'No. I won't have you that way.'

She pulled in a shuddering breath. 'Then you can have me in no way at all. I will not ruin your family. I will not ruin your name.'

'No,' he said again.

'What will you do when you hear of a man who has been my protector? What will you do when your mother is no longer welcome around her friends because of her association with me?' Her cheeks had gone red as she spoke. 'I will not trap you in marriage.'

'No,' he said a final time. 'Please, Lottie.' It was his turn to speak. 'I didn't simply come here to receive your answer. I have more I wish to say.' He held out the flowers, first the daffodils and carnations.

The tension on her face melted. 'These are like the first bouquet you ever brought me.'

'With one special exception.' He withdrew the small lily from behind his back and presented it to her.

She regarded the tiny flower with reverence, and the emotion on her face told him he understood its significance exactly. 'Oh, Evander, this is my favourite of all the bouquets you've given me.'

He breathed a sigh of relief, glad she enjoyed them. 'But that isn't all. I botched it yesterday. I have more to say.'

Lottie nodded and started to twist her fingers again. It was the perfect opening.

'You say you aren't the same women you were six years ago,' he said.

Lottie's brow furrowed, but he wasn't going to allow himself to be distracted this time and continued.

'I disagree.' He held up a hand to stop any argument. 'In some ways.'

He indicated her twisting fingers. 'You've done that for as long as I've known you. Whenever you're anxious or nervous.'

She stopped the action immediately.

He chuckled. 'You were considerate and kind when I knew you, and you still are now. It's why you're so adept at helping the young women you instruct. It isn't seduction you teach them, but confidence and self-worth.' He stepped closer. 'The Lottie I knew put others before herself, which is what you are doing now by trying to turn me away. Although I won't let you.'

She opened her mouth to speak, but he shook his head.

'I'm not done telling you about the woman you are now. The woman I love more than the girl I met six years ago. Because you're correct—you have changed.'

She swallowed and regarded him with a wary expression.

'You're a woman now—one who understands obligation above all else,' he said. 'You're a mentor who helps show others how to navigate through difficult waters. Something you had to learn on your own.' He put the lily in her hands and cradled them with his own. 'You're a mother who gave up every part of herself in an effort to save her child.'

She looked away, but he reached for her chin and gently drew her face back towards him.

'I'm in awe of you, Lottie. In complete and utter awe of how greatly you cared for our daughter.'

Her eyes searched his, as if she was looking into his soul and finding the truth behind every one of the words he spoke.

'You need to forgive yourself, Lottie,' he said as gently as he could. 'Would you do it all over again if you had Lily back and she needed you?'

She closed her eyes and a single tear ran down her cheek as she nodded.

'I know, my love.' He ran his thumb over her cheek and wiped away the tear. 'And that is why you need to forgive yourself. What you did was heroic and selfless.'

'Heroic.' she scoffed, opening her eyes.

'Yes,' he replied fiercely. 'What you did, you did for Lily—for our child. Never was there a purer reason than that of a mother's love.'

She shook her head. 'Your good name—I don't want you ruined—'

'I sacrificed you once for the sake of my good name.' Ire rose in Evander at his own youthful impetuousness. 'And I'm filled with regrets because of it. I will sacrifice anything to have you back in my life, Lottie. And not as my mistress. Not when I can think of no woman worthier of being my Countess.'

He plucked the ring box from the table, opened the box to reveal the ring that carried so much weight in its tiny stone, and knelt before her. 'Lottie, my one and only love, will you marry me?'

Chapter Twenty-Three

This was not the first time Evander had proposed to Lottie, and yet her heart pounded as frantically as if it were. The day before she had been resolved to turn him away. But she hadn't appreciated how fully he understood who she was. Now she realised he saw her better than she saw herself.

Heroic.

That was what he'd called her.

Never had she thought of herself in such a light. She'd only ever done what was needed.

He knew about her at her worst, and through his eyes saw her at her best. What was more, he had shown her how to see it as her best as well—as something not filthy, with broken morals, but something made resplendent with the truest form of a mother's love.

This was her second chance, and although she'd been inclined to cast it aside he had convinced her to take it.

And she would.

She looked down at Evander, kneeling before her, still handsome with his sharp jaw and deep green eyes, his auburn hair falling over his brow in a boyishly handsome way, and her heart gave in. Without restriction or fear.

In that instant, she released her concerns and let this be only about them.

A man and a woman in love.

She put her fingertips into his hands and nodded.

His nostrils flared and his eyes widened slightly. 'Was that a yes?'

She laughed and nodded. 'Yes.'

A squeal came from the other side of the door, followed swiftly by another bout of feigned coughing.

Evander looked towards the sound with an eyebrow cocked, then turned towards Lottie again, laughing as he leapt to his feet and threw his arms around her. He squeezed her to him and lifted her into the air, so her slippers dangled an inch over the floor.

After a joyous twirl, he set her down and caught her face in his hands. 'I love you, Lottie.'

'And I love you, Evander.' She leaned up towards him and pressed her lips to his.

He kissed her once, firmly, then gave her a second kiss, and a third. His hand cupped the back of her head and her lips parted in anticipation for the brush of his tongue. They held each other, savouring the freedom of finally giving in to their affection. Not through a need for comfort, but out of love.

'I'll never let you down again,' he said between kisses. His forehead rested on hers. 'I'll always be here for you. Whenever you need me.'

'I know,' Lottie said.

He pulled her to him once more, laying her head against his chest, where she could hear the thud of his strong heartbeat, as fast with delight as hers.

Out of nowhere, something banged against the door.

Lottie and Evander started as the doors flew open and Sarah tumbled in with a glass in her hand. She hopped up and looked around, clearly searching for some excuse to offer. Behind her stood Andrews and the cook, both equally as flustered as Sarah.

'Ah, this glass.' Sarah gave a nervous titter. 'I found it sitting in front of the door and was just taking it to the kitchen to ensure the scullery maid sees to it.'

'And I thought you'd be bringing it, so I came up to get it.' Cook gave a flash of a smile and reached for the glass. 'There was a shortage, and I wanted to be certain…er… that we had enough.'

Lottie nodded slowly, not believing a word.

One of Evander's arms remained around her shoulders.

'Don't let these two fool you,' Andrews said airily. 'They were using it to eavesdrop.'

Sarah huffed and thrust her hands on her hips. 'Don't go acting so high in the instep, Andrews. You started listening too.' She wagged a finger at him. 'And if you hadn't been trying to grab the glass—'

But Andrews was no longer listening. He pitched the tip of his nose into the air and strode from the wayward group with exactly the 'high in the instep' demeanour of which he'd been accused.

'Well, I supposed we needn't break our wonderful news,' Lottie said in playful chastisement. 'As it appears you are already well aware.'

Sarah gave a wide, eager grin.

'When shall we wed?' Lottie asked Evander.

'As soon as possible—so you don't change your mind.' He winked at her.

'That's the truth, my lord,' Sarah piped up, and folded her arms over her ample bosom. 'I always said Lord Westix was a smart man.'

Lottie laughed at that. Giddiness flowed through her, leaving her effervescent. 'How about this Saturday?'

In truth, she would have wed Evander right then and there. There was something so liberating about finally giving in to her desire to marry him, to love him. It was like throwing off weighted moorings and being left feeling light enough to float away.

'I can ensure the food is done in time,' Cook offered.

'I can take care of anything else that's needed,' Sarah said quickly. 'And Andrews will be most helpful with whatever might be required of him,' she called out loudly.

From somewhere down the hall came a quiet scoff.

'If you're serious,' Evander said to Lottie, 'I can secure a special licence in two days.'

'That would leave us with two days to spare in the event of any delay,' Lottie mused aloud.

'There won't be a moment of delay,' Evander cocked a brow.

'That's four days until we're wed.'

Evander furrowed his brow in an exaggeration of mock concern. 'What *will* people say?'

Lottie laughed. 'You're terrible.'

'Don't you mean I'm charming?' He beamed a smile at her that went straight to her heart.

'And wonderful,' she said dreamily. 'And perfect.'

'Oh, well, I didn't intend for you to elaborate, but by all means do go on.'

A long, wistful sigh sounded from the other side of the room where Sarah stood. They both turned to look at her, and found her watching them with a sentimental smile tilting her lips.

She stiffened, realising she'd been caught. 'Oh. I...' She looked about. 'Where did I put that glass?'

'Cook took it for you,' Lottie said, holding back a laugh.

'Ah. Yes. Well...' Sarah floundered for a moment, before throwing her hands up in surrender with a huff and rushing from the room, swiftly closing the doors behind her.

For all the good that might do in a house full of servants such as Lottie's.

But it was privacy, nonetheless, and Lottie found herself eternally grateful for those few moments with Evander.

He gazed down at her, his eyes sparkling once more the way they'd done when he'd met her for their walks on the little footpath in Binsey.

'In four days you'll be my Countess.' He stroked a hand down her cheek, his eyes tender with affection. 'My wife. After six long years.'

And they had indeed been long years, suffered independently of one another, but now they were brought together through happiness and honesty.

Why was it, then, that a little twinge of discomfort had lodged at the pit of Lottie's stomach? Perhaps it was simply the thought of marrying by special licence in only four days? Or the fear that his mother would be displeased?

Perhaps, too, it was anticipation of the ton's reaction to their union.

Regardless of what it was, Lottie pushed it away, tucking it neatly into the back of her mind. Whatever it was, she would address it at another time. For now, she simply wanted to be deliriously blissful.

And for that moment she was. She truly, truly was.

As it turned out, the special licence was not obtained in two days. Evander procured it in only one.

Wealth went a long way among the ton, despite their claims to be above such vulgarity.

In the four days they'd had to plan, a vicar had agreed to do the ceremony at a small nearby chapel, and Evander had placed a large order of flowers at Aphrodite & Cupid, purchasing arrangements for the chapel as well as Westix Place, where the breakfast would be held after.

Miss Flemming had never smiled so broadly, seeing the number of centrepieces he'd requested. He wanted all of Westix Place filled with the scent of fresh flowers for Lottie.

The four days had flown by, far more quickly than Evander had imagined they would—especially when he had been certain they would drag terribly. But with the swiftness of a blinking eye Evander was waking up to the morning of his wedding day.

The sun shone on the cool day, burning off the last vestiges of fog as his carriage pulled up at the small church. His mother sat opposite him, alternating between offering titbits of unsolicited marital advice and beaming proudly. By the time they arrived, Eleanor and Charles were already there.

While Lady Westix saw to the final touches of the decorations in the small church—white and silver ribbon with clusters of lilies and ivy—Eleanor went to wait for Lottie in the narthex of the church.

That left only Charles, lingering near the altar.

There had always been an underlying tension between Evander and his brother-in-law. First with the unfortunate business between their fathers coming between them, and then with the wrongs Evander had committed to both Eleanor and Lottie, in worrying them in the years of his absence. And, of course, for having ruined Lottie.

Evander would never forgive himself for those last two infractions either.

Being that they were the only two remaining without task in the church, Charles approached Evander, his brilliant blue eyes narrowed. 'It's your wedding day,' he said.

'It is,' Evander agreed.

'Your marriage will not be well received by all.'

Evander lifted a shoulder in a partial shrug. 'It's nothing I can't weather.'

'You'll protect her from it?'

Evander tilted his head in question at Charles' seriousness. 'That goes without saying.'

Charles exhaled a mirthless chuckle. 'You love her. I
know you do. God knows, she did her best to shove you
away, and you kept coming back. I admire your tenac-
ity—I do.'

'I would do anything for her.'

Charles nodded and glanced up the aisle to the closed
door, where Lottie would soon be making her entrance.
'I dare say I haven't ever seen her as exuberant as she has
been these last few days. Not since we were children.'

Evander was grinning. He knew it and he didn't care.
Let all the world know how joyful the woman he was soon
to wed made him.

Charles stepped closer and put a hand on Evander's
shoulder. The friendly look in his eyes turned hard. He
looked first to the door of the church once more, then back
to Evander, and squeezed hard.

'I swear on my mother's grave,' Charles ground out, 'if
you ever hurt her again, I will ensure you disappear once
more. Only this time you'll never return.'

Before Evander could react, the doors opened and Lord
and Lady Dalton entered, with Lady Caroline and Lady
Alice. Charles released Evander at once and smiled con-
genially as he waved to them with the hand he'd used to
threaten Evander.

'Strike it from your mind,' Evander replied under his
breath. 'I'll never hurt her again.'

'It pleases me to hear it.' Charles patted Evander on the
back and slipped away.

The vicar asked everyone to take their seats as Lord
Rawley and the Marquess of Kentworth slipped inside,
and then invited Evander to the front of the altar. Eleanor
entered through the side door and took her seat beside

their mother, who was already dabbing at her eyes with a handkerchief.

The doors opened once more and Lottie entered, wearing a pale blue gown. Silver tissue formed small flowers down the front of her skirt and along the hem. Her hair was bound back and secured by a silver-trimmed wedding bonnet, with several loose curls around her face.

She had always taken his breath away, but she did so especially now, on their wedding day, when she would finally be his wife. Her face lit up when she saw him, and her eyes locked on his as she made her way to him on Charles's arm.

Finally, she stopped before him, and extracted her hand from Charles, who gave Evander a nod. After all, their conversation had already been concluded.

The vicar opened the *Book of Common Prayer* and began reading.

It was a short, fast service—a perfect end to an interminable wait. Evander and Lottie spoke their vows and exchanged rings. Both were made of gold and engraved with their initials and the date, to commemorate their love for all time.

After a quick cheer from their guests, Charles and Lottie were led to the vestry towards the parish register book, to enter their marriage lines. With that, they were finally, *finally* wed.

He looked down at her and smiled. 'My wife.'

'Oh, Evander.' She threw her arms around him.

He caught her and lifted her against him, spinning her as he'd done when she had accepted his proposal. As they slowed he set her down and kissed her. His wife. His Countess.

His heart now finally made whole.

'I'm so blissfully happy,' she whispered. 'I never thought... I never expected to be able to allow myself to do

this. For so long I believed I had sacrificed any chance…'
She swallowed. 'Thank you for never giving up on me, for
loving me so much.'

'I do love you,' he declared. 'Far too much to ever con-
ceive of letting you go.'

The wedding breakfast that followed was a grand affair, with every sort of food one could imagine. There were
shirred eggs along with rolls, toast and thick, briny ham
slices, as well as the most exquisite pastries, glittering
with coarse-grain sugar and glossy with brushed honey.
All of it had been laid atop a white lace tablecloth edged
in silver beads, amid half a dozen bouquets of pristine lilies entwined with ivy.

Their guests celebrated with joyous wishes and em-
braces, until finally Lottie and Evander were left alone.
Even Lady Westix had planned to spend the evening at
Somersville Place with Eleanor, to afford them privacy.

Evander took Lottie's hand in his, marvelling at how the
rings on their fingers glinted in unison, and led her up to
his large bedchamber. Though their chambers were con-
nected, he fully intended that they should share the larger
of the two rooms together. He wanted the closeness of her
company, and most especially the intimacy of the same
bed. Night after night.

'I have a present for you.' His pulse raced with the anticipation of giving her the gift he'd purchased so long ago.

'Marrying you has been gift enough.'

She smiled up at him with a joy he would always sa-
vour. He meant to make her just as happy for the duration
of their lives together.

'You say that only because you haven't seen what I have
for you.' He winked at her.

She laughed. 'Well, now I confess I am curious.'

He led her into his room, where an envelope lay on the
table beside the door. But once the door clicked closed

behind Lottie she reached for him before he could even think of the envelope again. The tender kiss she gave him led to a deeper kiss, which led to him slowly undoing the small pearl buttons along the back of her gown.

As it fell from her, revealing her lovely body to him, all thoughts of Huntly Manor faded completely from his mind.

Chapter Twenty-Four

The first time Lottie and Evander were intimate, they had given in to youthful passion and infatuation. The second time they had been in need of comfort, to fill the chasm of loss.

This time, however, as man and wife, was so much different from the previous two. Each took care to undress the other slowly, exploring with hands and lips and tongue. There was nothing rushing them and nothing to pull them apart when it was finished.

They consummated their marriage with love, their eyes locked and their hands clasped as their bodies came together. Afterwards, they lay in one another's arms, their hearts beating in tandem as they leisurely traced invisible patterns over each other's damp skin.

Evander sat up on his elbow, as though he'd suddenly thought of something.

'What is it?' Lottie asked.

'I dare say I was distracted from my original purpose.' He glanced to the door.

'I dare say your original purpose was acted out quite well.' She smiled up at her husband and swept her hand through his mussed auburn hair. 'I certainly have no complaints.'

He gazed at her with so much love in his eyes that it made her heart feel as though it would burst in the close confines of her chest.

'I do love you so,' Lottie said tenderly.

He leaned over her, hovering over her. 'I could spend a lifetime hearing those words.'

'You will spend a lifetime hearing them.' She studied his face, from the lovely green of his eyes down to his sharp jaw. 'I spent far too long holding them back.'

'None of that matters.'

He kissed her forehead with a sweetness that made her ache in the most wonderful way.

'All that matters is the beautiful things we've shared and what we have to look forward to together.'

Lottie gave a wistful sigh. 'I like that.'

He pushed up from her. 'You'll like this even better.'

He strode across the room, entirely devoid of clothing. Lottie sat up and ran her gaze over his strong body, marvelling at the lovely movement of muscles beneath his skin. Long legs, narrow hips, broad shoulders and the fine, tight bum she'd enjoyed digging her heels into as they'd come together earlier.

'You're correct, my love.' She lifted her brows coquettishly. 'I do like that even better.'

He withdrew a large envelope from the table beside the door. 'You minx.' With a grin, he returned to the bed and handed it to her.

She sat up in the soft bedsheets, careful to avoid crinkling it. 'What is this?'

'A promise kept.' He lifted his shoulders as though it were nothing of import. 'Something I purchased for you as soon as I returned to London. I meant to give it to you earlier, but there was never a perfect time. I'm actually glad to have waited, as now is when I believe it will matter most.'

Lottie tilted her head in coy curiosity before sliding her

finger under the lip of the envelope to open it. Inside was a large sheet of paper, which she withdrew.

Her gaze skimmed the handwritten official document and she sucked in a gasp.

'This is the deed to Huntly Manor.' She turned her attention to Evander. 'In my name.'

'I told you we would buy it.' He settled onto the wall of soft pillows beside her, his naked leg resting against hers. 'I wish it could have been six years ago.'

She stared at the document, incredulous. Evander had made good on his promise. And even though she had shoved his affection aside, time and again, he hadn't sold it or had it transferred to his name. No, he had continued to hold it, as determined that it would some day be hers as he had been that they would be married.

'You were right,' Lottie said. 'It matters most now. Thank you for this generous, thoughtful gift.'

Suddenly she was thinking of Oxfordshire, of the small village of Binsey and the home she had shared with her father. While she was grateful that Charles had been at the ceremony to give her away, it did not mean she had not felt her father's absence.

She had missed him over the years, but never so greatly as the day of her wedding.

Evander ran a hand down her face. 'I know it won't be the same,' he said gently, as though hearing her thoughts. 'If you'd prefer never to go—'

She shook her head. 'No, I want to. Before my father's death there were so many happy memories there. Not only with him, but with you.' She replaced the deed in the envelope and folded her hand into his.

'I know we haven't had time to plan a wedding trip.' Evander tucked his free arm behind his head and leaned back into the plushness of the many pillows. 'God knows if anyone deserves a respite from their lives to celebrate their affection for one another, it's us.'

Lottie laid her head on his chest. 'Indeed.'

His heart thumped in a steady rhythm beneath her cheek. 'I wanted to ask where you wished to go. We could travel to India, as Charles and Eleanor did, or perhaps see the floating city of Italy, or...'

'Or go to Oxfordshire and stay at Huntly Manor?' she suggested, lifting her head to gaze up at him.

'That was exactly what I was going to say.' He smiled down at her. 'And exactly where I was hoping you would want to go.'

'Yes,' she breathed, returning her head to his warm, strong chest. 'That is exactly where I should like to go. There is a path near the vicarage that I am especially fond of.'

'I believe I know the one to which you refer.' Evander ran his fingers over her naked shoulder, leaving her skin tingling with pleasure. 'I'll see to the arrangements and I imagine we can be there within a week or so.'

Lottie gave a dreamy sigh as Evander removed his hand from hers to curl one strong arm around her, securing her to him in a tender embrace.

Never had she thought such happiness was possible. And indeed it was, when they were together. But despite Evander's assurances of his love, and the joy she felt at that moment, dread for the future pooled in the bottom of her stomach. Not for her marriage, but for how others would react.

Members of the ton were cruel, and she had married her way into society. She knew it would be a long time, if ever, before she would be accepted.

Even as she tried to force away such thoughts as she lay there in blissful contentment, they hovered in the back of her mind like a vulture. No matter the love of her friends and her husband, the ton's scorn was coming.

Evander spent the remainder of Saturday and Sunday enjoying life as a happy newlywed. Countless hours were spent learning Lottie's body—what made her breath catch, what made her moan, what made her grab him and pull him towards her. But at last Monday arrived and business had to be tended to. His lovely new Countess would oversee the blending of her small staff with his and co-ordinate the moving of her belongings into Westix Place while he set off to meet with the other investors in the mine.

Last week had brought reports that the largest deposits of silver yet had been uncovered, with the promise of more to come. True, Evander was beyond wealthy, but he never forgot the power of a fortune.

Nor how easily one could be lost.

Especially now that he had a wife, and hopefully a family soon to follow. He would ensure his line remained secure in their good name and wealth. And this was just the way to do it.

He entered the smoky library at Huffsby House, where the other investors in the silver mine sat around the large table. Glasses of scotch and brandy sat before the men, while several held cigarillos with tendrils of grey smoke coiling up from the glowing tips.

As one, the men stopped talking and turned to face him.

Evander continued towards them, a stack of leatherbound papers pinched between his elbow and torso. They held his ideas for how best to capitalise on selling the silver.

Lord Huffsby, the Earl who headed the investment, got to his feet and held up a hand.

As no one else was moving, it was clear the gesture was for Evander, who stopped in his tracks.

Huffsby narrowed his small grey eyes at Evander across the large table. 'Lord Westix, we've heard some disturbing rumours.'

'Maybe you should keep away from gossip circles and leave them to your wives,' Evander jested.

No one laughed.

Lord Huffsby cleared his throat. 'Is it true that you have soiled the sanctity of marriage and your own good name?'

It was Evander's turn to narrow his eyes as his stomach clenched with suspicion. 'I cannot say I know what you mean,' he said slowly. 'Perhaps you ought to be blunt in what you ask to ensure nothing can be misconstrued.'

Lord Huffsby's jowls quivered. 'Have you married a whore, Lord Westix?'

Evander was in front of the shorter man in only two short strides, one hand reaching out to grasp his lapel and his other cocked back as the leather folder of papers plopped unceremoniously to the ground.

'I beg your pardon?' he said through gritted teeth. 'I'll ask you to repeat yourself while reminding you to be respectful.'

'That woman earns no respect from any man here,' Lord Huffsby spat. 'And nor does any man who would deign to marry her.' He curled his lips around those last words, his disgust clear.

'"That woman", as you so crassly refer to her, is more worthy of her new title than any of you who were born to yours,' Evander said. 'I believe it would be best for this partnership to come to an end.'

'That is precisely what we meant to tell you, once you'd confirmed you'd tied yourself to that lightskirt.' Lord Huffsby gave an arrogant sniff.

Without bothering to think of the consequences, or caring for anything other than Lottie's defence, Evander released his cocked fist and let it slam into Lord Huffsby's piggish face.

The man reeled back, his arms spinning wildly for control, before falling to the floor and rolling back like a flailing tortoise in its shell.

Immediately several arms gripped Evander, pulling him back and away. Someone shoved his leather folder into his hands—a wealthy merchant named Mr Weatherby, who blinked at Evander with owlish eyes behind his round spectacles.

'Please just go, Lord Westix. Your staying here will do no good.'

Evander jerked his folder into the crook of his arm and regarded the men he had once referred to as his associates. Many of whom he had called friend. Their regard was cold and unwelcome.

'I see,' Evander said, with as much pride as he could muster. 'If you run out of funds do not seek my aid, for I will not be there to offer any.'

With that, he turned from the room and departed, with the blades of a thousand stares stabbing into his back.

He climbed into his carriage moments later, his heart thumping with rage and horror. While he had understood there would be retaliation against his union with Lottie, he had not been prepared for it to be so swift or so harsh.

Not that it mattered—truly. Evander had funds enough. He would ensure he received what was owed from the hefty sum he had invested in the silver mine venture. And there would be other ways to gain profit, with partners who didn't care what Lottie's past was.

Shipping would be an ideal place to start...

Yes, shipping would be a lucrative alternative. After all, he'd had his own experience of sailing foreign seas, not to mention his own ships. And there would be more friends to be had. Ones who were true.

When he returned home, he found his mother sitting in the library by the fire, with her head bent over a book of poetry.

'Mother, I thought you had plans to call upon Lady Stetton. Is she ill?'

'She is a woman of poor judgement.' The Dowager turned the page and focused her attention on her book.

'I beg your pardon?' He approached her and took the seat opposite her.

The Dowager Countess sighed and lifted her head from the book, 'Lady Stetton is an ignorant woman whose judgments are loftier than I realised.'

Evander's heart squeezed into his stomach. 'What do you mean?'

His mother cocked her head at an arrogant angle, appearing every bit the austere Dowager Countess she was. 'Lady Stetton has refused to see me and has cast aside years of friendship on the basis of prejudice.'

Evander exhaled a pained breath. 'Because of Lottie.'

His mother narrowed her green eyes. 'Had I known Lady Stetton to be such a viper, I would have broken our association years ago.'

'Mother—'

She shook her head. 'Seeing you happy after all these years matters more to me than a false friend.' She reached for him and squeezed his hand.

It was a curious thing, how his mother could often appear so frail, with her slender frame and delicate, papery thin skin. Yet at other times, such as now, she could possess such a fire within her.

'And besides,' she said. 'I've found other friends—such as the Dowager Countess of Dalton—who are far more entertaining and enjoy my company.'

He got to his feet and kissed the top of his mother's head.

She looked up at him. 'What was that for?'

'For being the best mother any earl could ever ask for.'

'Well, then, it's a good thing you're not a duke, or I might have fallen short.' Her eyes twinkled.

He chuckled and gently touched her hand before leaving her to her book.

Though his mother had played down her broken friendship, he was certain it had indeed hurt her. She and Lady Stetton had been friends for as far back as Evander could remember.

They had both known there would be trials to be faced after his marriage to Lottie, and they were seeing them realised now. While they had braced themselves for exactly this kind of retaliation, he knew well how Lottie would take news of their difficulties.

And so, above all else, he resolved to make certain Lottie did not, under any circumstances, find out.

Chapter Twenty-Five

As the days pressed onward, Evander was grateful to see Lottie remained blissfully unaware of what had transpired with the friends and associates of himself and his mother. And at night he held Lottie in his arms as they continued to make up for the six years that had kept their love at bay.

In the meantime, Huntly Manor was being prepared for their upcoming stay of a fortnight. Lottie's staff from her townhouse had been sent there, to organise its cleaning and supervise some much-needed renovations. The process was taking longer than anticipated, but the house would be ready in a week's time.

In the meantime, Eleanor was to host a ball at Somersville Place—one of the few she and Charles bothered with, given their frequent trips abroad. And although the invitations did not state its purpose, Eleanor told Evander it was to be a celebration of his union to Lottie.

Which meant there was no choice but to accept happily.

It would be their first official social event as man and wife. Fortunately, the attendees would be made up of friends, ensuring prejudice would not be able to infringe upon their enjoyment.

While Evander knew it was only a matter of time before they encountered people who would not welcome Lottie, he would have her rest easy in ignorance for as long as possible.

Time flew by when one was in love, and the night of the ball arrived swiftly. Lottie was a sight to behold in the new sapphire necklace and earbobs he'd given her, with a Spitalfields silk gown in patterns of the same vivid, deep blue, trimmed with slashes of white satin at her sleeves. Her most lovely adornment, however, was her smile—the one that had not left her lips since they'd exchanged vows.

Upon their arrival at Somersville Place, Evander's mother was introduced by the caller first, as the Dowager Countess of Westix, which meant he and Lottie were next. She stiffened at his side.

'No need be nervous,' he said softly. 'You're a countess.'

She glanced anxiously towards him, her smile faltering, and he could read the concern in her eyes. He covered her hand where it rested at the crook of his elbow.

'You are surrounded by friends here, my love,' he reminded her.

The caller announced them as the Earl and Countess of Westix and they strode into the room. Everyone turned their attention towards them and applause broke out, echoing over the polished hardwood floors and high ceilings.

To his delight, Lottie broke into a wide smile as she recognised so many of the faces around them.

'They're here to celebrate us,' he said in her ear.

Those standing on the dance floor moved aside as the first notes of a waltz began.

Evander extended a hand to his wife, 'May I have this dance, my love?'

She put her gloved hand into his and he led her out to the dance floor. He slid his hand around her slender waist, holding her as closely as one could hold one's wife during the waltz.

'Have I told you how beautiful you look?' he asked as they began to twirl across the floor together.

'Only a dozen times.'

She gave a lovely laugh that made his heart soar.

'Perhaps I shall tell you three dozen more times before we return home, then.'

'And will you not find me beautiful when we return home?' she teased, with that playful banter he'd always found so enticing.

'Quite the contrary,' he replied. 'But then, instead of telling you, I can show you.'

Her cheeks flushed as they twirled by one of the other couples who had joined them on the dance floor.

After a magical time, the music wound down to a close.

'Thank you for a wonderful waltz, husband,' Lottie said with a curtsey as he bowed.

'I assure you, my love, the pleasure was all mine.'

He saw her from the dance floor, and Eleanor greeted her with eagerness.

'It warms my heart see you both looking so happy,' Eleanor effused.

'Thank you for hosting this ball—even though it isn't supposed to be for us,' Evander said with a wink.

Eleanor laughed. 'Saying it was for you would have been far too much pressure.'

Lottie offered her a grateful smile. 'It's truly lovely, Eleanor. Thank you.'

But Eleanor waved her off. 'Come, you must try this cake. Violet says she's never had anything more decadent in her life.'

Lottie flashed a grin at Evander before she was whisked away.

Lord Kentworth approached him half a second later, a nearly finished drink in his hand. Evander was certain the glass did not contain lemonade, despite its innocent appearance.

'I daresay I've never seen you smile quite this much before,' Kentworth said.

Evander looked after his stunning wife with a pride that made his chest swell. 'I've waited a long time for her.'

'Was she worth it?' Kentworth studied him for a moment, then straightened. 'Judging by your face, I would say she was.'

'When can we expect you to wed, Kentworth?' Evander turned back to his friend.

The other man scoffed. 'No one wants this drunken lout for a husband, any more than I want a nagging wife. I'll be fine as I am, with my late-night jaunts and the like.' He lifted his brows in a suggestive manner. 'Though I did want to ask you about your mining investment. I hear it's becoming quite lucrative...'

Evander tried to hide his surprise. 'I didn't realise you were interested in investments.'

'I dally from time to time.' Kentworth lifted a shoulder. 'We've spoken on it before, I believe. After you returned from your travels.'

Had they? Evander prodded his memory. Ah, yes, there it was.

How shameful that he had forgotten and Kentworth had remembered. But now that he considered the chum he'd gone to university with so many years ago, he noticed how the other man's eyes were clear, his cheeks not yet flushed.

Clearly he was on his first drink of the night, and Kentworth always was a different man without liquor.

'I'm afraid,' Evander replied, 'it would appear my fellow investors found my current lifestyle rather disagreeable and we have parted ways.'

Kentworth's eyes narrowed shrewdly and Evander knew he understood to what he referred.

'That's rather unfortunate,' he replied.

'Indeed.' Evander kept his face blank in the hopes Kentworth wouldn't see how even the recollection tugged at his ire. 'However, prior to our parting of ways it was a profitable investment. One I'd recommend for certain.'

'I do hope that one disagreeable reaction is all you'll encounter.' Kentworth took a sip of his drink. 'The ton can be rather judgmental.'

'Rather, indeed.' Evander sighed. 'Unfortunately, my mother has lost a long-time acquaintance. Someone she once considered a friend.'

Kentworth nodded, his brow wrinkled. 'You truly do care for your wife. I hope she appreciates how far your love extends.'

Evander's eyes found Lottie in the crowd, where she stood with Violet and Eleanor, the three of them laughing and smiling.

'I'm certain she does.'

'What the deuce?' Kentworth stiffened, his focus pinpointing a tall, older gentleman who wove through the crowd. 'Who would possibly have invited Lord Finsby?'

Evander lifted a brow as he searched his memory. 'Lord Finsby? Was he not an associate of my father and the late Duke of Somersville?'

Kentworth continued to study the curious man with an affronted frown. 'Yes—and one of your wife's former protectors.'

The words slammed hard into Evander's chest with an impact that nearly made him stagger back. 'I beg your pardon?'

He kept his gaze fixed on the man who continued to walk towards something with purpose. Or perhaps someone. He was older than him. Quite old, in fact. Although his snow-white hair was still thick and brushed regally to the side, and his attire as stately as any other gentleman in the room. He strode without a limp nor the aid of a cane, appearing as hearty and hale as a man half his age.

Kentworth uttered a low curse. 'Forgive me, Westix. Usually Rawley is here to keep me from saying everything that's in my head.' He gulped down the remainder of his drink in one great swallow. 'I didn't mean—' He grimaced. 'I'll make it up to you.'

But Evander was scarcely listening to Kentworth. His entire attention was fixed on Lord Finsby, who was now only a few feet away from Lottie, his gaze locked with purpose.

There was no mistaking whom he intended to see.

Lottie popped the last bit of cake into her mouth. It was moist, with a thin layer of sugar over the top that seemed to melt upon her tongue and leave the slightest hint of rose. Violet was correct. It was perhaps the best Lottie had ever tasted.

Violet and Eleanor left to go to the retiring room as Lottie finished her cake. She'd turned to glance about the room, in the hopes of finding Evander, when her gaze settled on an entirely different familiar face.

Lord Finsby.

A torrent of memories rushed at her in that instant. The times they'd stayed up far too late talking, the laughter they'd shared, the fears he'd assuaged. Of all her protectors, he was the only one she'd told about Lily. The only one she'd told about Evander.

Lord Finsby hadn't been in the market for a lover. Not like her other benefactors. He'd simply wanted a companion—someone who understood him and with whom he could speak without rebuke or judgment. It was his personal physician who had seen to Lily the night her breathing went so terribly wrong. And when Lord Finsby departed for a trip that would keep him in Italy for some time, he left her with ownership of the townhouse in Bloomsbury and a stipend to see her settled until she obtained a new protector.

'Lady Westix.' He inclined his head respectfully towards her.

'Lord Finsby,' she said, with genuine delight.

'You look well, my dear.' His kind brown eyes crinkled at the corners as he smiled. 'Better than well, in fact. You're glowing with joy. I see miracles do happen and the fates have returned your love to you.' He nodded, more to himself than to her. 'Marriage becomes you.'

'Thank you.' She couldn't help smiling at his praise.

'It appears your travels have done you some good. I trust you are well?'

'Quite myself. And it is so kind of you to ask.' He

'Oh... I have found love.'

Lottie clasped her hands to her chest. 'Oh, Lord Finsby, that's wonderful.'

'She is widowed, like myself, and has the *joie de vivre* of someone half our age.' He chuckled to himself. 'You would adore her.'

Lottie glanced about. 'Is she here? I'd love to meet her.'

'Alas, she's in Venice still. I'm only here briefly on business.' He nodded towards Charles, who was standing some distance away. 'I saw Charles yesterday and he mentioned the ball and asked if I'd like to come.'

'I'm so glad you did,' Lottie said. 'It is good to see you.'

He bowed to her, maintaining the proper amount of distance between them, no doubt out of consideration and to ensure no one misconstrued their meeting. 'Likewise. It is truly wonderful to see you so happy.'

'Safe travels back to Italy.'

With a final nod of his head, he departed.

Only then did it cross Lottie's mind that perhaps they

ought not to have spoken so openly. Perhaps those with long memories might question her loyalty to Evander. Even those who were friends.

She glanced around, seeking out her husband, and her gaze settled on Lady Caroline and Lord Rawley, dancing. Both appeared lost in one another, their gazes locked even as the dance pulled them away.

Violet appeared at Lottie's side, her eyes sparkling with excitement. 'Oh, I've just heard the most wonderful news from Seth,' she said.

Lottie turned to Violet and Eleanor, who looked at one another and grinned.

'Lord Rawley has asked to speak with Seth.'

Surely that didn't mean…?

Lottie sucked in a gasp.

'Yes.' Violet bounced on her Caroline's have suspect Lord Rawley will finally ask for Caroline's hand. suspect Lord

'Oh, I truly hope that is the case,' Lottie said wistfully.

'As do I.' Violet shook her head with a little laugh. 'I remember last autumn we thought he'd finally ask to court her, but he'd simply come to ensure there wouldn't be any shrimp at a ball we were hosting. So when he finally asked to court our dear Caroline, we were beside ourselves with joy.'

Lottie remembered exactly how elated they had all been.

She didn't see Caroline or Lord Rawley for lessons any more. In fact, she didn't see any of her students. Well, none except for Alice, whom she could not bring herself to let go when the woman was still in such need of her own blissful future. And Alice wasn't even considered a student any longer. Now she was a friend and payment was no longer accepted.

It had been difficult to inform some students of the

termination of their lessons upon Lottie's marriage to Evander. However, parting with others—like the daughters of Lady Norrick and Lady Cotsworth—had admittedly given her a little thrill of pleasure. Indeed, it was delightful not to have to see some of the more entitled whelps of the ton any longer.

Lottie had the sudden nagging sensation of being watched from across the room. She looked about and found Evander on the other side of the dance floor, regarding her.

'Forgive me, ladies,' Lottie said. 'I see my husband.'

Eleanor flicked a glance to the right. 'I was just planning to lure Charles out for a dance.'

Violet waved at both of them. 'Do go on. I'll find Seth. I fancy a dance myself. I love my darling Juliette, but these nights of being with my husband are the ones I do cherish.'

Lottie squeezed her hand affectionately. It was still difficult for Lottie to hear of Violet's new daughter. Guilt niggled deep in her heart every time there was a mention of the babe. She couldn't hear about the little girl and not think of her own Lily.

Quickly, Lottie strode away. She was navigating around the dance floor when someone caught her by the elbow. She spun to see Lord Kentworth.

He bowed. 'Forgive me, Lady Westix.'

'Of course.' She turned to go, but he pulled gently at her arm once more.

'I require an audience with you.' The lemonade in h' hand was nearly empty, and smelled very strongly of s' its. 'Now, if possible.'

'By all means.' She tilted her head patiently and for him to say what he wished.

No doubt it was something about Rawley ar tionship with Lady Caroline. She knew poor was feeling rather out in the cold without h panion at his side. Rawley had made mention of it on several occasions—the fear that he was abandoning his closest friend. What was more, Rawley had confessed that he'd told Kentworth about his lessons with her. She wouldn't put it past the Marquess to mention it—especially when he was clearly in his cups.

'Is this about Lord Rawley?' Lottie asked.

Kentworth furrowed his brow. 'Lord Rawley?' He shook his head determinedly. 'No, no—of course not.' He leaned closer and said, 'Though what you've managed to do with the stodgy sod has been a bloody miracle.'

'I'm glad you think so,' Lottie replied warily, uncertain where this conversation might go. 'It's good to see him happy.'

Kentworth grunted and drained his glass.

'Perhaps you've had a bit too much lemonade?' she suggested.

'I assure you I haven't had nearly enough.' Kentworth curled his fingers more tightly around the glass, as though he was worried she might try to prise it from his grasp. 'I came to see you about Westix.'

'My husband?'

Kentworth gave a hard nod. 'Yes. I want you to know that the man has spoken of no one but you for years.'

He exaggerated the last word. So much so that the li-
~~or~~ he'd added to his lemonade now emanated from his
~~t~~h in a hot wash of alcohol.

~~tie~~ offered him a patient smile. 'I'm pleased to hear

~~orth~~ lifted a shoulder in a casual shrug. 'Truly,
~~sure~~ you understand how much he loves you.'
~~e~~ a little laugh. 'That is kind of you.'
~~een~~ a man so willing to put aside so much

scorn.' Kentworth chortled, and tried to drink once more, frowning when he found his glass empty.

Lottie's stomach rolled over on itself. 'I beg your pardon?'

Kentworth scoffed. 'Closed-minded snobs of the ton. You know how they can be.'

'I'm afraid I'm not certain what you're talking about,' Lottie said slowly.

'Westix was in a lucrative mining investment,' Kentworth pulled a flask from his pocket and put a finger to his lips as he poured something clear into his glass beneath the cover of his jacket. 'As soon as they found out he'd married you, they refused to do business with him.'

Lottie stiffened. Evander hadn't mentioned anything of the matter.

Kentworth screwed the top back onto his flask and deposited it into his jacket pocket once more. 'Apparently even his mother is learning not all of her friends are loyal.' He took a large sip from the glass without so much as a wince. 'They've begun to leave her side as well.'

Lottie's heart crumpled in her chest. 'I see,' she said breathlessly, suddenly finding it hard to draw in air.

'Do you, now?' Kentworth nodded, as though he'd proven a point 'The man loves you more than any man has ever loved a woman. I thought you ought to know the extent of it.'

Lottie blinked at him, uncertain what to say. 'Thank you,' she said at last.

He beamed a smile at her. 'Lady Westix, my dear, you are most welcome.'

With that, he staggered off, with the clear assumption he truly had done some good that night.

She remained where she was for a long moment, her mind spinning over what she had learned.

Evander and his mother had suffered because of their marriage.

They had accepted her, and loved her, and paid a hefty price.

Her throat felt too thick, the room too hot and suffocating.

How was it that even here, in a sea of friends, she still felt as though she was drowning?

Chapter Twenty-Six

Something was amiss. Evander had noted it in the way the light had dimmed in Lottie's eyes the second half of the ball. Yes, she still smiled and laughed when she was supposed to, but there was a flatness to her joy, implying that it was false.

He'd tried to bring it up while they were still at Somersville Place, but she'd brushed him off. Knowing it was pointless to ask in the carriage on the way home, he'd held his tongue until now, when they were finally alone in the bedchamber they shared.

Once the door was closed, the smile fell from her lips, replaced with a wounded expression.

'Was it Lord Finsby?' Evander demanded.

After all, she had been perfectly fine while dancing with Evander. It wasn't until they came together to dance a second time that he'd realised she was upset. During the space that had elapsed between the sets he had seen her speaking to the older Earl.

Though the man had kept his distance, Evander had noticed Finsby and Lottie had spoken at length. And, while Evander had tried not to feel anything, he hadn't been able to help the stab of hurt at their apparent joy at seeing one another.

'Lord Finsby?' She tilted her head with a frown.

That terrible ache throbbed in his chest once more. 'I know he was your lover.'

'He was my protector. Not my lover.' Now it was she who appeared wounded. 'You knew this was a possibility when we wed. I told you—'

'Forgive me.' Evander ran a hand through his hair. 'I... I didn't expect to feel so...' He sighed. 'Jealous.'

She came to him, her feet silent on the thick carpet of his bedroom. 'Jealous?' She shook her head. 'No protector I've ever had possessed even a modicum of what you have.' She pulled off her long, white satin gloves, gracefully plucking one finger at a time. 'Lord Finsby was a lonely widower who wanted companionship—'

Evander put his hands up and backed away, not wanting to hear any details, uncertain if he could bear it. 'You needn't say more.'

'I won't give you all the details of all my protectors, Evander, but I'd like you to listen to this one.' She took his hands in hers and lowered them. 'Lord Finsby wanted someone he didn't have to explain the background of his story to—someone he spoke to often enough that they would already know. He was not my lover, but over time he did become my friend. That was all that ever existed between us.'

'You spoke with him for a while.' Evander said the words before he could stop himself and wished he could snatch them back, hating how jealous he sounded.

Lottie did not appear upset. Instead, she smiled. 'He was telling me of his recent marriage to a woman he has lost his heart to and congratulating me on ours.'

'Then what is it that's upset you so?'

Her smile wilted. 'Lord Kentworth approached me tonight.' Suddenly she seemed to deflate, the energy going out of her. She sagged down onto a chair before the hearth. 'He meant well…in the way that Kentworth does.'

Evander took the chair opposite her, his body tense. 'What did he say?'

The fire popped and snapped. Lottie sighed, reaching for her hair and slowly beginning to slide free the pins. A tendril of black hair uncoiled from where it had been secured in an artful curl over her brow.

'The truth.'

'What truth?'

Lottie lowered her hands, with her hair still mostly locked in the intricate arrangement, and stared down at the pins gathered in her palms. 'About your mining investment. And about how your mother's friends have treated her.'

Anger coursed through Evander like molten lava. Damn Kentworth. Evander had confessed that information in confidentiality, not for it to be immediately regurgitated to the very woman he was trying to keep it from.

'That drunken dolt,' Evander growled.

'I think he thought…' A tear fell from Lottie's eye. 'I think he thought he was doing me a favour, by offering me proof of how very much you love me. So much that you would suffer such treatment.' She choked in a sob and her hands came up to her face, the pins scattering over the floor.

Evander put a hand on her shoulder and offered her his handkerchief. She looked up at him, her eyes wet with tears, and accepted it.

'Why didn't you tell me?' he asked.

'I knew it would upset you.'

His chest tightened—with rage for how others made her feel, with hurt that he had caused her such anguish, with the realisation of the predicament they were in.

Damn Kentworth.

'I hate that you are treated so because of me.' She dabbed her eyes. 'And I have no way to fix it.'

'Lottie, I have a confession to make.' He crouched down in front of her.

She watched him, her expression hesitant and filled with such hurt he felt it viscerally in his soul.

'I don't care what others think of me or who doesn't want to do business with me.' He smirked. 'That is not the only investment opportunity at my fingertips. There are plenty of people willing to do business with me and my money.'

'Your mother,' she said miserably.

'Did you see my mother tonight?' He lifted his brows.

Lottie shook her head and one of her partially pinned curls cascaded downward. Before she could reach for the pin, Evander got to his feet and slid it free. The lock of hair glided from its restraint and tumbled over her shoulder.

'The Dowager Countess of Dalton was at her side, along with her true friends.' He gently liberated one pin after another. 'I dare say with so many widows in one small cluster we've a good deal to worry after. One never knows what schemes may be afoot with those ladies.'

Lottie offered a weak smile as several more curls were released from her coiffure.

'Losing a false friend is no loss at all,' Evander said. 'My mother said that to my father when the adventure club fell apart. It stuck with me.'

'Perhaps she feels differently now that it's happened to her,' Lottie said softly.

Evander ran his fingers through Lottie's thick, dark hair, confirming that he had removed all the pins. 'Perhaps you ought to speak with her about it, as you have me.'

Lottie looked up at him, her lovely glossy hair falling around her shoulders like black silk. God, she was so beautiful it almost hurt him to gaze upon her.

'I don't want you to regret…' She twisted her fingers together.

He put his hands over hers to stop the nervous action. 'You never need worry after that. The King himself could give me the cut direct and I would still not regret having married you.'

'The King?' Lottie gave a little laugh at that. 'Truly?'

He drew her hands higher, encouraging her to her feet. 'Truly.' His arms came around her in an embrace. 'I swear on my life, Lottie, I will never regret loving you.'

He lifted her chin with his fingertips and gently kissed her.

Later that night, however, as he lay in bed with her sleeping on his chest, their predicament rolled about in his head with more insistence than he liked.

Whether Huntly Manor was ready or not, he would have their trunks packed for departure on the morrow. While a few days in the country wouldn't fix their situation, a much-needed break would do Lottie a world of good.

Lottie found Evander at breakfast already the following morning, with a broadsheet stretched out in his hands. Upon her entrance he lowered it, and smiled at her in the familiar way that set her heart fluttering.

'What would you say if we left for Huntly Manor today?' He set the newspaper on the table in a crinkle of thin paper.

A footman approached and held out a seat for her. Lottie sank into the chair and nodded her thanks at the young man. 'Have you received word that it's ready?'

'How can it not be ready?' he asked. 'They've had nearly a fortnight, which is plenty of time.' His hand reached across the table and took hers. 'Being at the ball last night made me realise how much I long for some time alone with my wife. In the place where we fell in love.'

Heat blossomed over her cheeks. 'I confess, it would be nice.' And indeed it would—to be away from the ton, from judgement and rumour and gossip. At least for a little while.

'We don't need the entire house,' Evander continued. 'Just a warm fire for chilly evenings. Coverlets and sheets on a bed that's had the mattress turned. How does that take a fortnight?'

She hesitated, knowing how displeased Sarah would be if everything wasn't in proper order. Let alone how Andrews might take their precipitous arrival.

'Imagine it, Lottie,' Evander said wistfully. 'Oxfordshire. Binsey. To be back in the village, to see the old vicarage. To walk our path.'

She couldn't stop her mind from wandering back, and her heart ached for its familiarity with a sudden pang.

'Very well,' she conceded. 'When shall we leave?'

'In the time it takes for our trunks to be packed for us.' Evander sat forward in his chair and kissed her cheek. Before all the servants.

Lottie flushed with pleasure and noticed one of the maids hid a smile.

'Good morning.' The Dowager Countess entered the room as Evander pulled away.

He regarded his mother. 'Did you rest well, Mother?'

'Heavens, too well.' She made her way to a chair as the footman quickly pulled it out for her. 'I slept later than usual. I fear the ball drained me of all my energy.' She smiled fondly at Evander and Lottie. 'Such revelries are better left for youth, I think.'

She poured a cup of tea and added two lumps of sugar, selecting the largest from the bowl with a pair of silver sugar tongs.

'It would appear,' Evander said gently, 'that Lottie has heard of your parting with Lady Stetton.'

Evander's mother rolled her eyes in a most un-countess-like manner. 'That wretched woman.'

Lottie watched her mother-in-law to ensure she wasn't simply posturing for her sake. 'I thought you were friends.'

'We were well-acquainted,' the Dowager Countess conceded. 'Truth be told, I never did enjoy her company overmuch. She always was a waspish woman—very critical of others and with a ready opinion for every matter.'

Evander raised his brows at Lottie, as though to say, *See there? It's as I told you.* He lifted his paper. 'I'll see to the arrangements for our departure to Huntly Manor.'

He bent to Lottie and gave her a kiss on the cheek before departing, leaving her alone with his mother.

Lottie fiddled with her toast, her appetite gone. 'I don't want you losing friends on my account.'

'Losing a false friend is no loss at all.' The Dowager Countess set her gaze on Lottie, her eyes sharp despite her otherwise frail appearance. 'I have many friends. I needn't worry about those who aren't worth my time. Anyone who finds fault with you has no room in my life.' She lifted her teacup. 'Frankly, I am too old to care.'

She took a prim sip of tea as Lottie gave her a grateful smile.

Her mother-in-law waved off her thanks. 'So, what is this I hear that you are leaving for Huntly Manor today?'

'I believe they are nearly done with the preparations for our arrival.' Lottie pursed her lips. 'Or at least Evander is confident they are.'

'They'll make do.' The Dowager Countess smiled. 'You'll have a grand time.'

Lottie reached for her toast, her appetite restored. 'I'm certain we will.'

Packing for the fortnight-long trip was done quickly, and by ten that morning Lottie and Evander were ready to depart. They sat on the same side of the bench in the carriage on the way to Oxfordshire, and chatted about Lottie's memories from Binsey and all the things she wanted to explore while they were there.

The journey took five hours before the carriage turned down the long road leading to the massive manor. Trees lined either side of the drive, framing the large white front of Huntly Manor, which featured a fountain and a cascade of steps leading up to the large wooden doors.

Lottie recalled seeing the exquisite home as a girl and imagining that a princess lived inside. Never had she considered that one day she might actually be the princess.

Together, they made their way up the steps, expecting the door to open quickly as Andrews had been notified of their arrival by the groom who had ridden ahead.

It remained closed.

How curious.

'It is a large house,' Lottie said, by way of plausible explanation.

'It is.' Evander put his arm around her as they waited.

Still the door remained closed.

After a long moment, Evander rapped on the brass knocker. No one answered. He lifted his brow, put his hand on the knob and opened the door.

What greeted them was pure chaos.

Servants ran about this way and that, the trunks that had been sent ahead lay in a heap, and orders were being shouted from the stairs.

Evander looked at Lottie, incredulous, and she began to laugh.

'Don't you be laughing now, lovey, when you've surprised us like this.' Sarah raced down the stairs, her silver-streaked hair coming out of its normally neat chignon. She paused at the bottom, her hand resting on the banister as she huffed for breath. 'We told you we needed only two more days. We've been taking the place apart in order to put it back together. I had suggested we do that after your visit, but *someone* insisted it be done straight away.'

'If it's worth doing, it's worth doing correctly.' Andrews appeared, casting Sarah a sideways glance. 'Do forgive me, my lady, as you can see, we were a bit surprised.'

Lottie shook her head. 'You needn't worry at all. We were simply so eager to come we were not overly concerned about the reception we might receive. Though admittedly we had not imagined this.' She laughed again.

Poor Andrews flushed red under his collar.

'I'm sure it will look perfect when it's complete.' Evander patted Andrews on the shoulder.

The old butler straightened stiffly. 'Indeed, my lord.'

'We could go to the village for a spell,' Lottie suggested.

Evander nodded and put his arm around her. 'It's been ages since we've visited.'

'Wonderful,' Sarah said, in an exaggeratedly bright voice.

A maid ran down the stairs and stopped short when she saw Sarah, then looked to Evander and Lottie. She gave a little squeak of surprise and darted in the opposite direction.

Andrews tugged at his collar and indicated the door. 'It is a lovely day for a jaunt to the village.'

Lottie and Evander allowed themselves to be ushered out of their own home.

'Well,' Lottie said on an exhale. 'It appears we will have an excursion to Binsey.'

'There is no one I'd rather while away the day with than you, my love.' Evander put his arm around her. 'This is why we're here. To simply enjoy our time together without obligation. This is the first day of our wedding trip and I mean for us to enjoy it.'

He led her to the carriage and together they climbed in. Lottie's heart racing in anticipation of seeing the place that had been her home for so many years.

Chapter Twenty-Seven

It had been six years since Evander had last been in Binsey. The village was larger than he recalled, no doubt having grown over the years. Despite the addition of shops along its main streets and alleys, it still appeared charmingly quaint.

Although it was not as familiar to him as it was to Lottie, it became so with each of her exclamations on what had changed or what new building had been erected. The eagerness with which she explored the village while on his arm made their early arrival entirely worthwhile. Especially when compared to how she had appeared the prior evening, after Kentworth's damn prattling.

The image of the servants running about like mad, however, was another boon. A chuckle tickled up his throat at the memory.

'What is it?' Lottie asked.

'I'm thinking of the servants at Huntly Manor.'

He laughed again, and this time Lottie joined him.

'Oh, we did give them a surprise, did we not? Sarah, I know, didn't mind, but I confess I did feel rather horrid for poor Andrews. Perhaps…'

Evander lifted a brow at his wife as she considered something. 'What is it?'

'Perhaps we should purchase them some cakes. In appreciation for their hard work.' She gave a playful grimace. 'And for descending upon them with such little notice.'

'A bribe?'

'Not a bribe. A thank-you.' Lottie tilted her head with a grudging look. 'Well, perhaps a bit of a bribe for their forgiveness.'

'Of course we can bring them some cakes.' He rubbed the back of her hand where it rested in the crook of his elbow. 'Your consideration is most admirable.'

She flushed in that way he loved, showing that genuinely humble nature of hers.

It was perhaps that humility that kept Lottie from noticing how people stared at her as they walked to the confectioner's shop on the main street.

All at once, she drew up short with a soft gasp. 'Mrs Williams?'

A woman with her grey hair in a simple chignon turned around. 'Lottie? Is that you, child?' Her gaze went down Lottie's gown and back up before settling on Evander. 'Goodness, but you've grown into such a fine lady. Your father would be enormously proud of you, God rest his soul.'

Lottie slipped from Evander's hold and embraced the other woman. 'Thank you, Mrs Williams. Allow me to introduce my husband Evander Murray, the Earl of Westix.'

'Lord Westix?' Mrs Williams brows shot up. 'The Earl who bought Huntly Manor some time back for…?' She covered her mouth with her hands. 'For the woman he loved. That was you, my girl?'

There was that lovely flush on Lottie's cheeks again.

'Indeed, it was,' Evander said, stepping forward.

'Evander,' Lottie said, 'this is Mrs Williams—the owner of Notions, the haberdashery.'

Mrs Williams curtseyed, and Evander inclined his head respectfully to her. 'It's a pleasure to meet you,' he said.

'The pleasure is mine, my lord.' Mrs Williams's chest swelled with pride. 'Our Lottie—a countess!'

Lottie beamed at the older woman. And it was that look on his wife's face that made Evander so glad he'd convinced her to come to Huntly Manor with such haste. In London, there were too many members of the ton eager to throw their scorn at her feet. Here, she had only ever been loved.

Mrs Williams waved over several friends, of all whom greeted Lottie with the same enthusiasm. These people were the ones with whom Lottie had been acquainted before being faced with the choices she'd been forced to make. These people knew her in her truest form—for her kind nature and for how she always thought of others before herself.

It was his hope that the affection she felt here would bolster her courage for when they returned to London, as they would eventually have to do. He wanted her to keep it in her heart that she was loved, that she was as pure and wonderful a person as there could be.

Once they had met nearly all of Mrs Williams friends— at least the ones she could pull aside with a wave of her hand, which proved to be a good number—Lottie and Evander continued on their way and placed an extravagant order at the confectioner's.

They returned to Huntly Manor. Upon their return to their new home they found the staff settled, albeit flush-faced and breathless, and the entire manor available to explore.

'Would you like to see your new home?' Evander asked.

'Oh, yes, please.' She gave a bashful smile. 'I loved to come here and look at this manor when I was a girl, imagining what a grand place it would be to live.'

'Now it's yours to make entirely your own.' Evander offered his arm to Lottie.

'Our own.'

She slid her hand into the crook of his elbow, but it did not remain there long. As they went room by room she ran about with unfettered delight, exclaiming at the painted ceilings, the plaster ornamentation surrounding the chandeliers, at each carved mantle and gilded sconce.

Evander had stayed at the country estate when he'd first met Lottie, borrowed from his university chum. At the time he had not appreciated its finery, seeing it as simply another aristocratic residence—a place to lay his head at night.

He experienced it now through Lottie's eyes, and respected the grandness of the home. It made him all the more grateful for these weeks they had set aside to enjoy a quiet life in the country, without the meanness of the ton and the cruelty that Lottie would face when they eventually made their return.

All the money in London wouldn't protect Lottie from that harshness, but in this lovely place she would at least be shielded from the vitriol.

If only for a while.

Two weeks passed swiftly. In that time Lottie had the opportunity to see nearly everyone she remembered and visit all her favourite spots—with the exception of her former house, as the vicar who lived there now was in Yorkshire, seeing to his ill father.

Even with him out of residence, Lottie could not bring herself to go to the vicarage that had been her home for so many years.

Every day she walked with Evander on that small path between Huntly Manor and the old cottage, and every day they stopped at the corner where he'd met her so many years ago. And every day, he asked if she wished to go further, towards the vicarage.

She never once hesitated as she shook her head.

Their time in the country was precious. There were no fears of running into women like Lady Cotsworth or Lady Norrick, who would greet her with kind smiles and then hurl insults at her back.

Going to the cottage where she had lived with Lily had been difficult. There was a place inside her that was still raw with the effects of that emotional day. As such, that same place inside her harboured a fear that seeing the vicarage might hurt just as badly.

On the last day of their stay at Huntly Manor, however, Lottie hesitated before declining to go further than the corner.

'I'll be with you,' Evander said encouragingly.

Lottie looked at him as she vacillated over her decision. Being in the country had been as good for Evander as it had been for her. The lines on his brow had been smoothed away and there was a lightness in him that made his smiles ready and left his eyes sparkling. He looked as happy as she felt.

Did she truly want to put an end to their happy time together by seeing the old vicarage again?

And yet once they were in London they might not be able to return to Binsey for a while. What if something happened in the meantime? Buildings burned down all the time. Or they were damaged by something falling on them in a storm. Or…

She was being ridiculous.

She nodded and clasped his hand more tightly in hers. 'Let us go. Together.'

He smiled and allowed her to lead him around the corner and down the path that ended at the vicarage.

The whitewashed walls soon became visible through the slender tree trunks and Lottie's pulse quickened.

Evander followed her down the path, stopping short

alongside her as the house came into view. It looked exactly the same, with a small white fence framing the garden, the whitewashed walls clean and stark against the sun. The sweet scent of the thatched roof was carried towards them on a light breeze that caused the flowers under the windowsill to rustle against one another.

It was so familiar that she half expected her father to walk out at any moment.

No sooner had the thought entered her mind than the front door swung open and a man strode out into the sunshine. The breath she'd locked in her chest whooshed out as she realised it was not her father.

This man was around the same age her father had been when he died, but was much shorter, with fair hair. Clearly he was the new vicar having returned from Yorkshire. He gave them a broad smile.

'Good morning,' he called in a jovial voice. 'I trust the day finds you both well.'

'It does, thank you,' Lottie replied, slightly breathless.

Evander glanced down at her, his worry evident, but she gave him a reassuring smile. There was comfort in knowing that the old vicarage was still standing and in good condition, its garden tended and the home well-loved. The way it was meant to be. The way her father would have wanted it to remain.

The vicar who had replaced her father, Reverend Richards, approached them, his expression open and friendly. 'Is there something I might help you with?'

'I...' Lottie flushed.

'My wife used to live here,' Evander said. 'Formerly Miss Charlotte Rossington. Now Lady Westix.'

The vicar's smile widened, if such a thing were possible. 'I thought you seemed familiar. I hope you weren't in need of anything in my absence.'

'Not at all.' Lottie shook her head. 'I hope your father is much improved.'

Reverend Richards nodded and his thick hair fell into his eyes. He absently brushed it away. 'He is, thanks be to God. I appreciate your concern.'

'I simply wanted to come and see the house.' Lottie's cheeks warmed. 'It's been six years since my father passed.'

'God rest his soul.' The vicar's expression eased into one of sincere sympathy. 'I've heard he was a good man.'

'Thank you.' Lottie smiled softly to herself as she recalled those sweet, wonderful memories of her father. 'He truly was.'

Suddenly Reverend Richards straightened. 'I found a box belonging to your father last year, when I was going through the attic. It was nestled so far at the back I'd missed it in the many times I'd been up there before.' He hesitated. 'Actually, would you like to come in for some tea?'

The idea of going inside, of seeing the same furnishings in her old home belonging to someone else, made her freeze. It was too much, too soon.

Lottie shook her head. 'Another time, perhaps. We are departing for London shortly, but thank you for the offer.'

'I'll retrieve it for you.'

Reverend Richards quickly turned and disappeared inside the house, emerging moments later with a medium-sized plain wooden box.

'It must have fallen for it to have been so out of sight. I tried to find you, but the forwarding address you'd left at Huntly Manor no longer seemed to have occupants. I was unsure where to find you after...'

'Thank you for having gone through the effort,' Lottie said, reaching for the box.

Before she could put her hands on it, Evander took it with a wink. 'I'll carry it.'

She nodded her appreciation to Evander and thanked the vicar once more. Her gaze remained fixed on the box as they departed.

'Is it heavy?' she asked, after a long moment of burning curiosity.

Evander shook his head. 'Not terribly.' They rounded that familiar corner. 'Do you want to stop and open it?'

She laughed. 'Am I so obvious?'

'I know that if I received a mysterious box, I would want to know its contents.' He raised his brows.

'Mysterious box, indeed.' She laughed again. 'It simply fell behind some others. As Reverend Richards said.'

Evander held the box out and Lottie lifted off the lid. 'Just a peek,' she conceded.

A quick poke about revealed an old christening gown that had gone yellow with age—most likely hers—a wooden rattle and lock of dark hair tied with pink ribbon. She did not recall them from her youth, but it was just the sort of thing her mother would have kept.

Evander peered into the depths. 'There's another box at the bottom.'

Lottie moved aside the full skirt of the christening gown and discovered there was indeed a smaller box. Something heavy and solid shifted about inside, and it was tied with a bit of twine and labelled with a familiar name.

The Duke of Somersville

Lottie frowned. 'This is odd. It's for the Duke of Somersville. Not Charles, obviously. His father must have been Duke when this box was placed with these other items. Though it must have been done so by mistake.'

'Why do you say that?' Evander asked.

'Father was meticulous.' Lottie smiled at the memory. 'All these items were placed together. He would never have combined them. Perhaps this was one that had belonged to my mother.' She put down the box, careful not to disturb whatever it contained, and replaced the lid. 'We'll give it to Charles when we return to London. It may hold something of value for him.'

'Aren't you the least bit curious?' Evander asked as they walked on.

'About the box for the Duke of Somersville?'

'Yes.'

Lottie slid him a glance. 'From what I recall, the old Duke's adventure club had enough backbiting between its members that I scarcely want to see what is involved with this.'

Evander gave a laugh, knowing of his own woes with his father and Charles's from the damn club. 'That is an excellent point, my love.'

She put the twine-bound parcel from her mind as they continued on the path. Her steps slowed as Huntly Manor came into view. Their time there had been like something out of a fantasy tale. There had been no gossips to disparage her, no associates to cast their disdain at Evander for having married her. For the first time since the cottage, she had truly been happy.

She didn't want it to end.

'We don't have to return,' Evander said.

Lottie hadn't realised she'd stopped walking until he spoke. 'I beg your pardon?' she said.

'We aren't so terribly far from London.' He looked at the estate with the same wistful joy that warmed her heart when she regarded their home. 'If I was needed for an important vote in Parliament I could be there within five hours. All other matters could be handled through the post.'

Lottie's heart raced at his words. 'What are you saying?'

He turned to her, the box still in his hands. 'I'm saying I should be amenable to remaining at Huntly if you are, my love.'

'Are you in earnest?' she asked, breathless with the excitement of what he said.

'I've never cared for London.' He smirked. 'Too many gossips, too many people who believe themselves better than others. I was only ever there for you.'

'Truly?' she asked, unable to believe her ears.

He laughed. 'Truly.' He bent to set the box down and pulled her into his arms. 'Let us retire from London and enjoy our life here.'

She nestled into his embrace, revelling in his strength and his familiar scent, beyond grateful for this husband who understood her so well.

'Yes.' She tilted her head back to gaze at her husband. 'Nothing would make me happier.'

A grin lifted the corners of his mouth. 'I know.' He indicated their carriage in the distance, which was being packed for their departure. 'You stay here. I'll return to London to secure arrangements to have the remainder of our effects brought to Huntly and inform my mother of our decision.'

'I do hope she'll join us,' Lottie said. 'Do you think she will be terribly distraught?'

'Most certainly not,' Evander replied, with enough confidence that it set Lottie's mind at ease. 'She always enjoyed our summer estate. Binsey will charm her.'

'I'd like to return with you,' Lottie said, realising she had business to tend to in London before their long departure to Huntly. There were good friends to bid farewell to, for a while, and of course the little box for Charles to be delivered.

Upon their return to London, she made her way to Somersville Place to meet Charles. Whatever curiosity Evander harboured about the box's contents would be soon satisfied, and soon she and Evander would be back at Huntly with his mother and a whole life ahead of them.

Lottie sat in the quiet drawing room of Somersville Place, the small box for the Duke set on the table before her. Whatever it was, the label must have been written some time ago, as the box's wood had darkened with age and the ink had faded to a pale brown resembling weak tea.

Eleanor and Charles entered, and Lottie got to her feet to embrace her dear friends.

'I didn't expect to hear from you so soon after your arrival back into London,' Eleanor said. 'But I'm glad for it. I imagine you had a lovely time   you are simply glowing with good health.'

'Did you enjoy Huntly Manor?' Charles asked. 'It's said to have some of the best hunting in the area.'

'You know I don't hunt,' Lottie chided him. 'But the pathways surrounding it are truly beautiful and it was wonderful to be back in Binsey once more. Indeed, we will be staying there indefinitely after this brief trip in London.'

'Oh, Lottie, that's wonderful news,' Eleanor said with a smile. 'I'm pleased to see my brother has not only won back your heart, but clearly knows how to keep it.'

'I only returned to bid farewell to my friends before our departure.' Lottie reached for the small box. 'And to give you something. The current vicar discovered something he said belonged to my father. There were some old items of mine, from when I was a baby. And this.' She handed it to Charles.

He quirked a brow as he accepted it. 'This was for my father?'

Lottie nodded. 'I presume so.'

'Perhaps it's another adventure,' Eleanor said, with more enthusiasm than Lottie had exhibited at the idea. But then, Eleanor now held an affinity for adventure—a newly discovered passion she and Charles enjoyed indulging together with their exotic travels.

Charles did not complain as his wife peered over his shoulder while he pulled the twine free, lifted the top and drew out several papers. 'It appears to be a letter, though not in my father's hand.'

His gaze skimmed over it, along with Eleanor's. Suddenly she sucked in a breath and looked at Lottie.

A knot tied itself in Lottie's stomach. 'What is it?' she asked warily, uncertain if she should want to know.

'Did you read this, Lottie?' Charles reached for something else in the box and withdrew what appeared to be a small *Book of Common Prayer*.

'No, of course not. Why ever would I do such a thing?'

'Because while this is written to my father,' he answered slowly as he opened the book and scanned the first several pages. 'It also concerns you.'

'Me?'

Charles lifted his head from the book and stared at her incredulously. 'Lottie, you're my sister.'

Chapter Twenty-Eight

While Lottie was visiting with Charles, Evander went through the stack of correspondence on his desk. Most were reports from his steward, as well as several accounts to be reconciled. At the bottom, however, was a missive from the Captain of a ship travelling to the Far East in three days' time, agreeing to Evander's offer to become an investor.

Captain Billington's ship was newly acquired, and he required a good amount of capital for his first few voyages. However, he promised a large return on any investment by way of silks, spices and other goods to be procured on his travels. It was for that reason Evander ended up at an old wooden building by the wharf to meet the Captain that afternoon.

He was not the only investor to do so.

Lord Kentworth entered through the door with a wide smile.

'Westix. I wondered if you might be the other investor. This seems to have your name all over it.' They clasped hands in greeting. 'Welcome back from the country. I trust it wasn't too dull?'

'We enjoyed it so much we have decided to relocate.'

Evander looked around the simple room, taking in the

stained walls and the upturned barrels being used as chairs. The Captain would need some capital indeed—but, based on his itinerary, his journeys were carefully planned, with consideration for weather and other disasters. In all, it had the designs of a solid investment.

'You can't be serious,' Kentworth said as he settled on one of the barrels.

'I most certainly am. I've merely returned to settle my accounts and ensure I'll have proper correspondence for important matters such as this.' Evander took a seat opposite the Marquess. 'I assumed you were going with the silver mine.'

'Not after the way they treated you. I do have scruples, you know.' He winked.

Evander had forgotten what a good man Kentworth could be when he wasn't drinking. Unfortunately, that wasn't often. 'Oh, I do know. Thank you for being a true friend.'

'Of course.' Kentworth chuckled. 'And a good thing I didn't too. They got what was coming to them after their treatment of you.'

Evander glanced out through the dirty windows for any sign of the Captain. 'How so?'

'Just yesterday the entire mine collapsed,' Kentworth said.

Evander's attention snapped back to the Marquess. 'Good God. I hope not too many men were injured.'

Kentworth ran a hand through his thick dark hair. 'Not a soul. It happened some time at night. By the time the men went to work in the morning the whole thing was sealed up tighter than a virgin's—'

The door opened and Captain Billington's broad shoulders filled the frame. 'Sorry to have kept you waiting.'

He approached the table—two barrels with a plank laid over them—and set down a pile of papers. 'These are the contracts to review with your solicitors. I can meet with you both separately on the morrow, to finalise whatever needs be done.'

Though he was young to be a captain, his weathered face told the tale of a man who'd spent a life on the sea.

'I'll review this today.' Evander stood up from his seat to shake hands with the other man. 'Future correspondence will go through my solicitor, who will forward it on to me in the country.'

'As you wish it, my lord.' Captain Billington's hazel eyes crinkled at the corners as he accepted Evander's hand in his warm, callused grasp.

Kentworth did likewise, and the two exited the old wooden building together.

'Do you fancy a fireball or a measure of whisky?' Kentworth asked.

Evander shook his head. 'Perhaps another time.'

'Ah, yes.' Kentworth nodded. 'Your wife is no doubt waiting for you at home.'

'You should get one at some point.'

'A wife, or a drink?' Kentworth chuckled.

Evander grinned at him and waved as he made his way towards his carriage.

Upon his arrival home, he discovered not only Lottie in the drawing room with his mother, but also Charles and Eleanor. Several old documents lay on the tea table, rather than a tray of refreshments, as well as an old book.

Ah, yes, the mysterious box…

'Oh, Evander,' Lottie gasped. 'You'll never believe it.'

He grimaced. 'Please tell me it isn't another gemstone our fathers fought over, that will require another lengthy search through those abysmal journals.'

'No,' they all said at once, in equal agreement, before laughing.

And they were truly laughing. The kind of bubbly, exaggerated sort that came from good news.

Evander narrowed his eyes at their curious behaviour. 'Dare I ask what it is?'

'I'm Charles's sister.' Lottie rushed to stand by Charles with a grin. 'Well, half-sister. Do you see it?' She pointed between them.

Evander looked between them—*really* looked between them. Of course, he had always known Lottie had stunning blue eyes, and that Charles's were a relatively similar colour, and that both had dark hair. But never had he truly studied them side by side, looking for familial traits.

Both had high cheekbones and full lips. Their jaws were sharp, though Lottie's was more pointed at the chin. But, yes, when comparing them side by side, and understanding that they were indeed related.

Evander blinked in surprise. 'Good God.'

'My father married her mother after mine passed,' Charles said.

'When I was born, our father thought she had not been faithful, and insisted I be removed from his sight,' Lottie continued. 'Without anywhere else to go, she went to stay with a sister in Wallingford whose husband had recently accepted an appointment as vicar in the village of Binsey.'

She lifted the papers, settling them one on top of the other, and carried them over to Evander.

'Mother—my aunt—wrote everything here, you see?' She handed them to him. 'My mother died soon after my birth and so my aunt, who had stayed behind to tend her, claimed me as hers. But she had my mother sign this note. And there is this.'

She reached for a *Book of Common Prayer* and opened the battered volume, revealing the details of not only a marriage but also a child being born.

'Then your father...?' Evander looked to Charles and then Lottie.

'Yes, my father was truly the Duke of Somersville and I was his legitimate daughter.' Lottie touched Evander's hand. 'And the man and woman who raised me were my aunt and uncle—yet they treated me as if I truly was their daughter. Their love...' She paused, taken for a moment with emotion. 'Their love for me was so pure that I never suspected.'

'Lottie.' Evander pulled his wife into his arms and held her, knowing the impact this would have on all her memories of her childhood.

'I must say this—because someone should.' The Dowager Countess held her cane out at an arrogant angle and a slow smile crept over her lips. 'The ton will be tripping over themselves when this news comes out.'

'Oh, and it shall,' Eleanor said. 'I feel quite certain that the *Lady Observer* will be making a special reappearance to publish a column quite soon, regarding this very juicy titbit. At least once Violet receives the missive I sent her prior to our departure from Somersville Place.'

Evander grinned in anticipation of all the tabbies, such as the likes of Lady Norrick, learning of Lottie's true lineage. It would indeed be a sight to behold.

Lottie held the latest copy of *Society Journal* in her hands two days later at breakfast, reading through the very special edition from the previously retired scandal sheet author the *Lady Observer*.

Violet's story in *Society Journal* was wonderfully detailed, sharing the information about the Duke of Somersville's marriage to Lottie's mother, which was recorded in the *Book of Common Prayer*, and how Lottie had been raised without an inkling of who she was. In the end, confirmed unequivocally by the parish register in Binsey, Lottie truly was the legitimate daughter of the late Duke of Somersville.

Lottie sighed and set the paper down beside her plate.

'What do you think?' Evander asked. 'You've been quite close-lipped about the lot of it.'

'It's bittersweet,' Lottie admitted. 'The people who I thought were my parents truly were not.'

'How do you mean?' Evander poured himself a bit more tea and took a careful sip.

Lottie shook her head. 'They weren't my parents, but all that time they never told me.' The thought of her father—or rather her uncle, whom she couldn't help but think of as her father—burned in her chest. 'Nothing could make me truly theirs. I was the daughter of a duke who didn't trust my true mother and left her to die without his support.'

'I disagree.' Evander set his teacup on the saucer and leaned back comfortably in his chair. 'The Duke of Somersville was never a father to you in any way. Not the way Reverend Rossington was. And your poor mother never had the chance.' He tilted his head sympathetically and reached across the linen tablecloth to take her hand. 'You have always considered them your parents. Why change that now?'

Lottie let his words sink in and nodded to herself. 'You bring up an excellent point. What does it matter?'

'The only difference is that now we'll enjoy watching the ton trip over their tongues as they try to retract their harsh words.' He chuckled. 'On that note, shall we attend the fashionable hour at Hyde Park?'

She laughed. 'Oh, you are wicked.'

'Me?' He put a hand to his chest in mock offence. 'Truly, it will be a lark. Say yes.'

He cocked his head at a rakish tilt and winked at her, setting her laughing once more.

'Very well,' she replied. 'But this changes nothing of our intention to remove to Huntly, does it?'

'Why ever would it?' he queried. 'I assure you, the pompous ton finally accepting you to their bosom does not endear me to people I never found agreeable. This changes nothing.'

'Forgive me, my lord.' Edmonds appeared between them with a missive on a salver. 'There is a message for you.'

Evander took it and thanked him. He scanned the missive and scoffed.

'What is it?' Lottie asked.

'It would appear Lord Huffsby would like to offer me a place in the mining investment once more, claiming it will be just as lucrative once it's been cleared out.' Evander refolded the note and tossed it carelessly onto the table. 'It appears my "considerable business acumen" would be of great value to their operation.'

It was not the last letter to come. On and on they arrived, from various lords and ladies who had slid snide glances in Lottie's direction or never bothered to speak with her, now offering invitations to soirees and balls. Lady Stetton even came by to see the Dowager Countess of Westix, who claimed she was otherwise engaged and would not be available for tea.

The fashionable hour came upon them quickly, and both Lottie and Evander dressed in their finest—Lottie in a stunning blue silk dress trimmed with delicate white lace and a bonnet with several ribbon forget-me-nots adorning the band of blue running along its sides. This time they did not take the carriage. Instead, Lottie took Evander's arm and they ambled along the slow path lining the Serpentine.

'Lady Westix,' called a cheerful, familiar voice from Lottie's side.

She turned to find Alice, with a tall, handsome blond-haired gentleman at her side. One sleeve of his fine jacket hung empty and pinned to his shoulder.

George.

'Forgive me for having not welcomed you back to London,' Alice said with a wide smile. 'George and I...' She looked at him and bit her lower lip excitedly. 'We've married.'

'That's such wonderful news,' Lottie exclaimed.

An ecstatic Alice made the proper introductions to George.

'I've heard very agreeable things about you,' Lottie said to Alice's new husband—a very handsome young man who couldn't keep his gaze from wandering towards his new wife.

He flushed. 'As I have about you, Lady Westix.'

'Felicitations on your union,' Evander said. 'I must say, love reclaimed is even more blissful the second time around.' His hand gently squeezed Lottie with affection.

'On that we can agree,' George replied. 'Especially when the one you love is so persistent in ensuring you know they care for you and how much they value you.'

'It takes a special person to be so determined,' Lottie said.

'And a considerable amount of love,' Alice finished.

'We truly are so happy for you,' Lottie said.

'As I am for you.' Alice edged slightly closer to Lottie. 'When I read the article this morning, I planned to come to Hyde Park with the hope of seeing you. I thought you might be persuaded to do it.' Her gaze slid to Evander.

He held up his hands in surrender. 'I couldn't help myself.'

After a fond farewell, Alice and her new, happy husband departed, still smiling at one another.

'Did I mention we received an invitation just before we left this afternoon?' Evander asked.

Lottie cast him a wary look. 'Which one?'

There had been, oh, so very many. Especially in comparison to the few they received upon their union.

'From the Dowager Countess of Dalton,' he replied nonchalantly. 'For Rawley and Caroline's wedding.'

Lottie gasped and looked up at him. 'You are cruel to have kept that from me.'

'I feared if I told you before we left you'd insist on going to Dalton Place at that very moment to speak with Lady Caroline.' He gave her a knowing look.

Lottie chortled at that. 'You know me far too well.'

'Which is why I love you so dearly.'

She looked up at him, letting herself become lost in his handsome green eyes.

'Lady Westix,' a shrill voice called. 'Oh, my dearest Lady Westix.'

Lottie and Evander both turned to find Lady Cotsworth hurrying towards them at a pace that set her ample bosom swaying. She huffed as she caught up and lightly fanned herself, smiling despite her ability to breathe properly in that moment.

'It has come to my attention that the invitation I sent you for our ball this Saturday was somehow lost in delivery.' Lady Cotsworth pouted. 'I wanted to smooth over the offence of our footman's carelessness by extending you a personal invitation to our ball.'

'I see,' Lottie replied slowly.

'Well?' Lady Cotsworth dabbed at her broad forehead. 'Do you think you'll be able to attend?'

'We have a prior engagement,' Evander said.

Disappointment was evident on Lady Cotsworth's face. 'Oh. I see. Well, you needn't worry. I have a soiree coming up as well. I'll ensure that you receive—'

'While it's kind of you to consider us, Lady Cotsworth,'

Lottie said, as gently as possible, 'we are removing to our country estate.'

'Why on earth would you do such a thing?' The older woman was flustered.

'Because we prefer to be where people are kind,' Lottie replied.

Lady Cotsworth's flushed cheeks went redder still.

'Good day, Lady Cotsworth.'

Evander steered Lottie away from the vile woman.

'You, my dear, were far kinder to her than she deserved,' he said to Lottie when they were out of earshot.

'I don't wish to be cruel,' Lottie replied. 'But nor will I lower myself to feign friendship.'

'Your strength is one of the many traits of yours I find so admirable.' Evander smiled down at her. 'You were worth waiting six years for, Charlotte Murray.'

'I'm only sorry I put you off for so long.' She moved her fingers over his forearm and held on to him, caressing him tenderly. 'To think we could have been so happy for all that time when we were otherwise so miserable.'

'But it wouldn't be as sweet as it is now.' He stopped and gazed down at her. 'Because now I know what I lost before and I will never, ever let you go.'

'Don't you dare even try,' she teased. 'Or you will find I can be just as persistent as you when it comes to something that I want.'

A wicked gleam shone in his eye. 'And you want me?'

Desire pulsed through her at the suggestion in his tone. 'Oh, I do.'

'Do you feel we've accomplished our goal in this promenade?' Evander began to steer her in the opposite direction.

'Quite,' she replied. 'I believe I should like to return home.'

And that was exactly what they did, where they loved one another in the light of day and lay abed dreaming of a future together. A future neither one of them ever thought they would have.

Lost and finally found once more.

Epilogue

August 1820, Huntly Manor

Everything was in order. Or so Lottie hoped.

Sarah took one look at her and chuckled. 'Don't you worry, my lady, everything has been seen to.'

'By one of us,' Andrews muttered as he strode by.

Sarah cast him a pointed look. 'The house party will be an enormous success and everyone will have a grand time.'

'Did someone say a grand time?' Evander asked loudly, swooping in from the drawing room with a dark-haired little boy perched on his shoulders, who erupted in a giggle.

'A grand time,' their son parroted.

'We love a grand time, don't we?' Evander asked.

'Yes,' Rory cheered.

Lottie laughed at their antics. The two were always making a ruckus, filling the house with a loudness that made her shake her head and chuckle.

'Come now, Rory, get down from there.' Lottie gave Evander a chastising look. 'You're supposed to keep from getting too excited.'

'I'm afraid that is not possible,' Evander said, even as he lowered Rory gently to the ground. 'As he was already enormously excited before I picked him up.'

Rory hit the ground and tore off with a roar towards Silky, who strolled casually in the opposite direction.

'Heaven help me, that boy has energy in spades,' said Sarah with exasperation, before racing off after him.

'Rory,' Lottie called. 'You must be calm if you want syllabub later.'

The pounding of his feet came to an abrupt halt.

'Thank you,' Sarah panted from the other room.

Lottie and Evander looked at one another and laughed. 'Thank goodness for the promise of sweets,' Evander said.

'And for wonderful little boys who bring so much happiness.' Lottie tilted her head grudgingly. 'As well as a bit more noise.'

'A bit?' Evander arched a brow. 'I think we need to try harder.'

Lottie put her hands on her hips in feigned anger. 'Don't you dare.'

'Or what?' Evander pulled her into his arms.

His embrace was comfortable and familiar in all the best ways.

'Or I'll have to kiss you so much you won't be able to make a peep,' she threatened playfully.

'There are worse threats in this world, my love.'

He leaned forward and captured her lips.

Even after all these years she loved his kisses, craving them with the same intensity as when they first wed. She leaned into him and deepened their kiss with a little flick of her tongue. He drew her more tightly to him and Lottie's blood went hot in her veins.

Someone cleared their throat and they leapt apart like guilty children. Andrews stood primly by, with his hands folded behind his back. 'Forgive the interruption, my lady, but it appears your first guests are arriving.'

Lottie and Evander shared a sheepish look at having been caught, and dutifully moved towards the door.

'Yes, I see,' Evander said. 'Thank you, Andrews.'

Andrews gave austere nod as the gravel outside crunched under the wheels of a stopping carriage. A cacophony of voices came from outside—the occasional agreement of a man's voice and the incessant chatter of a small feminine one.

'Presumably Lord and Lady Dalton,' Andrews said dryly.

It was an accurate guess as Violet's daughter, Juliette, was notorious for speaking almost without stopping. Lottie hid a smile behind her hand and the corner of Andrews' lip flicked upwards before swiftly disappearing.

'Go on and open the door,' Lottie said. 'We don't need pomp and formality when it comes to friends.'

The quirk of Andrews' eyebrow indicated he did not agree, but he obeyed regardless.

No sooner had the door opened than Violet and Seth were there, with little Juliette, stepping into the house along with their son, James, cradled asleep in Seth's arms.

'The thing about violets is that they are such lovely flowers,' Juliette said. 'More than peonies, yes?' Without waiting for an answer, she continued, 'Violets are perfect for pressing.'

'Yes, I have always been partial to violets.' Seth winked at his wife.

Juliette beamed up at Lottie and Evander. 'Lord and Lady Westix, thank you so much for having us.' She scanned the hall. 'Is Rory here?'

'I'm certain you can find him,' Lottie said.

'Rory,' Juliette called out.

Her nursemaid gasped. 'Juliette, a young lady shouldn't—'

But Juliette was already running past them all into the next room.

Violet sighed with a smile and shook her head.

Lottie embraced her with a laugh. 'I assure you, it's nothing Rory isn't already doing. They're just excited.'

'I know.' Violet smiled. 'Thank you so much for inviting us. Binsey is such a lovely village. We drove through it on our way to the manor. I can see why you two enjoy your stays here so much.'

James shifted against Seth's shoulder and lifted his head. His dark hair was mussed, with the left side jutting upright, and he slowly blinked his dark blue eyes open.

'Are you still tired?' Seth asked softly.

The boy nodded.

'Do you want to rest?'

James lowered his head to Seth's shoulder once more in response.

'I'll take that as a yes,' Seth chuckled.

'Come, I'll show you to the nursery, where we can speak of masculine pastimes like teething and tantrums.' Evander waved for Seth to follow him.

Outside, another carriage arrived.

Within minutes Eleanor and Charles were striding through the door, confident and smiling, their skin tanned golden from their latest adventure. Their son, Simon, walked in front of them, leading them into the house with his nursemaid hovering nearby.

Perhaps it was the fact that their little Simon travelled with them around the world, but the boy was incredibly independent, always insistent on doing things himself.

Lottie and Violet embraced Eleanor and Charles.

'Thank you so much for coming,' Lottie said. 'It's so good to see you again.'

'Thank you for having us, little sister.' Charles grinned at her, his teeth bright white against his tanned skin. 'It's been an age since I've visited Huntly.'

'Where's Rory?' Simon said.

'Juliette is here as well,' Violet said, and Simon's eyes lit up.

'You can go and find them, but mind yourself,' Eleanor said.

The little boy nodded and darted off to find the other two. A feat easily accomplished, based on the chatter and giggles coming from one of the back rooms.

'Should we be worried about them?' Eleanor asked.

'Most likely,' Lottie replied, and they all laughed. 'Especially once Alice and George and Caroline and Rawley arrive with their little ones,' she added.

'Oh, I'm so pleased they'll be joining us,' Violet said.

'Yes, but not until this evening,' Lottie replied. 'Evander's mother will arrive tomorrow as well.'

Evander and Seth appeared on the stairs and Charles regarded them with a wave. 'I suppose this means I won't be left alone with the ladies after all.'

'Pity for you,' Eleanor teased him with a smile, which earned her a playful wink in return.

While the children played, the newly arrived couples found their rooms and freshened up after their travels, leaving Lottie and Evander alone for a brief moment.

He drew her into his arms once more. 'Thank you for co-ordinating this. I believe it will be the most successful house party of all time.'

She smiled up at her handsome husband. 'I'm so happy to finally have everyone at Huntly Manor at the same time.'

'I know how much you love it here.' Evander ran a hand down her cheek and she turned into his touch.

'At one time it was simply coming here that made me happy, but now it's more than that.'

'Is it?'

He lowered his head, nuzzling her neck. Chills of pleasure danced over her skin.

'Mmm-hmm,' she agreed. 'It's you. And Rory. And the way you two make me laugh.'

Evander leaned back and grinned at her. 'I'll remind you of that when we next engage in a game of tag.'

'Not in the drawing room again,' she admonished with a tease.

'No, not again.' He pulled her towards him. 'And maybe next time you'll join us.'

'I confess it did look terribly fun.'

'The best.' Evander kissed her. 'I love you so very much, Lottie.'

'And I love you, Evander.' She cradled his face in her hands. 'Thank you for this life and for such happiness. Thank you for never giving up on me.'

'My love, waiting for you was worth every moment. I'm just glad I was finally able to convince you to marry me.'

Lottie melted into his embrace. 'As am I.'

* * * * *

*If you enjoyed this story, be sure to read
the first two books in Madeline Martin's
The London School For Ladies miniseries*

How to Tempt a Duke
How to Start a Scandal